ADVANCE PRAISE FOR *TEN*

There's something special about givi...
and that's exactly what happens in this unique collection.

 —*Dan Szczesny, journalist, author of* The White Mountain, *Manchester*

This volume is rich and diverse in its content and craft. I loved reading it because of the surprise element—not knowing what was around the corner. The anthology strikes a perfect balance between poetry and prose as well as interior and exterior landscapes.

 —*Sarah Anderson, author, co-founder of The Word Barn, Exeter*

Ten Piscataqua Writers does kaleidoscope right. Style, subject, and emotional range is exciting and inviting, but each of the writers has the gift of enough pages to be fully accessible. Rather than ten little windows opened and slammed shut, the reader discovers the beautiful play of this year's literary shape and color.

 —*Maren C. Tirabassi, author, former Portsmouth Poet Laureate, Portsmouth*

This is a project that deserves revisiting, if only to preserve the voices and stories of the lives in our region.

 —*Jan Waldron, artist and author, Rye*

The concept behind this anthology is a veritable GPS of the imagination. It inverts the go-broad, free-range sense of a typical anthology, finding the expansive in a small area. Offering this on an annual basis is also a very fine idea, suggesting that one geographic area can be returned to repeatedly to mine its creativity.

 —*Alexandria Peary, author, New Hampshire Poet Laureate, Londonderry*

Impressive writing chops gathered into an exceptional collection. Don't miss it!

 —*Bill Paarlberg, editor and artist, Kittery Point*

The seacoast is home to so many talented writers, an annual anthology would be a wonderful way to get to know them all.

 —*Jennifer Richmond, Ceres Baker, South Berwick*

Not a clunker in the bunch!

 —*Andrew Periale, editor* Puppetry International *magazine, Strafford*

I have lived closely with all the stories, essays and poems, traveled through eras and locations. The book has broadened my tastes.

—**Pat Spalding**, *writer & storyteller, Rye (& Harrisville)*

I loved the choices of works for this book. The poetry too. A beautiful compilation.

—**Laura Stutz**, *painter, cook, baker, South Berwick*

How wonderful to see new work by writers I was familiar with, and to find others who suddenly feel like old friends by way of the landscape, both literal and emotional. These stories and poems take us on that search through an array of unforgettable, compelling episodes. I couldn't put it down.

—**Ann Joslin Williams**, *Director MFA in Writing, UNH, Durham*

I know and love the Seacoast more deeply thanks to this collection.

—**Denise J. Wheeler**, *writer, educator, activist, arts maven, Greenland*

Ten Piscataqua Writers is a very impressive and varied collection, the best selection of local writing I've seen gathered in one place. I feel a sense of pride to see their high quality work in print, and the whole book makes me proud to be from the Seacoast.

—**Roland Goodbody**, *actor, writer, director, Portsmouth (& UK)*

Ten Piscataqua Writers takes a unique approach to showcasing regional talent by bringing together a collection that spans genres, styles, and themes. This is an anthology that celebrates a vibrant writing community and introduces readers to significant new voices and new work.

—**Katherine Towler**, *author of* The Penny Poet of Portsmouth, *Portsmouth*

Impressive and highly recommended.

—**Brendan DuBois**, *New York Times bestselling author, Exeter*

Writers like to hide out, so they really do need to be discovered. A yearly anthology is a wonderful place to begin.

—**Mimi White**, *award-winning poet, Rye*

A sparkling collection of fiction, nonfiction and poetry allowing ten writers plenty of space to show their stuff.

—**Andrew Merton**, *journalist and poet, Durham*

TEN PISCATAQUA
WRITERS
2022

PAPERBACK WRITER SERIES
Ten Piscataqua Writers 2022

STUDIO TO COFFEE TABLE BOOK SERIES
Ten Piscataqua Photographers (2019)
Ten Piscataqua Painters (2022)
Ten Piscataqua Makers (forthcoming)

TEN PISCATAQUA
WRITERS
2022

An Anthology from the Watershed

EDITED BY

Phillip Augusta

Rebecca Rule

Gerald Duffy

Jessica Purdy

◆

Ten Piscataqua • PO Box 1354 • Portsmouth, NH 03802 • *www.tenpiscataqua.com*

Photograph of Todd Hearon courtesy Cheryle St. Onge

$25.00
ISBN 978-1-7379723-1-0

TEN PISCATAQUA
PO BOX 1354
PORTSMOUTH, NH 03802-1354
www.tenpiscataqua.com

Set in Minion
Book design by Phillip Augusta
Cover design by Brenda Riddell

Printed in the USA

About the Writers

Merrill Black

I moved to Portsmouth from New York City in 1978 and then again, after many years away, in 2013 to marry Seacoast artist Russell Aharonian.

During the intervening years I earned a master's in creative nonfiction from UNH; was a New York Foundation for the Arts fellow; and taught writing at the City University of New York, Southern New Hampshire University, and the Arthur Ashe Institute for Urban Health.

I gave a TEDx talk and had essays published in *The New York Times*, *New York Press*, *UnderWired Magazine*, and *Autobiographical Writing Across the Disciplines* (Duke University Press) and *Becoming Portsmouth: Voices from a Half Century of Change* (The History Press).

I'm currently writing a memoir on the legacy of substance abuse, hoping to bear witness to the power of connection to place and community, and the surprising moments of joy that can emerge from addiction, recovery, and loss.

Mary Duquette

I'm a graduate of the MFA program in Writing with a concentration in Fiction at the University of New Hampshire. I am a member of the New Hampshire

Writers' Project, and won the Dawkins Prize at the University of New Hampshire. My work has been published in *The Good Life Review*, *Epiphany*, and *Ginosko Literary Magazine*. I was included in a pulp fiction anthology entitled *Murder Ink 3*.

I've recently completed two novels, a short story collection, and a poetry collection. I'm currently at work on another novel. www.megermanottaduquette.com, maryelise555@gmail.com

Bill Burtis

My first published poem, "Night Fright," appeared in the Hartford *Times* when I was about the age of 10. I've since published in magazines and journals including *Aurorean*, *Aspen Anthology*, *Chelsea*, *Glint*, *Nine Mile*, *Paris Review*, *The Poet's Showcase: An Anthology of New Hampshire Poets*, *PORT smith*, *Seneca Review*, *Sou'wester*, *Three Quarter Review*, and *Tower Journal*. My one full-length collection, *Liminal* came out from Nine Mile Books in summer, 2021; a chapbook, *Villians*, was published by W. D. Hofstadt in 1978.

I earned a BA from Hobart College and an MFA in poetry from the Iowa Writers' Workshop. Pre-COVID, I was a frequent reader at open mics in the Seacoast region, and I'm a long-time member of the City Hall Poets workshop. I served multiple terms on the board of the Portsmouth Poet Laureate Program (PPLP), including as PPLP co-chair in 2017–18.

I live in Exeter with my wife, the poet Nancy Jean Hill.

Cathy Wolff

As a kid, I wrote poems and puppet scripts. (The most notable involved a Russian Sputnik dog crash landing in the U.S.) Then I went to journalism school (University of Missouri) and abandoned "creative" writing.

I came to New Hampshire in 1974 to work for the Associated Press. Left that job in 1976 to relax and collect sunsets, but instead became intensely involved in protesting the Seabrook nuke. Also picked apples; married, had a kid, and divorced; and worked as a writer and in PR for UNH, Dartmouth, and Tufts.

My freelance efforts include a couple of essays in *The Boston Globe* and a how-to-juggle story in *Boys' Life*. For the past 20 years, I've been part of a writers' group convened by writer/artist Jan Waldron of Rye, NH. (See the book *Ten Piscataqua Painters*). That group is the reason I submitted essays for this book. So don't blame me.

Clark Knowles

I moved to the New Hampshire Seacoast in 1989 and made my home in Portsmouth. I live with my family in an old farmhouse in what was once the outskirts of town. I received my MA in Writing from the University of New Hampshire in 1999, and I've been teaching writing there ever since. I earned my MFA in Writing and Literature from Bennington College in 2005. The NH State Council on the Arts awarded me an Individual Fellowship in 2009. You can find my fiction in lots of small journals, both online and in print, and I'm thrilled to have my work appear in this anthology with these brilliant, geographically linked writers. The short-short stories that make up "Emporium" are explorations and inventions about a life similar to mine. They take place in the landscapes that make up the bulk of my adult experiences. I hope you'll enjoy reading them. For more information about me, or the sorts of things I'm writing, please visit www.clarkknowles.com or email me at clarkknowles@gmail.com.

S Stephanie

In and out of foster care, I grew up in NH and Maine with many definitions of "home," "love," "family." At 15, I left that childhood behind, poor but with a thick dictionary in my back pocket and a love of reading and writing. I believe it is that rocky childhood which motivated me to read life and people from a variety of angles. I believe words saved me. Books saved me. I built a life around those.

I studied poetry under Charles Simic, Mary Ruefle, Dave Smith, Nancy Eimers, William Olsen and Betsy Sholl, all poets I respect and am grateful to. I married W. E. Butts, who became a NH Poet Laureate. Together we helped create the early poetry scene in Portsmouth NH, published a national literary magazine, and gave and organized readings and workshops all over New England. It has been an exciting life! NH is blessed with so many good poets, artists, and musicians. I am grateful to be part of the community.

Currently I work in a small hardware store, am an adjunct for the Institute of Art and Design of New England College, and live in Rollinsford, NH. I write, being careful not to disturb my two cats.

Mary Ann Cappiello

For the last twenty-eight years, I've been a literacy and humanities educator for humans of all ages. Currently, I am a Professor of Language and Literacy at Lesley University, where a Russell Fellowship and a Faculty Development Grant supported my research on Dinah Tuck. I'm the co-author of *Text Sets in Action: Pathways Through Content Area Literacy*, *Teaching to Complexity: A Framework for Evaluating Literary and Content-Area Texts*, and *Teaching with Text Sets*. I've been a guest on public radio and a consultant to public television, and my work has appeared in *English Journal*, *Language Arts*, *School Library Journal*, and more. I'm a co-author of "The Classroom Bookshelf," a *School Library Journal* blog and, *The Biography Clearinghouse*. I live with my husband, Tim Horvath, and our daughter Ella in Stratham, New Hampshire. You can find out more about my work at www.teachingwithtradebooks.com, and you can reach me at cappiellomaryann@aol.com.

James Patrick Kelly

Although I grew up in the suburbs of NYC, I atoned for my upbringing by moving to New Hampshire in 1976, the year after I sold my first story. I've been on the Seacoast for the past thirty-two years.

At this point my writing scorecard features six novels, over a hundred and fifty stories, a dozen or so plays, a handful of poems, and twenty-five years of my regular column "On The Net" for *Asimov's Science Fiction Magazine*. I write mostly science fiction and fantasy and have won several of the genre's awards. The short fiction has been reprinted in many Year's Best anthologies and overseas in fifteen different languages. Among the other accomplishments of my checkered past are fifteen years teaching at the Stonecoast Creative Writing MFA program and eight years serving as a councilor on the New Hampshire State Council on the Arts. Free stories and essays of mine await you at jimkelly.net.

Todd Hearon

For my chapter, I've pulled from my work in poetry, drama and songwriting. A few years back, I collaborated with my friend, the composer Greg Brown, on a piece about the Quabbin Reservoir in western Massachusetts, the source of the water supply to Boston at the expense of four Revolutionary-era towns that were disincorporated and "drowned" in order to create that body of water. That piece forms the first part of my chapter and debuted in Philadelphia with the chamber choir The Crossing (www.crossingchoir.org). The second piece in my chapter comes from when I lived in Boston, working with an independent theater troupe; it was produced at the Boston Center for the Arts. The third part of my chapter comes from my new album, *BORDER RADIO* (2021), a collection of original songs that hearken back to my roots in traditional American music. You can find more of my work at www.toddhearon.com and can email me at toddhearon@yahoo.com.

Christina Keim

I have a passion for writing nonfiction because I believe there is beauty in sharing true stories that make an impact, inspire hope, and influence change. As a narrative journalist and travel writer, I have focused primarily on telling other people's stories, as seen through my lens. The two essays I have the opportunity to share in this anthology are a departure from my typical work. They are deeply personal yet reflect universal struggles. Many individuals have entrusted me to share their inner truths through my writing. Their bravery has inspired me to now tell my own story, in my own words. My writing has appeared or is forthcoming in a wide variety of digital and print media. I hold both an M. Ed and an MFA from the University of New Hampshire. Please visit me at www.christinakeim.com or contact me at christinakeimequestrian@gmail.com.

About the Crew

Phillip Augusta ◆ Editor

I began publishing local with photo postcards of the region in the late 70s, one of which became that tugboat in the fog poster you used to see everywhere. Not long after came *re:Ports.*, an arts and entertainment calendar that became a voice for the regional music, writing, and arts community in the early and mid-80s, just when alley galleries and ad hoc cinemas were popping up as Portsmouth's transformation from blue-collar military town to upscale cultural hotspot got underway. An arts weekly was really about discovering and promoting local talent—live music in the pullout 7-column calendar for the fridge, visual artists on the cover, and local writers of fiction, nonfiction and poetry inside as the pages grew. Hail Re: ! I've since worn a variety of hats for small and medium press in the book industry, and now editing the Ten Piscataqua books is about finding a sustainable way for the community to again discover its homegrown talent.

Rebecca Rule ◆ Fiction Editor

When Phillip Augusta floated the idea of *Ten Piscataqua Writers*, I embraced the opportunity to help put world-class writing by local writers into the hands of readers. The task turned out to be a daunting one—in a good way. So many generous writers sent in their work for consideration, it was hard to choose just three pieces. Really hard. With any luck, this is just the first anthology of many, so readers can enjoy the work of other fine Piscataqua writers as well.

For ten years I hosted the *New Hampshire Authors Series* on NHPBS. Now I host *Our Hometown*, also for NHPBS. I also write regularly for *New Hampshire Magazine* and *New Hampshire Home.*

My books include collections of short stories, nonfiction, two picture books for children, and—most recently—a memoir, how-to, and compendium of Yankee humor called *That Reminds Me of a Funny Story.*

Gerald Duffy • Nonfiction Editor

It was no surprise to me that this project would produce some fine writing. The Piscataqua basin has long attracted talented, creative people to the region. The authors of the four winning nonfiction submissions took me on a rich journey, from far-off places to deep corridors of the psyche. As their editor, I was grateful that the writers made my life so easy; often, there were only minor elements to discuss and resolve. The pieces already had good shape and came alive through insight and detail. There are scenes from each piece that have etched themselves into my mind: a child's painful encounter with a parent, a young slave woman laboring in a kitchen on the Isles of Shoals, a hiker struggling to climb out of a deep gorge, a punch not altogether reluctantly landed, and a woman tussling with a Wi-Fi password in a cafe. It's been a pleasure working with writers who love their language, are willing to dig deep, and who know how to tell a good story.

Jessica Purdy • Poetry Editor

I have lived in New England all my life. Having majored in both English and Studio Art at UNH, I feel drawn to the visual in both art and poetry. I received an MFA in Creative Writing with a concentration in Poetry from Emerson College. I have worked as an art teacher and a writing teacher. Currently, I teach Poetry Workshops and Creative Writing at Southern New Hampshire University. I also teach Creative Writing in an EXCEL program for middle and high school students. In 2019, I was the Esther Buffler Poet-in-Residence at Portsmouth High School here in New Hampshire. In 2015, I was a featured reader for Finishing Line Press, who published my chapbook *Learning the Names,* at the Abroad Writers' Conference in Dublin, Ireland. My poems have been nominated for Best New Poets and Best of the Net. My poems and reviews have appeared in many journals, including *One Art, Dream Pop, Feral, Hole in the Head Review, Museum of Americana,* and *Gargoyle.* Anthologies my poems have appeared in include *Writing the Land, Covid Spring I and II, Except for Love: New England Poets Inspired by Donald Hall, Nancy Drew Anthology,* and *Lunation.* My books *STARLAND* and *Sleep in a Strange House* were released by Nixes Mate in 2017 and 2018. *Sleep in a Strange House* was a finalist for the NH Literary Award for poetry. I was honored and humbled to be able to select the poets' work for this anthology.

Adi Rule ◆ Copyeditor

I write books for teens, most recently *Why Would I Lie?* (Scholastic). I am also a freelance editor and assistant manager of the Wentworth-Coolidge Mansion in Portsmouth. Visit me online at www.adirule.com.

Lynn Davey ◆ Website Administration

I have worked as a creative for over 18 years in a variety of industries including print shops, a local newspaper, a signage company, and an upscale home and garden magazine. I ultimately found my home as the owner of LD Creative Designs, a marketing agency based in Newfields, New Hampshire.

I am passionate about the conservation of land and spend a lot of my free time roaming around local trails or hiking mountains in the North Country. I am also a proponent of animal rights and welfare.

Peggi McCarthy • Advance Publicist

I first encountered Phillip (and Bill Paarlberg) in the early 1980s, through the weekly 11-by-17 arts sheet *re:Ports.*, for which I became the 100-word reviewer of local plays. I'm a lifelong maker of writing and theater, so *re:Ports.* provided a wonderful opportunity to express my dual loves under a deadline. In the decades since, I've worked in my disciplines at a good number of local academic and arts institutions. I've sat behind desks to write, to teach, to do non-profit administrative work; and walked stages to direct, to perform, to teach. It's great to get re-woven into the fabric of the Seacoast community, engaging the locals to support one another through Ten Piscataqua's admirable mission.

Brenda Riddell • Cover Designer

My career in the creative industry as a designer, educator, and entrepreneur spans over two decades. Through my work at both in-house and agency settings, I've refined my skills in print design, brand identity design, web development, and integrated digital strategy.

Since 2007, I've been the creative director and proud owner of Graphic Details, Inc., a design agency based in Portsmouth, New Hampshire for over 30 years.

I believe that teaching design is the best way to remain focused and on-trend. Consequently, I've taught graphic design courses for over 16 years, most recently for the Graphic Design Department at New Hampshire Institute of Art.

I am also passionate about animal welfare. I volunteer with several animal rescues and founded *artfortheunderdog.com* and *straightoffthastreets.com*, initiatives that aim to raise awareness of animal homelessness and neglect.

Table of Contents

Merrill Black

Girl Walks Into a Bar & Other Essays

In her reflections, Merrill contrasts the Portsmouth of today with a much grittier version of itself. She evokes bars, clubs, and hangouts, most of which are long gone. It's hard to imagine Portsmouth's current prosperous, gentrified cityscape as a rougher world of motor-cycle gangs, day laborers, and a lot of alcohol. But the author's skillful storytelling takes us into its smokey rooms. She also takes us deep into her interior landscape with stories of early struggles, addiction, and relationships that hurt but can't be released. Merrill doesn't flinch from the hard details; her accounts, including one of deep personal loss, are brutally honest. Throughout, we realize we're in the company of a compassionate woman who has lived through pain but still loves the world and all its stories. G.D.

Girl Walks Into a Bar

There were two bars at the intersection of Daniel and Penhallow, streets in Portsmouth.

The backroom of a Chinese restaurant, the bar on Penhallow felt like an afterthought. No windows, just a back door flung open, letting the twang of jukebox country-western music and the funk of beer and cigarettes curl out into the street. There was beer and bourbon, but you could top off a day's drinking with a frilly sweet Dragon's Skull from the restaurant, tricked out with tiny paper parasols, nourishing with cream and probably the same orange sugar syrup that coated the sweet-and-sour pork. There were lines of motorcycles parked outside. Afternoons, the bar was largely empty, but from five to closing, the small Formica bar was banked with big guys talking loudly, wearing denim cutoff vests with "Iron Horsemen Motorcycle Club" on their backs.

The bar on Daniel was a brick building with paned windows. A carefully designed sign hung over the door, picturing a vintage typewriter encircled with the name "The Press Room," homage to the owner's former career as a journalist. Inside was a long, polished wooden bar underneath a painting of a nude woman. There was live folk music, good Scotch and Guinness, lots of lively talk.

I know less about this bar. In 1978, when I was looking for a home-base bar, I was drawn to its intellectual atmosphere—Dylan Thomas, or any of the people I drank with in college, would have chosen this bar. But what would I say to all these people who had taken root in interesting lives of art and writing, gainful employment, and family-making? I'd just escaped the reboot of six weeks in a psychiatric hospital in New York City, which in my mind cancelled out any promise I had shown as a young adult.

Imagining gun barrels over a department store makeup counter and receiving coded messages through the radio, only I knew of the revolutionary takeover menacing from the edges of day-to-day life. As life became more hallucinatory, madness had not been the genius-triggering release I'd hoped for. Rather, it became a chaotic disorientation where everyone who cared about me leaned in to ask, "Are you all right now?" I interpreted their concern only as expectation, as *Can we get on with it now?*

I moved here with a man I'd dated for six months because he gave me an escape route—the poor bastard just happened to be sleeping with me when the bottom fell out of my world. Internalizing the stigma associated with hospitalization, ashamed of my duplicitous relationship to my lover, I did not feel worthy of the Press Room. I snuggled instead into the anonymity and novelty of the China Empress. No one expected anything of me. It was a guilty comfort, a free ride into an unknown world, like joining a carnival, a source of curiosity, which at the time felt redemptive.

When I imagine a rewritten past now, I ask friends to meet me at the Press Room and let them introduce me around, let someone else explain how I came to be there. I can laugh at the witty repartee around me and eventually find a way into conversation—as long as I kept people talking about themselves, I'd discovered in the hospital, no one cared too much about what was up with me. Maybe I'd meet The Man, a life I could attach myself to, grow within, contribute to, and maybe eventually move beyond once I discovered my own momentum.

Or maybe I could have made a lasting connection with the man I am now married to. He was there—a day tripper in bars, not really a drinker. He made his own party wherever he went out of whatever he found there. And yet there was a stable core anchoring his crazy. He went off to his construction job in an art car he created, embellished with erotica, feathers, and colored foam. His wife was the head nurse at a local hospital, reporting for duty competent and in charge, with sparkle still in her hair from the night before.

It would not have gone well then. We were both involved with other people; he never wanted children and being a mother was the only thing I knew for sure I wanted; sex, often indiscriminate, was for each of us a necessary escape hatch, an essential life force, our way of being in the world. Who we were then would not have led to where we are now: fulfilled, connected, and sane.

Smashed

Excerpt from *Saved by the Ever-Ready Kid: A Mother's Memoir of Bereavement, Recovery and Redemption*

Ships docking in Portsmouth in the '70s sent agents to the China Empress to hire day workers to unload cargo. The base of operations for the fledgling New Hampshire chapter of the Iron Horsemen Motorcycle Club, the bar provided a standing supply of able-bodied, unemployed men. Falling out the side door into the blinding afternoon light, the rowdy hulk of drinkers would stagger down to the docks a block away. Bull-rushing back in around five, they returned red-faced and noisy, covered with sweat and sugar, sawdust, or road salt, revived by work, rolls of bills in their pockets. Before I started hanging out at the China Empress, I didn't know anyone with a tattoo or missing teeth, or who had fought in Vietnam or served prison time. Within six months, this would describe everyone in the support group I'd come to count on.

No one cared that I was fresh out of the nuthouse. For a long time, I hadn't felt as though anybody was ever glad to see me, so it was easy and comforting to be in the presence of these undemanding men. The club's president, Dusty, was my protector and companion, taking me for long drives, buying me donuts. Tall and barrel-chested, his long greasy hair flowed from under a leather top hat he wore. He rode a Harley with an old saddle for a seat. The biker women in the bar supported themselves and their children by working at massage parlors, running drugs, or performing at local low-budget sex shows. I looked after their kids while I drank—happy to be around children, teaching them to read the jukebox or build houses out of bar supplies.

In my mind, I had no future, but I had found a space and company where I felt anonymously safe and marginally alive. My hope was that the boyfriend I'd moved to town with would leave me, taking the moral high ground, the only parting gift I could offer. My relationship with the suitable boy who had seen me through the worst year of my life was over and I felt nothing.

One of the bikers, Jack, had wild red hair and spider veins lacing his ruddy cheeks. He was a raconteur and could imitate exactly every kind of motorcycle or power tool manufactured in the United States or Japan. Bent over a placemat in the bar, he drew cartoons or made sketches for work.

I still have a drawing Jack did of me the summer before we married, when we talked about having children. In the drawing, my sleeping face turns toward my curled hand, amid a riot of mismatched bedclothes. It is an astonishing likeness I kept for our son, evidence to counter all the chaos of the home we made together—that his father once loved me, watched quietly while I slept, and bequeathed a slender legacy of his untutored and unsung talent.

The crises of life with Jack provided a structure that gave me daily marching orders, just as my mother had while I was growing up. It did not make me happy, certainly, but I had stopped seeing happiness as an option. I craved purpose, order, knowing what to do next—all of which this relationship's disarray amply provided. On a roughly monthly cycle, Jack and I had to find a new place to live, and a new job for him.

By Christmas that year, all the earmarks of subsistence living seemed commonplace: the phone and electricity disconnect notices, eviction, kiting small checks at the local grocery store, avoiding driving in certain towns because there was a bench warrant out for my husband-to-be. We lived in motels and on friends' couches. And I had finally found a job I could hold since leaving the hospital. Ricco's Cafe did not sell mixed drinks—just two sizes of beer, 35 cents or "frosties" for 50 cents. The cash register was broken so accounting was easy. In Portsmouth's ecosystem of bars, the Starlight Club and Ricco's were vestiges of the old town, before the malls and the fern bars. Most of Ricco's patrons were older working men, divorced and bitter toward women, bristling that no one seemed to recognize the value of being able to bang nails, haul nets, or fit pipe into their fifties. Bartending consisted mostly of nodding, smiling, and listening to their stories.

The main tasks were opening and closing the bar, and crowd control in between. In the Starlight, where I went after work, there was a handwritten sign taped to the mirror over the bar that read, "If you are on medication and shouldn't drink then don't." My response was to stop taking the medication prescribed in New York. Being my husband's advocate and support was a consuming avocation. I didn't have time to be crazy.

Working at Ricco's anchored me in regular hours and a known community. It allowed me to emulate the hostess skills I'd learned from my mother with a new proficiency. I broke up fights. I'd leap over the bar, throw my arms around the aggressor, pinning his arms to his side while I looked up into his face. In a quiet voice, I'd catalogue the consequences he might face: being barred, breaking parole, facing Ricco's ire, queering chances for child visitation that month. It always worked. I felt more competent than I had since college. Ricco would come in every night to close out the register. "How'd it go?" he'd ask. I'd regale him with stories and updates on customers, relationships, court cases, mental states. Standing behind him as he counted out the change, I sometimes saw his broad back jiggle as he'd chuckle and shake his head.

The bar became a safe space for Jack and me, public enough to give respite from our own fighting and a community with its own comforting rhythms and rituals. In the fall there was always a rash of petty crimes committed by those who couldn't find a job or a girlfriend to see them through the winter. The local jail provided three hots and a cot for the brutal winter months. After smashing several windows on State Street, one of the old-timers bribed guys with beer to break his jaw. As an indigent, he could count on a month's convalescence in the county farm—it would take him through the holidays.

When nights got longer after Halloween, tinseled swags festooned the streetlamps. Fluorescent-lit store windows reflected wrapping paper and cheap ornaments onto the cold blue-dark sidewalks. A street-corner Salvation Army Santa rang a bell. If you were unwelcome elsewhere, you could always come home to Ricco's.

During the holidays we served a free full-course dinner: turkey, ham, side dishes and pies, like a church supper except with a lot of beer. The guys washed up for the occasion. Some wore ill-fitting suits saved for funerals. Ricco led grace to a long table of bowed, pomaded heads. Careful, awkward, and proud, some guys sat next to the children they saw only on holidays— little girls gift-wrapped in party dresses and combed little boys in clean, starched shirts. Grim-faced ex-wives arrived briefly after the allotted hour of visitation to pick up the kids, glance around the bar, and shake their heads.

When Jack asked me to marry him, the idea that anyone could want me that much, for that long, was the sliver of evidence I needed to prove I had value, that I could take root in the world again. I said yes.

He hit me the first time about a month after that. Afterwards, I found him back at our rented room, shaken, silent and sorry. He cried all night, his broad shoulders shaking the foldout bed. In the morning I held his face in my hands and said, "You're a lot bigger than me. If what happened last night happens again, someday you're going to really hurt me." He nodded, unable to speak. Now we had a secret to take to the altar, an intimate, unspoken bargain.

We thought we could just get on with our lives, that the secret had bonded us, and that it would never happen again. His word became my gospel—I suspended all disbelief, siding with him as he walked off job after job in construction work. He argued with my customers in the bar, with landlords, and with employers. I cleaned up after him as best I could. He trusted me to witness his unstoppable pain. I believed in his resolve. We were a tiny nation in a dangerous world, with an iron pact of mutual protection and solace.

All the drama gave my life a trajectory, a story I could tell myself of overcoming the odds and ending up okay. We would look back from our stable middle age, I imagined, and laugh together about these rough early days together. This imagined marriage would be an accomplishment.

The summer before our wedding, Jack sustained a disabling back injury while working as a temporary laborer. The rotted surface he was breaking up with a jackhammer collapsed. Having defined himself in terms of his physical strength his whole life, Jack did not do well with having to explore other, more cerebral avenues of employment, but he found a vocational program that offered drafting. He was glad to provide some income with his disability checks.

Occasionally, I would take new day jobs, but they never lasted. I would show up late, distraught after a fight the night before. The workday was punctuated by highly charged phone calls from Jack, who now had more time to think about ways in which I and everyone else had wronged him. Sometimes flowers arrived, a grandiose gesture that never failed to move me, even though often the next day the florist would call the office demanding payment from me. Ricco's was the only job I could stay with—a demanding relationship, it occupied me full-time.

One afternoon Jack came into the bar to tell me that we'd been evicted again. To soften the blow, he brought my guitar, with a hat tied onto the case's neck, and our only painting strapped across its body. He called it something funny—maybe "home in a box"—I don't remember. The guys in the bar laughed like hell—our marriage had become a standing joke. I laughed too, snapping a lit cigarette from the lips of one of my customers and taking a drag for the first time in six months, the first since learning I was pregnant.

It had taken a while for this new knowledge about the pregnancy to sink in. Initially, I thought I'd just contracted a hangover that wouldn't go away. My periods had been erratic for years and I was used to throwing up in the morning. I abruptly stopped drinking and smoking once I knew for sure, afraid that the cocaine and booze had already damaged the baby. Without my drinking, our bar life made the pregnancy seem like a long stay in bedlam's waiting room, with no magazines to read but *Arizona Life.*

Driving

When I was little my mother would take my unblemished palm in hers. "My hands were already so callused by the time I was your age," she would say. There is a picture of her as a girl standing with her father, brother, and sister in front of the family car, a battered and snow-covered Ford Model A. Their gloveless hands clench each other's against the New England cold. She talked about getting chilblains as a child, a word I had only seen in nineteenth-century novels. She talked about how much she hated chores on her family's chicken farm.

Her adult life was one long repudiation of this childhood deprivation, a way of thumbing her nose at everything she'd grown up with and refused to let define her. She delighted in everything that went with the middle-class professional life she'd made. The only woman in our Virginia neighborhood with a job, she also had her own car.

Neighborhood wives were out by 8 a.m., watering their lawns, wearing pedal pushers and crowns of pink foam curlers. Coiffed and made-up, wafting clouds of Miss Dior, her high heels clicking out a staccato on our porch steps, my mother would jangle her car keys on her way to the driveway. Swinging her stockinged legs under the wheel of her blue '65 Dodge station wagon, she'd wave at her detractors as she drove off to work.

The first car she bought herself, years later, after leaving my father, was a Cadillac. She waved from the passenger seat of our beat-up Pontiac as my husband drove her to the dealership. She came back after a few hours, at the wheel of the biggest car I had ever seen, with my son in the front seat beaming, and his father in the back, clawing at the roof to steady himself as she swerved into the driveway.

From that point on, our own car filled our three-year-old son with disgust. His chubby legs just meeting the passenger seat's edge, he would fold himself in half to crank down the window and, exasperated, say, "You really"— crank—"should get windows like grandmother has."—crank—"You just"—crank—"push a button."

While its push-button windows worked, the new Cadillac soon revealed a fatal flaw—a vapor lock. At any time, without warning, the car would just not start, sometimes for a few minutes, sometimes an hour or so. Trips that involved multiple stops—running errands, picking up children at daycare, gassing up—were particularly risky.

My mother was not a patient person, but the Cadillac could do no wrong. She began to tuck needlework projects into the car's console to pass the time until the car was ready to start. I still have a little car key purse she did in cross-stitch over the course of one winter when the Cadillac was particularly crabby. The purse's color scheme matched the autumnal colors of the Caddie.

In her sixties, my mother and her long-term partner Mike bought an eighteenth-century tavern in Germantown, New York to restore together. She started referring to all new purchases as her last. *This is my last house. This is my last winter coat. This is my last vacuum cleaner. This could be my last artichoke, you know.* She bought her last Cadillac over Mike's derisive references to pimp cars—an enormous satiny black model with silver trim and red leather seats.

There is a long, steep hill between Hudson and Germantown. Every time she drove the Cadillac down this hill, Mike and she would act like a couple of kids on a roller coaster, even pausing in the middle of a howling fight only to resume it when they reached the bottom. It seemed emblematic of their relationship—there were certain sensations, tastes, aesthetic experiences that trumped, if only for an instant, their mutual need to savage each other. They would ride out these brief, shared moments of delight, then resume where they left off, almost refreshed, ready to return to battle.

My mother was diagnosed with cancer a few years after they bought the tavern. Mike and I spent a lot of time in the Cadillac, driving her to Albany for treatment for three years before she died.

She asked that her ashes be buried in a little circle of aspens they planted behind the tavern.

The morning of the burial, before anyone was up, Mike drove the unwieldy car over the long back lawn and parked it at a respectful distance from the circle of trees. As we buried her ashes, the morning sun glinted off the Cadillac's hood, as it stood like a fallen knight's steed, or a Viking boat, ready to serve as a floating pyre.

Boys Will Be Boys

Weekends, my son, Josh came first for the pile on, delighted to be waking the grown-ups, then stayed for the warmth. My partner Dan's king-sized bed was jammed up against the uninsulated wall with windows. Sunday's paper would be spread out over the bed, coffee cups cooling on the windowsill. After the ambush, Josh and I would burrow back under the covers, me spooned around him with Dan reading the paper and stroking my back. If Josh had a friend over, the friend would pile on too, astonished at the ritual, the heady experience of breaching an adult sanctuary. I grew up in such a formal household—I loved waking up on weekends into this mess, this laughing, this closeness. The summer after third grade, the sleepover pile on suddenly involved squirt guns. A few squirts, lots of laughs, pile on, snuggle, done.

It intensified one weekend when Dan wrested the gun from the boys and started squirting back. They were all laughing still, but there was an edge. It was one of those red flag moments you can't see when you're newly in love with someone.

When Dan first started hiding a loaded squirt gun next to the bed I was amused—such a serious man, it was fun to see him so playful. The boys loved the escalation and reconnoitered the following weekend. I heard their giggling approach, then a metallic clattering as they leaped on the bed wearing saucepans on their heads, holding cookie sheets as shields, squinting their eyes shut, squirting with renewed energy. Dan retaliated and suddenly the sheets were a lot wetter than you want.

The boys found more inventive ways to augment their tactical gear: garbage bags, umbrellas, dish pans. Somebody else would have been able to say, "It's not funny anymore." But I couldn't. We were all dripping. The paper was tangled up in the wet sheets. The boys looked like the Tenniel drawings of Tweedledee and Tweedledum. It was still funny, but the cozy laughing winding down seemed harder and harder to achieve.

Dan disappeared during one attack. I thought he was just leaving me alone with the boys because he knew that I loved this ritual. But he came back holding a pot of water with two hands. Feeling bested by two eight-year-olds, he needed to up the ante. Maybe he rationalized, "If that was fun, this will really be fun." I yelled *no* in my sharpest mommy-no-more-nonsense voice, pointing not at the boys but at him. He stopped and came back to his adult self, pot poised, like after one of those cartoon slaps that knocks someone out of hysteria.

I did not recognize playful exchanges like this as the technical run-throughs for the larger conflagration. The conflict between my partner and my son did not reach critical mass until Josh hit adolescence. When testosterone clashes, men and boys seem to commit at a cellular level to bringing more firepower to the generational battle of who will be left standing.

Mourning Person

If there was ever a time *not* to buy clothes, it is now. Yet I've never felt under more pressure to pass as a professional woman. I just took a new job after years of working at home. It is not just the bad economy muting my urge to shop—a little over a year ago, I lost my only son, Josh. I am told religious Jews observe a year of mourning, avoiding all public events. I'm not Jewish, but this year I've found solitude and the ritual of wearing black comforting. However, as a fifty-six-year-old, single, self-employed woman with a mortgage and bills to pay, when a client offered me a job, I took it.

The dressing gene skipped a generation in my WASP family. My mother and son always looked effortlessly pulled together. My son Josh used to look me up and down before we went anywhere, sighing, "Mom, just look down—if you see socks, go change." I always look like I just walked across one of those old-fashioned funhouse air vents. Luckily, my friend Sally Ann has great taste and gives me her castoffs. Pant length is still a problem. I am about three inches taller than she is. Before, when I worked for myself, I could leave meetings before it registered that my pants were too short.

Now I need five viable ensembles a week, and it can't be the same five week after week. I am one of two white women in the Brooklyn office. My Black colleagues are dauntingly elegant and discuss sample sales the way I imagine seasoned hunters track their prey's scent. The standing compliment is, "You better hold on to that—I have my eye on it." My white colleague and I surreptitiously check each other each morning, tucking in flyaway labels and straightening seams. It's an uphill struggle.

I checked the three thrift stores in my neighborhood, thinking I would extend my Sally Ann Hard line with some more black pants, scarves, and earrings, and maybe a "signature" jacket or two. When it didn't matter, I always found things that could pass office muster. In New York City, everyone wears black, no matter what the season. Now that I care, everyone is looking for affordable options. East Village thrift stores are starkly picked over, leaving hoochie mama tops with dangling sequins, spandex slacks explicitly forbidden in our HR manual, and flowery dresses with shoulder pads so extreme they should come with a complimentary set of Tammy Faye eyelashes.

It's not just the procurement, it's the upkeep. The suiting-up for work is relentless. I used to stroll to the bodega in the morning dark for coffee, leisurely watching my neighborhood come alive, listening to the birds on the rooftops. Getting up early is not my problem. It's what gets done with those first precious, sparkling hours of the day. Day in, day out now: laundry and dry cleaning, button-sewing, sock-finding, shoe polishing—a seemingly endless string of things that must match—and all that before I even get into makeup, nails, and hair.

Returning to work now feels like the occupational rehabilitation I imagine they offer at adult daycare centers, stringing macaroni necklaces or moving beads between Dixie cups. Given the current economy, I am fervently grateful to have a job. I am becoming a folk hero among friends who still work from home. Jan sent me an email the first weekend after I started, "You SO deserve it, you daily-commuting-salaried-employee-warrior you!"

I just have to remember how I used to fit life into the margins around a job. Getting ready Monday through Friday gives me some foothold within this "new normal," while I sweep my scattered life into different shapes, waiting for that jolt of recognition signaling what comes next. Besides, the new commute gives me time to take mental notes about what people are wearing.

Generation Sex

Being single on Valentine's Day as a middle-aged woman used to make me sad. One year I was checking into a hotel and the twenty-something clerk cocked her pretty head and said, "Just one key? It's Valentine's Day!" Our eyes locked. "I know," I said, quietly sliding the key card across the desk and slinking back to my room defeated.

I'm not sure when it shifted, but I've started planning to celebrate the lovers' holiday as a festive day of unexplored possibility: I'll try on clothes I wouldn't normally wear, torch-sing into my hairbrush to new music, fix broken things in my apartment, and write gratitude lists of the life gifts received from past relationships.

But there is one new frontier I won't be crossing, although I haven't yet decided how to tactfully decline. My son's childhood friend Corey sent me an "event announcement" on Facebook inviting me to a "Girls' Night In." The "Passion Party" apparently "presents tasteful and informative presentations, featuring lotions, lingerie, and adult toys that are purchased in a confidential setting."

I need to back up here to say that all contact and invitations from my son's friends are especially precious to me because, two years ago, at twenty-nine, my son Josh died of an accidental overdose. We held a memorial in New Durham, the small New Hampshire town where he grew up, and I was overwhelmed by how many friends showed up—many of whom he hadn't seen in a decade. Josh played Peter Pan in fourth grade and Captain Hook, Wendy, and a string of Lost Boys, now grown up with children of their own, all took me aside to tell me how much they would miss him.

Facebook facilitates our staying connected. Girls I didn't know existed tell me about their enduring crushes on him. His friends regularly post new pictures from high school and tell me when they dream of him. Some of these relationships are taking root beyond condolence and the connection to Josh. I am flooded with Farmville gifts and photographs of toddlers, new cars, and first houses, and delighted to be invited so open-heartedly into their daily lives.

At Christmas, Corey had written on Facebook how worried she was about money with two kids and a recently laid-off boyfriend. She alluded to a new business venture. She is now a "Passion Consultant," with a hostess party franchise "enhancing the sexual relationships of our clients with sensual products designed to promote intimacy and communication between couples."

Product parties are big in rural areas where jobs are now fewer than ever. Several women I've known piece together a financial existence from Tupperware and Pampered Chef parties. Although I'm not generally a big fan, I've driven through snowstorms to attend just for that glimmer of human warmth, during the long winters when the video store shelves are empty and plumbers are working twelve hours a day to unfreeze pipes. For once, I'm glad I'm not living in New Durham now—I know Corey's sunny energy. She'd drive over to invite me personally and I wouldn't know what to do with my face.

I like to think that I was a "sex positive" parent, not stigmatizing sex, willing to discuss intimacy and safety comfortably. I am flattered that she feels so at ease with me, but a quick scan of the guest list shows that I am the only mother invited who is over fifty. The habit of thinking of myself as a grown-up and them as kids dies hard.

"Why me? " I ask my college roommate over the phone.

"You still got it!" she suggests, but I can hear her stifling a chortle.

Wanting to help Corey out, I perused her online catalog at Christmas and decided I could safely order some gold dusting powder. Then I noticed it was flavored. Call me old-fashioned, I just don't want Corey to have a visual in her memory banks of me being licked. I'm not a prude—although, come to think about it, the one time I went into a sex shop, I wished I could spontaneously combust when a young man my son's age asked me if I needed help. I just can't get my mind around being assisted on "a personal journey of sensual discovery" by somebody whose coat I used to zip up.

I want to encourage Corey in her endeavors, but I break out in a sweat thinking about games with "dirty dice" with the girls who used to skulk across my living room barely making eye contact, who are now married to the boys who used to take my car for joyrides and return it "secretly" with the grill packed with mud. I think I'll send regrets and just visit the next time I'm home. Maybe I'll bring a batch of cookies, just to remind us both of who is who and what is what.

Pandemic Day

When the bakery where I work closed, I was relieved. I miss my weekly hit of comradely cooking and laughing with young people. But so many of our regulars are older and more vulnerable to the virus, and I feel that cooking in the close quarters of the bakery is like making pizza in a petri dish. The owner is itching to reopen. I know I'll have a job when she does. I still have work from New York that I can do online. This remote work also keeps me connected to the city I love even as the spreading pandemic turns its epicenter darker and darker.

I feel like a quarantine underachiever. I have not done a jigsaw puzzle, made masks, baked bread, or learned a language. I have enough to eat, a working vehicle, secure housing, stable income, and health insurance. I live with someone I can touch, who I love and even still like after three months relatively confined to a small apartment.

Even without the pandemic, being married this time around has been like a geriatric do-over of kindergarten: art time, music time, naptime, snack time, little field trips. We've established some daily rituals: I write as soon as I get up, have coffee with my husband when he wakes (which is earlier and earlier). We do *qi gong* with Mimi, a YouTube instructor we like. Sometimes I walk around the mill pond. On Mondays, I Zoom into my old AA group in New York. My husband Russ suits up to go downstairs to get the mail, usually reporting back on the neighbors. "Judy is having coffee at the picnic table." "I think there's a leak in the basement." "Is that guy at the end of the hall Frank or Bob?" "Angela wants a ride to Market Basket." So far, our senior housing home is intact. Nobody got sick.

We each call friends daily. This is a time when having nothing of interest to report is a good thing. I love sleeping now even more than the too-fat food I can't seem to stop making.

The *PBS NewsHour* reminds us at the end of our day that a disaster rages outside our comfortable life. My husband doesn't care about politics and rarely swears. But the pandemic has changed that too; as we watch the news, he whispers, "What an asshole." I have a crush on all the newscasters, love seeing their pets. I am worried but also a little relieved that Judy Woodruff seems crankier.

The news brings home the fact that I can't do anything about the pandemic out there that affects the world, my country, my friends. Knowing that the disaster could leak into our lives at any minute, I can only tinker away at doing small things: cook, connect, contribute what I can, create something daily. Every passing day, things seem more precious, more fragile. If we make it through, we will have made a habit of delighting in the small moments, leaning into any instance of reprieve, recognizing each opportunity for engagement, and feeling deep gratitude for human connection. I will take these habits into whatever comes next.

Mary Duquette

And That Divine Eye

Novels are tricky to excerpt. Sometimes readers need to get fifty or more pages into one before they figure out, well, how to read it. What we needed for this anthology was a novel that established its world quickly, with compelling characters who had a lot at stake from the get-go. Mary Duquette's And That Divine Eye *whirls into being. Yup, it begins with a tornado. Georgia remembers (or maybe she doesn't) being taken by a tornado as an infant, and surviving, physically unharmed but orphaned. This girl (!), now aged fifteen, doesn't speak, but how she sees the world and navigates it is a revelation. Set in 1967 in coastal New Hampshire, it seemed to me this taste of Duquette's yet-to-be-published debut novel was a perfect fit. R.R.*

Chapter One

July 15, 1967
Dear Violet,
This is what I remember:
    1. The gray field.
    2. The wind.
    3. The rain.
    4. The river.
    5. Nothing at all.

Here's the thing. The clincher. I may or may not remember any of it. Maybe it's just a dream I had, a hazy wish, fingers crossed in the middle of the night, whispering words on a shooting star. A longing to be exceptional. Maybe I just pretend I remember. Okay, I was only a baby. It's a long shot.

So, what I imagine happened is this: The wind pelted the earth with rain and marble-sized hail. It skittered across my face like a caress. The rain—first a sprinkle, then a torrent, then a drizzling spit, adhered to my skin in a glaze, the soak of it in my pores creating a union, breathing into me and making me the essence of it so that any kind of aggression would have been almost cannibalistic.

Of course, I was too young to contemplate such a thing, too soft to retain it. But the grass held me, and the wind rocked me, and I was saved. Not in any religiousy kind of way. God wasn't involved in this one at all. If there is a God in all this. You could say I was reclaimed. Somebody standing over me saw the whole thing. Or, hearing my cries, wandered over. Or maybe it was a group of them, rescuers in their shells, protective suits and helmets floating around on their bodies like hermit crabs—moving sideways to get a look at this little wet bulb of a baby, this aberration. Picked me up and carried me to wherever home was. I don't know where home was. You see, I don't remember.

I didn't want to leave, though. That much I'm sure of. I was taken with the earthy flora and the fallen light and the green sky and the tornado that lifted me and set me so gently down. A silent symphony. It was buried in me by that time. Already sucked inside, a creature inhabiting a creature, part of my breath and my blood. I wanted to ride that tornado again and again. To be forever linked to it and up in the air and spinning around. They say I was lucky to be alive. Lucky, although I don't know if luck had anything to do with it. Lucky that it lifted me up and transported me for miles. They say I was carried over the Mississippi River and into that field, where it lay me as tender as a mother laying down her baby in a crib. Like that. Of course, I have to reiterate that I don't remember.

It's with me still, somewhere. Whipping like a cascade, like one of those things at the fair. What are they called, Violet? The Funnel Rocket. You get in one of those and you feel like you're being shot all the way to the moon. For a quarter you can spread your pseudo-wings and fly like the most complicated bird in the world, or at least go a few feet in the air while stuffed into this electronic device that turns and twists as you rise. They had it at the Spring Harvest Fair last year—the one in North Comstock. I sat in that thing and closed my eyes and imagined I was in the tornado. When it was over, I acted dumb, like I didn't know my ass from my elbow, and clamped down in the seat. They couldn't get me out of it, no matter what they did. They didn't dare touch me. They probably thought I was contagious, like they'd catch whatever I had. The dreaded nonspeaking-weirdo disease. I sat without moving and I heard them talking.

"Get her the hell out of there."

"She's dumb. I don't even think she understands what we're saying."

"Don't call her that. Christ, she's just a kid."

"I'm not calling her anything. She can't talk. She's that O'Shea girl—the one what lives past the Eldridge place, down across Bainbridge. She's honestly dumb. As in the dictionary definition."

I heard them pause. They were looking at me, I'm sure of it. One thing you can always count on is people treating you a little softer once they believe you're a halfwit with nothing but seventy-five cents and a licorice whip in your pocket.

They stood around like seagulls on the beach waiting for someone to leave behind their potato chip bag, wondering if they should move me. I pressed my eyes closed tighter, so the lights from the arcades flickered behind my eyelids and disappeared. I could sense them there—they didn't know what to do with me and it drove them crazy.

"Leave her on," I heard one of them say. "Let her have one more ride."

The moon's shifted, just now, and something's different about the air. The storm is getting nearer, as certain as the sound of Louise the goat braying like a small, tufted madwoman, running in circles in the yard until someone strokes her wiry back and says, "There, there." I can feel it coming from the ocean, in my marrow, cataclysmic, egging me on to jump out and join it. My fingers tingle and I wiggle them like I'm playing some unseen piano. I'm sure there'll be hail the size of small chipmunks and Bridger will put down her paintbrushes and scream at Joey in her British accent to *go the hell outside and get her she'll die out there why does she have to do this every single time she's going to drive me insane one of these days I'll be in the nuthouse I swear.* And Joey will plod out in his hat and his big boots and look for me in the tall grass, but I'll be behind the barn, reaching my arms up as far as I can, wanting to be spirited away like before so I can fly—really soar, as if I have no reason to be stuck on earth. I'll wait on the edge of the wind for the storm to transport me, lie down on the grass with whipping dirt flying in my eyes and hair, until Joey comes and lifts me up in his arms, his careful eyes troubled, and so kind that I am almost sorry for being the child of the tornado—sorry that he is compelled to find me and carry me back inside again.

Joey

"Where is she?" Joey murmured as he brushed past Bridger toward the cupboard for a glass. He filled the glass with water from the faucet and took a long sip.

Bridger filled the coffee pot with water and took out the cream and sugar and two mugs. "I don't know," she said. "In the back? Amongst the trees? Over to the marsh? She's been spending a lot of time there, I reckon."

"By herself?"

"Yes, by herself."

"You sure?"

"Damn it—aye, I'm sure." Bridger's British accent became stronger the angrier she got. "Why, you think she's meeting someone back there? You think she's got some secret society back there?

Subversive meetings and the like? You think she's in a witch circle, maybe got some kind of anti-government, hippy thing going on? You think she's meeting with hippies back there?"

"Or a boy."

Bridger turned crimson. "Listen here, Joey O'Shea," she said slowly. "Don't you ever say nothing like that again."

"My saying it isn't making it true. But don't you think it's possible?"

Bridger looked out at the yard from the kitchen window and sniffed. "No," she said. "I don't."

Joey found Georgia past the inlet by the marsh, near a small clearing. She sat on a tree stump, the one he cut down last year because of Dutch elm. Her head was tilted slightly, her face caught in the sunlight, the angle of her chin, the light on her face. And she laughed—not aloud, but silently, as she did—a hand to her mouth.

She turned, seeing him. A finger moved to her lips, and she went back to whatever she was watching beyond the trees in the clearing below.

He looked where she was looking. A boy about her age walked the perimeter of the clearing. He was singing. He held a stick in one hand. His eyes were closed. He sang a song Joey was unfamiliar with, one of the popular ones—maybe the Mockingbirds or Jon Carter. He had a good voice. It was sultry. Georgia smiled, her fingertips still resting on her lips, as if to remind him to be quiet and to contain her laughter. Her eyes rested steadily on his face as if trying to make sense of the tiers of emotions that rose in him as he looked back at her—confusion, happiness, fear, admiration. Pride. She questioned him with her eyes, expert at the art of nonverbal communication as she was. She couldn't help it, her expression said back to his. She was a girl who wanted to watch a boy sing. All she desired in that moment stood crooning in that clearing, and Joey wouldn't stop her.

"Georgia?" Bridger emerged from the path, her feet crushing the moss and forget-me-nots. "What's going on? It's time to come home."

Georgia made motions with her hands, her finger at her lips in a plea of silence. She shook her head, holding her hand up toward Bridger as if she were erasing her, her face flickered off like a light switch. She turned again toward the boy in the clearing, who had stopped and was listening, stick hovering in the air.

"What in hell..." Bridger penetrated the brush and pulled back a branch of a young oak. "Hey!" she called. "What are you doing? Get out of here!"

The boy scrambled for his backpack, which was lying on the ground, and bolted away in the opposite direction, past the abandoned canoe and into the woods heading toward the Old North Road entrance, the bottoms of his shoes streaking the dark moss, the stick dropped near the base of a Canadian birch.

Georgia rose from the trunk. Her face was closed, but the tips of her ears were pink. She strode past them, pushing through Bridger's arms, shoving into them harder than necessary. Bridger fell back and watched her go and shrugged.

"She'll understand, one day," she said.

"Understand what?"

"She's better off."

"She needs to expand her horizons."

"To hell with horizons. She'll do to just stay in the yard. We can fix it up better. Get rid of the tiles, clean up the garden."

"You're not hearing me." Joey bent down and picked up a piece of moss that was stumped away from the rest. "She needs friends," he said, weaving the moss through his fingers. "Other kids. Socialization. I'm sure you've heard of it. Maybe school."

"No. I been schooling her since she came to us. She's fine. There's not a reason to—"

"Yes," Joey said. "There is a reason. You saw the way she looked at that boy. She has to feel what that's like. To be with other kids. To have friends. Even boyfriends."

Bridger crossed her arms. "What are you saying?"

"I'm saying," he said, "that this is a letting-go time. For us. A time for her to expand into herself. Don't you get that?"

Bridger stared at the ground. "She can expand into herself," she said. "But she'll do it here. At home. Plenty of room for expansion, and at no price." She kicked at the dirt and turned from him, walking back down the path toward home.

He held the moss loosely in his grip and threw it away into the leaves. He knew Bridger would resist the thought of Georgia going to school. It was an inevitability, but Bridger wasn't hearing it. She was like her mother, fearless on the outside, terrified inside—stubborn, and with a firm idea of what she wanted and what she didn't. But she would never admit it. She was either hopelessly unaware of herself or in a constant state of denial, possibly both.

He studied the part of the wood where the boy ran off, and thought of Georgia and her need to immerse herself in a normal life. She needed to feel what it meant to have a regular schedule and to rise every day with the security of knowing what was going to happen. As it was, she was too wild—like an animal—she needed more stability. She needed normalcy. And Bridger wasn't helping.

Bridger's opinion of Georgia was resolute. "Georgia's not an idiot," Bridger said on the phone to whomever she happened to be speaking. "But I have to say, she's not quite there. She's fine, but she's not there." Joey disagreed. He thought Georgia was more present than anyone else he ever knew. She was more than present—she was omnipresent. And that might have been the thing that she clung to, the reason for her withdrawal, her only salvation in that quiet world of hers. It may have been all too much for Georgia, the world. But she had to learn how to navigate it. That was his job. To make sure she could be a part of the world without hesitancy or reservation. This complicated world—more gray than black and white.

Joey picked up a stick and threw it toward the clearing. It landed in a bush and hung there, balancing in the thick bulk of branches. He gazed at the path where the boy escaped and glanced once toward the Old North Road path and turned, heading back toward the house. He thought he ought to check and make sure the faucet was quiet and leak-less, ought to patch up the hole that Louise had made with the butt of her horns and see if Bridger needed any help with breakfast while Georgia sat on the front steps in her usual spot, facing the yard with an intensity that made Joey want to look himself, to stop and stare where she stared, as if there were something he might miss.

Bridger

"So, I'm packing up and he's there, home from work, and he says, 'Let's goooo,' real loud-like, the way he does when he's ready to get on somewhere, and I say, 'Look, I'm not ready,' and he says, 'Why not?' and I say, 'Because I'm still laundering and doing all the other things I have to do,' and he says, 'Of course, I'm kidding, you know,' and I say, 'No, you're not,' and he says, 'What do you mean? Of course I am,' and I say, 'Listen, you can't come sauntering along home and tell me we have to go this instant when I been running around like a crazy person trying to get everything together and whatnot, and bloody packing and picking up after all you lot,' and he says, 'Well, now it's getting late because we've been talking about it this whole entire time and now it really is time to go, isn't it?' and I say, 'Go along without me,' and he says, 'What do you mean?' and I say, 'You heard me—go without me, and I mean it. I'll stay home.' And he says, 'I can't go along without you. Who will look after Georgia?' and I say, 'Oh, so that's all I am, is it? Just a child-watcher is what I am, no more,' and he says, 'No, no, that's not what I meant,' and I say, 'Sure it is, it's exactly what you meant. It's not, oh, but I'd miss you, Bridger, or oh, it wouldn't be as fun without you, Bridger—it's, who would watch Georgia?' And he says, 'For God's sake,' and leaves to go clean out the car. And I think about it as I'm making up the beds and realize, yeah—that's just what I am. He's said it, and it's the truth. I'm a bloody child-watcher and not nothing else. What else do I do? Launder. And cook. And now he's on about sending her to school with no regard for what it might be like for her."

Bridger took a breath and switched the phone to her other ear. She realized she had been talking for at least five minutes without pause (she checked the time and thought it was five, maybe even six minutes) and wondered if Francine had hung up on her. But there was breathing on the other end, so Francine was, indeed, there, and apparently alive.

"Francine?" she said tentatively, winding the phone cord around her finger like a long strip of hair.

"Yes."

"Well?"

"Well. What do you mean?"

"What do you mean, what do I mean?"

Francine was silent some more, and Bridger thought about hanging up on her and getting on with her painting. She had started a new one that morning, a landscape of the beach during a hurricane, with thoughts of Georgia. It was unsatisfying to have an obtuse neighbor who wouldn't even give you the dignity of calling around every once in a while, let alone responding when you asked a simple question, such as did she think Joey was being frustrating.

"So, what do you think?" Bridger prompted. "I mean, about Georgia's schooling. And Joey."

"What do you want me to say? That he's no good? That he needs to pay you more attention, do more around the house, stop pushing you to get packed when you go away together? Honestly, Bridger, he doesn't drink or run around, does he? He works every day and is home every night and is kind to Georgia. He takes you on trips. What more can you want?"

Bridger stared at the floor. "It's not more I want in that respect, see," she said. "I just need a bit of understanding. It's the understanding I'm not getting. The devil with trips if there's no understanding. See?"

"Bridger, I have to go. I have to get ready for the Grange ladies and the SMILES group. They'll be here at ten with dumplings." SMILES was short for Sundrops Mission in the Lord's Eternal Sanctification.

"Just a bit longer?"

"Sorry."

Francine rang off, and Bridger was left holding the receiver. She placed it gently back on its cradle against the wall, wondering when they would join the twentieth century and get a regular phone with a dial, rather than a hand-cranked one. She leaned on the kitchen counter, realizing she was pathetic, begging Francine to stay on the phone with her like she had nothing better to do than complain about her husband to obviously uninterested parties. She supposed that Francine would tell the Grange ladies and SMILES about her as they immersed themselves in dumplings, and they would smirk behind their dumpling-stained hands at the transplanted Brit who could talk a person's ear off, really. Time was a commodity that Bridger knew Francine could wrestle to her own liking. Nothing else to do but what she wished. This was how Bridger knew that Francine really didn't want to listen anymore. Francine didn't have many obligations—she had nothing but time. Her children were all in school. And she chose to leave Bridger out of her well-constructed morning.

Bridger looked out the window at the yard. The roof tiles became a part of the landscape of the garden and shone like small diamond-studded rectangles in the sun. She thought that she really ought to have gone out and removed them. At least they'd be out of sight, although she was used to them. And Georgia liked to use them for stepping on. She spent countless minutes jumping from one tile to the other.

In truth, Bridger was surprised when Joey suggested the trip to Boston. Boston wasn't all that far, and she knew it wouldn't cost them much. And they had been going on more trips lately, with Georgia being older and more easily transportable and able to be by herself more. Still, the fact that it had been Joey's idea to go was unexpected. He typically kept his money balled in his fist. It irritated her, his propensity for stashing. He was meticulous, hiding pennies away, carping about money like it was a jewel to be contained rather than a resource to be exploited.

And now Joey brought up the subject of Georgia attending school, and she was afraid that he couldn't understand why that was so frightening to her. Georgia, although intelligent, was strictly book-smart and knew nothing about the social aspects of school, which was so important, almost more so than academics. Extracurriculars, games, clubs, cliques, dances, and boys. She couldn't imagine Georgia alone in the middle of that. She was terrified for her.

She stood in silence, contemplating the idea of Georgia going to a regular school, riding the bus, eating lunch on a tray, joining the yearbook committee and the equestrian team. She just couldn't see it. She looked over at the half-painted canvas and picked up a brush, absently touching it with some Prussian blue. She added it to the canvas.

She didn't know why it was that Georgia always seemed so young, perpetually small. She even had her period now, for God's sake. Bridger's talk with Georgia about becoming a woman had been stilted and half-ridiculous, as if Georgia could honestly comprehend a word she was saying. She knew Georgia understood her words, but doubted she really got it—the implications of such a thing. She was able to get pregnant—she could be a mother. Have sex with a boy. The last thought horrified Bridger, and her impulse was to hide Georgia away until she had a better grasp on it—until her mind caught up with her body in its maturity. But that was impossible. Georgia would not be contained. She made that quite clear, completely without words.

She knew Georgia's lack of experience and common sense was partially her fault. Her freedom was her one nonverbal request, and Bridger tried to allow it although it made her sick to her bones. Georgia was an anomaly. She was both self-possessed and naïve, independent and reckless. A child, but not. A young woman, but only a girl. Stubborn and unwieldy and perfectly quiet. Georgia's eyes contained such mysteries, Bridger was often obliged to sit and talk until she was hoarse just to fill in the gaps, waiting like madness for a response so she could at last understand what it was Georgia wanted—what her core was.

And now, both Georgia and Joey felt a million miles away and Bridger thought she might be losing them both and she felt small and insignificant in her old bathrobe and slippers, clinging to a need to be understood. And neither of them understood her. And because of this, she might lose them.

She surveyed the work on the canvas and put down the brush. As usual, painting helped her think and sort things out in her head. She held onto the brush as if it was her lifeline, the secret to her resilience, the conduit to her world. In actuality, it was.

Chapter Two

July 29, 1967
Dear Violet,
They thought I couldn't hear them, but I could.

"I read she was the only one left."

"Who's that?"

"Georgia. I remember reading the articles about how the tornado lifted her up and how they found her two days later in that field. Two days! How can that be? How did she survive? Quite the miracle."

There was a pause, and I imagined Bridger's face, blank stare, maybe reddened. I imagined her shifting around in her chair and pulling at the ends of her hair like she does when she's nervous. "I..." she started. But didn't finish. She must have been upset if she couldn't find the words.

"I mean, how can someone survive something like that? Especially a baby. I just can't get over it."

"You're going to have to." Bridger's voice softened, her tone even—like it is when she's really peeved. Bridger's funny that way. She seems irritated when she's actually happy, calm when she's angry.

"And the rest of her family—gone." The guidance counselor had an accent—what kind, I couldn't detect. She went on as if she didn't hear anything. She didn't know about Bridger's incongruity. "They all perished. Didn't they? I think that's what I read."

"They did."

"All of them?"

Joey cleared his throat. "My sister, Violet," he said, his voice murky from a whole lot of not talking. "And her family."

"Oh. I...I'm sorry."

"Just her, and her two kids," Bridger said. "Her husband was already gone. All dead but Georgia."

"I'm sorry. I shouldn't have pushed."

"They say the rain sustained her. She drank the rain," Joey said, so quiet I could barely hear him.

"I'm so sorry. I didn't mean to pry. I didn't know."

"Now you know." Bridger squeezed the words out like butter. From the sound of it, she was furious.

"Yes." The screech of a window being opened. "It's getting warm in here," the guidance counselor said. "Mind if this is open?"

"No," Joey said. "Now, can we get back to it, please?"

"Of course. I know you have concerns about Georgia attending our school. But you don't have to worry. She'll be fine. We have lots of kids with handicaps. Lots of slower kids who need a little extra help. We're capable of handling almost anyone."

"Georgia's not handicapped," Joey said. "She's as smart as anyone else. Way smarter."

I imagined the guidance counselor working this one out. Wrapping her mind around it. "I'm sure," the guidance counselor said slowly, "that she's very bright, but…well, we'll need to do some tests. You say she can hear, is that right?"

I assumed somebody nodded because the guidance counselor continued like she had her answer. "Well, as I said, we'll be able to conduct a series of tests."

"What kind of tests?" Bridger's voice was so mellow and sweet, I was surprised she wasn't busy knocking things around in there. Breaking knickknacks. Throwing drawers open. Tearing curtains from the rods with her teeth.

"Just the standard tests we use to see where a child might fit. We'll need to get an idea of her grade level."

"I don't think you'll need to do that. Georgia is right where she needs to be. She's been schooled by me. I taught her everything she knows, which is quite a lot. I can tell she knows a lot because she's always reading, sometimes until late at night—past ten o'clock sometimes, and she'll just stay up until two o'clock sometimes, sometimes later. Sometimes, I come downstairs in the morning and she's sleeping with her head on the table and a book open in front of her. That's Georgia. She's a reader. And I know she can do multiplication and the like because lots of times she helps me in the kitchen, and I can tell she's dividing and adding and measuring. So, you see, she is well caught up in all she needs to be caught up in. There's no reason for testing. Just put her in where the others are, in her age group. She'll be fine."

Bridger stopped her relentless soliloquy. I could hear them all breathing in there. There was a breath-break. Which was fine with me because I was sick of the talk. All they did was go around in circles, with me at the center, and no one bothered to give a crap whether I had a say in the matter. They didn't even bother to include me in the frigging room, which was just perfect—the perfect example of how little they saw the need for me to orchestrate my own life.

"Mrs. O'Shea," the guidance counselor said. I thought her name might be Zelda. Anyway, that's what I decided to call her. "Where are you from?" Zelda asked. "England, isn't it?"

I winced at this and shifted uncomfortably in my seat. It was a kind of seat for two, a love seat, with red leather-like cushions and silver studs. I don't know if it was actual leather. Probably not, considering we are in semi-rural, coastal New Hampshire where extravagance is rejected and is the work of the devil. You know, those Puritans. So, it's leather-look all the way.

"Yes," Bridger said very slowly, drawing the word out of her mouth like a long, stiff question mark. "What's your point?"

Zelda laughed. "Well," she said, "I don't mean to offend you. But in America, we do things differently." I imagined Zelda leaning forward, trying for familiarity, comradery. "We have tests that we must carry out. It's mandated. By our bylaws. Don't worry. If what you say is true, Georgia will pass with flying colors."

There was more breathing in there. I became fixated on the little phrase Zelda coined: by our bylaws. It almost sounded like it should have been a song. A jingle. "By our bylaws," if said quickly and with enough resonance, could be the name of a very important politician. I would vote for him.

"I've been in America for twenty years," Bridger informed her. "Twenty. Not counting the years I spent visiting friends in Canada and going to university there and the like. You don't need to tell me about being American. I know all about being an American.

And pardon my saying so, but you got an accent, if I'm not mistaken. I'm assuming that means you haven't been here all that long yourself, unless I happen to be hearing incorrectly. Which I doubt."

"I apologize if I've offended you, Mrs. O'Shea. I just didn't know if you understood the bylaws. And, by the way," Zelda went on, her voice lowering, "I meant to ask you before. Have you tried sign language? Why doesn't she know sign language?"

More silence. Since they didn't answer, I wished I could tell her why. That sign language would mean I would have to reason with the world, to be accountable and beholden to it. That sign language would force closed the gap between me and other people and would give me no excuse for those little quirks that Joey and Bridger have come to accept in me. I realize the irony. That if I did know sign language, I could have told her what I feel. Which might go either way. I could have told her that I don't want to be answerable, that I hate being obliged to the human race, that I don't want to be a part of it, that I don't even consider myself human, sometimes. That, in a way, I am terrified to be a part of this world, with all its imperfections and limitations.

I heard the sound of a chair scraping across the floor. "Let's bring her in," Joey said. "It's time. Why not?" The door swung open and I was besieged by the three of them looking at me, Joey standing like a game show host, Bridger sitting with ankles crossed and an enormous grin on her face, Zelda behind a hulking desk. It was worse than I'd suspected.

Zelda turned out to be a younger woman with long, dark hair pulled back into a tight ponytail who wasn't half bad on the eyes. In fact, you could probably have called her kind of gorgeous. She smiled a lot at me, and I sat on the leather-look gazing back at them with the most idiotic expression I could muster.

"Come on, Georgia," Zelda said, like I was a little dog. I obediently stood and squeezed through the door. There was hardly any room in there, so I tried to fit myself into the corner until Joey jerked his head toward the chair he'd abandoned, and so I sank into it with as much grace as possible. Which wasn't all that much. You remember, Violet, about my awkward limbs.

"Hi Georgia," Zelda said. The nameplate on her desk said Julia Kalahashi.

"I'm sorry it took us so long to bring you in," Zelda went on. "We've been talking about your introduction to our little school. I think you'll love it here. Please call me Ms. Kalahashi. Or if that's too hard to remember, you can call me Ms. K." Her smile was as true as the ocean.

I tried to smile back at her. Just the right corner of my mouth moved, a stiff upward turn.

"'Ms.?'" Bridger was once again zealously focused on Zelda and her erroneous choices. "You one of them feminists?"

Zelda laughed in a way that you might have called breezy. "I'm not sure I'd describe myself as a feminist, Mrs. O'Shea. I don't really believe in labels. But, yes, I do believe in equal rights. For everyone. Don't you?"

"No," Bridger said pleasantly. "I do not."

"I think we need to decide about this test," Joey said. "When does she have to take it?"

"She's not taking any test." Bridger's tone was melodious. She was smiling so hard I thought her face was going to break.

"Actually, there's a battery of tests," Zelda said. She began to stack the papers on her desk, patting the edges until they were neatly aligned. "She can begin to take them as early as next week, if you'd like. We usually recommend no more than two at a time, to keep the child from becoming overwhelmed. I think Georgia will do fine."

"A battery? What?" Bridger's state of sweet fury was temporarily trumped by a need to understand what the hell was going on.

"It just means a bunch of tests," Joey said. "A set. Isn't that right, Mrs. Kalahashi?"

"Ms. Kalahashi," Zelda said. "And yes. That's right."

"Ms.," Bridger said to no one in particular. "Battery."

"Mr. and Mrs. O'Shea." Zelda swept her arms across the desk. "Could I talk to Georgia privately? I'd love a moment to get to know her a little better."

"Certainly not." Bridger grinned maniacally.

"Of course," Joey said. He took her arm. "Come on, Bridger. Let's go see the trophies. There's a case in the hall."

"What? No!"

"It would be so very helpful," Zelda said. "Please." Her beautiful face was pleading. She was Helen of Troy. No one could have denied her anything.

"I've no interest in trophies." Bridger crossed her arms. I pictured Joey picking up the chair and carrying her out in it like she was a Chinese empress in her litter. But, after a moment, she got up and left the little office room as if it had been her idea all along. She turned at the door. "Coming?"

Joey followed her and they wound into the hall, out of sight. Zelda got up and shut the door.

I felt like the room was closing in and I was afraid I'd fall onto the floor in convulsions like one of those ladies Freud treated, the ones with those monstrous episodes of hysterics. Although that was probably just because they were overly-corseted and lacked oxygen.

"How are you, Georgia?" Zelda placed her hands on the stack of papers she had so methodically organized. "I'm glad you're here. Now, how old are you again? Fifteen?"

I nodded.

"It must be quite nerve-wracking thinking about starting in a new school, but I don't want you to worry. You'll do well, I'm sure of it."

I didn't know how she could be so sure of that, but I didn't react.

"You know, I don't know how to say this, but the moment I saw you, I felt as if there was something about you—something special, I guess you could say. Is there? Is there something special about you, Georgia? Something extraordinary?"

I just sat there, not certain what she wanted from me. I don't know if I'm extraordinary. I don't know if I'm a shitload of magic stardust shooting its way to Neptune's outer galaxy, or Susie Shmoe from Plainville, USA, getting knocked up in the back of a Chevy station wagon and working as a cashier at the local Shop N' Stay. Or maybe, Violet. Maybe, I'm both. I tried to come up with a response when she threw another thought at me.

"So, I wonder. How can I get you to communicate? What do you do at home when you want to tell your mother something? I mean, your aunt. Do you have your own unique way to talk to her? Do you write things down?"

I nodded. I write all the time, in a journal (of course), and sometimes I use pen and paper if I want bacon instead of liver or want to listen to Bach instead of Beethoven or whatever I want to tell Bridger. Bridger pretty much lets me dictate whatever I want to eat or do. I usually go for ice cream, but lately it gives me pimples, so I've stopped eating that so much. Being a teenager now, I have to look out for things like pimples. It's a pain in the ass.

"Can you write something down for me now? Anything? I'd love to know how you're feeling. What you think about all this."

I nodded, and she handed me a pad of paper that had been sitting on her desk near the phone. I grabbed the pen she gave me and began to scribble down words. I finished and handed it back to her.

She read it, staring at the paper for a minute or two. She looked at me, her expression indecipherable. "Einstein," she said. "One of my favorites."

I nodded and shrugged. She was sort of making me claustrophobic, and not because the room was small. It was like she wanted a part of my soul, or my firstborn, or something, and I didn't know if I wanted to give it to her.

Bridger bounced in, Joey at her heels. "That's plenty of time," she announced. "What's this?" She picked up the paper on Zelda's desk and read aloud, "Only two things are infinite, the universe and human stupidity, and I'm not sure about the former." She looked around like there was someone else there, hiding behind the drapes or in the closet. "What the hell is that? What does that bloody mean?"

"It means," Zelda said, "that not only is your niece well read but she's deeply profound."

"Well," Bridger said, her smile brilliant. "I already knew that."

Joey

Joey listened for the wind. He strained for the sound of some hint of a hurricane that was slated to pass through. The threat of a storm always left him open-eared and edgy, waiting for the moment that Georgia would bolt. It didn't happen every time. There were nights she didn't wake. But he wasn't certain she was asleep and unaware of the wind. He thought she might be downstairs, at the table with a book—alert and agitated at the possibility of a storm. He couldn't find room in his head for external sounds, the tap of soft slippers on the stairs, a bang of a glass on a tabletop, the droning hum of Bridger's breath as she slept. His thoughts were too jumbled and there wasn't room for anything else. No creaks. No windows banging or tree branches scuffing or barn doors flung open. And Bridger, probably asleep—the only time she would let her body slow to an aching halt. The only instance when she'd will her arms and legs into oblivion, her mind turned off and allowing the rest of her a necessary break from herself.

There was never a moment, in Joey's recollection, when Bridger appeared completely rested in her skin. Joey imagined that even as a child, Bridger faced her share of discomfort. Her very name, Bridger—the outcome of the print on her birth certificate having been smudged into obscurity, the "t" transformed to an "r," her then six-year-old sister, just new at reading and eager to read everything, exclaiming, "Bridger! It's Bridger!"—must have driven her to fits of frustration, having to constantly correct those who insisted it be something else. Her parents, choosing the name "Bridget," found the mistake adorable and oddly hysterical—and it was Bridger from then on. "Not Bridget. Bridger," she sighed on the day she met him, that summer afternoon in Little Bay, the pronouncement of her name shared reluctantly, almost wistfully.

And as he lay awake in their bed, stabilizing his breathing so he wouldn't wake her, he wondered when it was that she had become so inflexible, where the little artist went, what had become of her, that undeniable spirit. Her sophistication, the way she made him feel, like he was her fool and he would do anything for her. She could make him bow to her will or feel like he was the protector. She was complicated, a contradiction. A mystery. And he loved that about her.

But lately, her staunch arm-folding and jaw-clenching when it came to Georgia was frustrating. He wondered why she struggled so hard against him when he only wanted to free Georgia—let her experience, for once, the joy that was childhood, with all that being a child meant. Experimentation. Flight. Falling. Getting up. Failure. Ability. Resistance and submittal. It was human experience that Georgia needed. The chance to be a girl, a teenager, and to figure out what that meant to her. This Bridger, the one who fought against him, who would rather have her niece bound to the house in a sort of imprisonment, confounded him. He didn't know who she was, the emerging Bridger. And he wasn't certain if she'd, at some point, fully replace the Bridger he knew. And if that was the case, he didn't know what he'd do about that.

He stirred, turning slowly so he could catch a glimpse of her in sleep, maybe ascertain something in her face, something soft that would make him forgive her. But her side of the bed was empty, the covers thrown back.

He considered the abandoned side of the bed, his face near the corner of her pillow, and wondered why he imagined he could hear her breathing. The pillowcase smelled like the fruit of her shampoo. He briefly let himself sink into the suggestion of waking alone every morning, every middle-of-the-night, without her. It would be both a relief and a devastation, being without her. He wondered if she ever thought of it—leaving him. Taking her small, worn suitcase she kept under their bed and leaving him for her England, her Dover. Multiple canvases under her arm. Taking Georgia, or not taking Georgia. He pictured what life would be like with only him and

Georgia inhabiting it. How silent it would be—no more of Bridger's prattling, its crescendos and decrescendos, those fluid cadences like patterns on the wall. How a mute home might edge its way into him, make him different—older. Serious, and implosive. Bridger's incessant chatter somehow bound them all together. Sometimes it seemed like she was the only one who had something to say about them all and their existence.

He inhaled her pillow once more before rising and stepping to the door. He crept down the stairs and into the front hallway. The grandfather clock indicated that it was two in the morning, too late for anyone to be up—except maybe Georgia, who seemed to relish the dark hours, transposing the night from rest to investigation, practicing an exploration of this, her narrow world, with her books spread out in front of her in a fan shape.

He found Bridger on the porch, hovering over the floorboards in the swing. Her legs were tucked up underneath her like a child and she was staring at the moon. He sat next to her and his first impulse was to take her hand, to pull her close—but instead, he stayed on his side of the swing.

"It's late," he said.

"Or early. Depending on how you look at it."

"It will be all right," he said, not completely sure what he was referring to.

"That's what you think."

"Yes. It is. I have to think that. What's the alternative?"

"You don't understand me."

"It's not that I don't understand you. I just can't see why you're fighting this thing. Why do you want to keep her home? Don't you think it'd be good for her to explore things in the world? What are you afraid of?" Joey fought to keep his voice from rising. He didn't want to appear angry, or worse, didn't want to anger her. He suspected that, in reality, he didn't understand her any more than he understood any person. That she was just another human, complex and difficult, and that he would do much better if he could go and try to reason with Louise the goat, bleating and stomping around in the barn.

"You think I'm being ridiculous." Bridger ran a hand through her hair and stood, the swing shaking from the sudden motion of her body moving away toward the railing. She walked to the edge of the porch with her back to him, and reaching out her hand, plucked a flower from one of the rhododendron bushes. "You've never been a girl," she said. "You don't know what it means. I'm telling you she'll get hurt. Certainly, these days. Drugs, sex, experimentation with various dangers. And who'll be there to pick up the pieces? You?"

She turned to face him. He saw in her eyes something like terror, but more than that, a resignation. Although she was fighting it, she knew it was going to happen. She had no choice. "Everyone gets hurt," he said. "Everyone. Girls and boys, it doesn't matter. It's life. You can't keep her in a bubble. And don't put your own personal biases in her head."

"I am not putting any personal biases in anyone's head. I'm simply being realistic. You think she's ready to socialize with other kids? You think she'll be sweet and demure, let a boy hold her hand, look down to the ground and show her pretty eyelids whilst some gangly teenager tries to slip his hand under her shirt? You think she'll join the cheer squad? Smile for the crowd? Bare her perfect teeth, the top of the pyramid? You see her walking the halls of school laughing with her friends and wearing miniskirts and pink cardigans and flirting with the boys in the gym and joining the marching band? You see her playing the piccolo?"

"God, Bridger."

"No, listen. You listen. I can't see her in that school, Joey. She's not normal. And there's nothing wrong with that. But she's not. She never will be."

"Who are you to say what normal is?"

"Normal is normal is normal." Bridger's voice rose to high levels, almost a shriek, but it was muffled by a strong surge of wind that drove cloudy dusts of dirt and sand onto the porch floor and blew the petals off the flower in her hand, the sound of ocean waves overtaking the crickets, and Bridger stopped and stared into the black of the side yard and looked at the empty leaves in her grip.

"Jesus, Joey," she said. "Did you know a storm was due?"

"I did—but it's all right. She's inside. She's at the table."

"Are you sure about that?"

"With the big book. I'm sure of it."

"Did you see her?"

"Well. No."

A roll of thunder edged its way from south to north. It was heading through, crawling over the southern grasslands, over Route 1 and into Portsmouth, gaining momentum as it prepared to spring on them. Joey sat in the swing, considering their options. He could lock the doors with the skeleton key, but he wasn't sure that would contain Georgia. Or he could creep in and see if she was sleeping at the table, in which case he could lift her and carry her upstairs. He hadn't done that in a while, but he was certain she wouldn't be too heavy; she was still such a slight girl.

Bridger bolted toward the front door before he could tell her to calm down. She disappeared into the house, and he followed her into the hallway and past the stairs to the kitchen, where the Big Book of Lists was open and dog-eared to page 151, one of Georgia's favorite passages, "Were the Pyramids Built for Extraterrestrial Beings? Twenty Theories of Egyptian Lore." An almost full glass of something pink, probably lemonade, sat next to the book, along with a plate of uneaten macaroons. The record player was making a skipping sound, having stopped and needing to be flipped over, the album cover on the table, the Brandenburg Concertos performed by the Ars Rediviva Ensemble. Bridger swung by him back to the hallway. He could hear her feet pounding on the stairs, and she came back down quieter, like something got sucked out of her. "Hell," she said, shaking her head.

Bill Burtis

Liminal
& Other Poems

This selection from Burtis' book, Liminal, *reveals emotional under-currents envisioned in unique imagery taken from a lifetime of roaming the natural world and familial relationships. From imagining the nature of angels, to night swimming, to Death's footwear, these poems take memory and spin it into pure sunlit wisdom. Looking and listening, they ask us to witness those moments that take place in between consciousness and lost time. From Pushcart-nominated, "Owl": "When the owl leaves the branch, he becomes/ the wind and the soundless dark,/threads the hem of branches with a faith/before knowledge, safe in the space between things."* J.P.

The Nature of Angels

If there were an angel on the stairs
you would not move aside.

An angel on a bicycle
flickers like sunlight on wavelets.

An angel does not remember
where it came from, but longs to return.

The thought running along the edge
of your consciousness is a signal shard

of angel radio. You suppose
you know no angels.

When you have wandered out of the storm,
an angel is leaving.

It is in the nature of angels
not to show their wings.

Children

Standing before a bench
in the small town park,
the man clasps the handle
of a stroller where his son
is about to begin crying.

Ribbons of sunlight cross the damp grass,
snake up the trunks of maples
along the blue, stone-dust paths.
One touches the man's leg
but he cannot move. At night now

he hears things flying
in the woods, tries to answer
but only dreams of falling. If he is lucky,
his skin will rise off him, a shroud
revealing the boy left bargaining in prayer.

The Woodsman

An enchanted forest is an easy place
for a heartless, inedible fellow.
I'd never a care a Brillo bath and a few
shots from an oil can couldn't cure.
Life was simple: see a tree, cut it down.
My evenings were spent rattling around
from stack to stack, counting.

That was before the rain.

Slowly, soundless as time, it grew to mist;
I was already going stiff before I heard
the pattering on my funneled pate
like bees when I've made a bad choice of tree.
By then, it was too late; the can out of reach, the joints
grinding tighter, until that final Pompeiian moment....
You spend a few decades standing
stock-still, with an ax frozen
over your head and it makes you think.

So, by the time the girl showed up,
I was ready. Of course, if I'd known
what life was going to be like afterward,
I might have told her to spare the oil
and leave me thinking. Not to mention
I'd stand in the woods forever
just to miss those monkeys!

But as luck would have it, I got a heart.

Once in the boiler of my tin chest a thought
echoed like a boy shouting in a cistern,
round and round and down and down

until dying in a whisper. Now there's a cauldron
where musings are heated into notions,
whose fumes rise to warp and spin
in the crazy winds of passion. Suddenly
I see things in a long and lovely light, wish
I knew the words to songs, and lie
awake at night, with the anguish of the lover, poised
above, but not quite ready for, a dream.

The Bat Hunter

A bat has eight fingers and loose thumbs.
When you hit a bat,
the wings clench like fists:
three small stones hit the ground at once.
When the bat hunter finds him,
the brittle wings still row with his breathing.

As he kneels to hear this dream of death,
the boy is pure sound in the pale evening sky.
Down the street, a dog howls.
In the hutch, his mother's china
quivers into a corner.

The blind, black eyes shine
like jewels in the velvet skin,
stare down the gleaming, raised barrels
to the eyes of the hunter.

Hard, glistening, man-like eyes.

Swimming Before Sunrise

I pull the moon slowly from her bed
high in the shoreline hemlocks.

The quarrels of the crows continue
variously with worry and accord

all lost to me, on my back, listening
only to the rustle of the water sweeping by.

I swim out past where I can see
the tops of the tallest pines.

Soon the silhouettes of pines on the island
rise against the color blooming in the eastern sky.

The moon is far adrift now; I turn
and with an earnest stroke, drive her slowly back

to nest between the pointed caps of hemlock.
I grasp the cold steel of the ladder and realize

a whole year's turning must pass
before the moon again waits

between these trees at this hour,
a precision unmatched by any human measure.

The loons call, announcing presence
and loss, presence and loss.

Somebody Else's Shoes

for Liam

When I cleaned out the house
where my parents lived for 25 years
I found a pair of Docksiders
on a shelf above the basement stairs.
They looked right, and when I
slipped them on still tied, they fit.

I wondered whose they were
because since I was a child I'd thought
my father's feet were bigger than mine
and my mother's so much smaller—
not to mention she'd have worn
a grass skirt sooner than Docksiders.

I meant to ask. Instead I learned
that things known too long
may not be known at all. I found
Death sleeps with one eye half open, his teeth
resting gently on his lower lip.
He does not walk the streets,

and his shoes are the white of light
seen through the avalanche,
the white the angels use to convince us.
Finally, bending to kiss him, I stop,
lips a breath away, feeling the cold.
None of this is expected.

View from a Third Story Window on a Winter Afternoon

"Sometimes at night I light a lamp so as not to see."
–Antonio Porcia

I am looking over the roofs of Dover,
New Hampshire, listening to the children
on their sleds below the empty trees
on the icy bank of the railway.

It is impossible to decipher the language
they are speaking, the way
the song the orchestra will play
is lost in all its pieces
until the instruments find their tune.

There are things that turn
against us without meaning to.
Look at the fathers.
Listen as their children try to speak.

After the Last Train

In the old ceramic subway hall,
too early or late in the day, never
any weather but the storms
brought in and out by trains,

one now just sifting down
behind the departure
of the last train, the one
the man has missed,

he rocks uncertainly
heel to toe, hands pocketed,
listening, noticing again
the blunt brown smell

of a place so long
without sunlight, full
of used breath and skin dust
and earth filling in.

Here there is, too,
a palpable waiting of souls,
left by so many eyes
peering into the tunnel,

having felt the push of air,
to see the shine on the curving wall,
hear the first faint clicking,
feel the slow thunder in their feet.

But he knows none of that is coming,
sees the next hours same as this one.
After a while, he will turn to the stairs
for solace, for the change and direction they offer.

Owl

When the owl leaves the branch, he becomes
the wind and the soundless dark,
threads the hem of branches with a faith
before knowledge, safe in the space between things.

There is a boy running through hemlocks
faster than he can think, out on the windy edge
where he is only his body moving, not conscious
of the rough bark, the whole hurt of a tree.

He makes no sound, breathes
between the pounding pulses of his heart
and his feet. Flying over
the crest of a rocky hillock, he slows

slightly out of fear
not that he will hit anything or fall,
but that he will leave the earth
and the company of his kind.

White Pine

On an October day, my daughters and son chirping around me,
minds quick as the mouths of baby birds: Why are the hickories
and beeches gold, birches bright as lemons, the maples gaudy?

These are the true colors of trees, the eldest states,
the rest of the year hidden—like the stars—by too much sunlight.
But with a sudden sadness she questions the yellowing of the pines,
a sure sign, she says, of bad air, bad water, bad things. But I

strike a familiar pose, arm raised in protest against bad things and,
taking a sprig of pine, I show them what my science-teacher father
showed me: the deep green needles at the tip, followed by a scar,
followed by another year of green, another scar and then

this oldest now-brown year of needles, how they drop off dry,
mimic the whole tree, whose lowest branches, brittle and barren,
break off, making room—and they are amazed I am this wise.
But I confess I know this only because my father told me and that
someday they will tell their children. Perhaps because she knows

how families are trees, this eldest, wisest daughter looks
through my words, past the scars, into my heart, and then away.

At the Aquarium

A hammerhead swims close to the immense, clear wall,
the eye on the nearest lobe of its terrible, eons-old head
pivoting at the boy of six or seven who has suctioned himself
against this window with as much of his flesh as he can mold
to it, his own starfish, to become a part of that other world.

He is breaking the rules, of course, but against what monstrous
rule breaking, the capture indoors of an ocean, can we measure
what is clearly only enthusiasm, a child's desire to be in there
swimming with this kaleidoscope of languid harmony, the wing
of the gliding ray, the mighty pulse of the blue fin, or the idle

power of the tiger shark, its effortless thread of the water?
What failure of our nature could fault this child's desire
to touch, to feel, perhaps to ride, these utterly other creatures,
to be one? I can see the glass beginning its transubstantiation,
its slow surrender to the boy's warmth and eagerness,

how it bends at each point of pressure to begin to admit him
and I wonder whether he will become a fish, another creature
entirely, or if he will simply learn to breathe underwater, and
I am about to connect this with my own speculation about crossing
over, how much will be gained and how much will be lost,

when his mother, coming suddenly as if from a great distance
out of her own Piscean reverie, registers the calamity of the wall
surrendering, whether to admit her son or to disgorge suddenly
the twitching, snapping mass upon him I cannot say, but her eyes
and voice convey a terror commensurate only with the latter.

Girls on a Swing

for Lily

The old post-frame swing set
rocked on its back legs
as if it might gasp in upon itself
and fling the flying pink and blond
giggling sisters onto the mud
of the footpaths
dragged below their seats.

So I stopped pushing, watched
my daughters lying flat back,
hair streaming, legs stretched,
their tiny hands gripping the ropes,
as they arced through speckles
of sunlight and shadow cast
by the spring buds of the maple,

sawed and split and burned
winters ago now. I understand: I could not
spare those girls either sun or dark
but pray always that each discovers
the peace to tilt back laughing
in whatever light she finds.

Chase

for Martine

1.
One day, leaving the park
by the ocean beach, I looked
up from installing your sister
in her car seat to see you
running toward the park gate,
arms outstretched, after a car
that looked like ours.

I knew everything at once—
what you believed, your spirit
like you, bent and staggered by your tears.

2.
Today, a boy that small, three perhaps,
still young enough that his intention to run
outdistances the capacity of his legs
to carry him at such speeds,
is chasing pigeons in the park
endlessly turning
to find a new pigeon.

Remarkably, they do not fly
but run on their little legs just
ahead of him as if understanding
perfectly this child's game.
He runs and runs, turning
to one pigeon after another.
There is nothing else in his world.

I scan the park and find
the grandfather, wisely,

like a grandfather, keeping
his distance, giving
this boy his rein, his realm.

Pneumonia

The lines of my face redrawn with a grime of urban dust
the coal-seam contrast of an Arbus image, I do not move
from the couch when they arrive to lug it into my lungs,

carefully setting one end in the left lobe, the other in the right.
The movers wait while I dig a few coins from my jeans, an effort
that causes a thudding in my chest. After they leave,

I protest that the world I've created does not comport
with this new arrangement. Backstage there is laughter;
when I angrily part the curtain there is a night more immense

than the edge of memory; a bone tossed there is never heard
from again,
a probe finds no other life, a needle pushed through the chest wall
to drain the fluid reports nothing, for better or worse,

but the grayness shown in scans, swelling slightly in a wind
across small northern seas where a dory rocks and a man stands
to hoist a sail. He hopes to reach land before nightfall but pauses

between each haul on the halyard, sweat gleaming on his face,
running down the black creases, almost like tears.

Liminal

1.
My children grew up in a house
without thresholds
between door bottoms and floors
to impede the progress
of rodents and cold, keep
the chaff in the threshing room.

So when my toddling daughter discovered
the hard barrier with her staggering feet
she fell. The scar from those stitches
and the ills of the world
are there still. And from that moment
of betrayal her new life began
hurtling on its singular path
rising and falling like river winds.

I don't remember how we staunched
the bleeding or tried to soothe the pain
and shock, or that dreadful moment
between her sharp gasp and the wail of pain,
how long we waited before going
to the clinic for stitches. I imagine

the child on my knee as I hold an ice cube
inside wadded paper towels, softly
against her chin. I missed keeping that
in my memory, as we do, not seeing
those moments for what they are.
But I have it now.

2.
I can tell you my life's choices
were not decisions, paths taken,

but outcomes, a person, place or job
to which I drifted, an empty canoe
on an irresistible current. What did I learn
as the butcher at the beach store,
the reporter at the Upstate daily? How
did I get there or end up with this
person or that? In the house by the river
or the hovel where the snow blew in?

On the road crew I met the ex-con
whose quiet deliberateness would become to me
a way of being under the force of change.
From the podium of the classroom, I heard
the voice of the young immigrant son
telling stories better than any I had yet read
or written. On the beach with a dying man I saw
his vision beyond the veil he faced and felt
his conviction. So when I sat beside the lake
with the knowledge of what would kill me
and when, I thought to ask only for peace
and got it. I shifted then into another space
I am often tempted to leave but learned
to take with me, along with all the rest.

3.
On a path in deep woods we often come
to change, pure and simple, where
for reasons known to the trees alone
they change in type and hue and take the ground
with them in texture and rhythm. Or a wall
of stones piled long ago to make a field for crops
gives way to a path or woods road and we know
we've gone from some use to another but nothing more
except woods are like that and no one really
owns the land any more than time.

Sometimes we stumble and sometimes we fall.
Some doorways pass by us unnoticed
like the source of a sweet scent or slight music
we sense later but looking back cannot discover
what it was or ever find it again. Move on.
For whatever the moment is, whether
there is a memory or a lesson, it has no meaning
without the future, the chance to see
how it works, as if under our feet the world is moving.

At night the wind may be time rushing past the window.
Stand on the ground that is traveling a thousand miles an hour
and if you can feel a silence and hear a stillness, find a peace
that is real, a heart-serene space where your vistas
make sense and the music comes back to you
and even, for a moment the sweet scent,
on an airless wind. You cannot stay.

Apple Seed

1.
It was a long day on a long road,
straight through the cold November
dawn to dusk, measuring from pavement
to the height of land on the other berm
of the roadside ditch, every time
the foreman said, "Here."

I'm sure we would have stopped
for coffee and for lunch, picking
a place to sit for dryness
or out of the wind that came
down off Ontario, cold as Canada,
but I only remember the end,

where we finished at an orchard
and there was one last apple
forgotten by the migrants or,
hanging alone, appearing
by some magic at that
unimaginable moment.

Regardless, I picked it
and lay on my back beneath the tree
and ate it, cracking with its coldness
and a juice so sweet and rich
I had to look again and again
to confirm its appleness

and at the end I gnawed close along
the stem to harvest every morsel
of this complete form of apple, every
succulent bit, drawing out the seeds

and spitting them upwards, watching
as they arced into the brown fall grass.

Warmed by the cold apple and my
own surrender to the fatigue
of all-day walking and bending,
closing my eyes, I dreamed
and all around me sprung up
apple trees in full blossom.

A little dream, seconds
only before I was wakened
to get in the truck
for the long drive back
crammed in with men smelling
of mud and cigarettes.

2.
At the end of some road
north toward the lake,
if you could find it, you
may come upon an orchard,
if it's not all houses now.

At the corner a little copse
of younger trees; their apples
the sweetest of any field.
Who are we to question
the possible, when a seed
so small can hold all

the green, the white and pink,
the gold and red
tumbling on as certain
as the sun's horizons?

What packed that gift,
and drew the ribbon, tight,

tighter, pulling all time
wisdom and beauty
into a bundle
so small
a man
could spit it in an arc?

I cannot argue
whether that dark seed,
pulled tighter, into the densest
point of all matter, everything we
have so far known or guessed,
was not ordained.

How close are we now
with our engineering
to the moment when
our cup will be ready
and we prove infinite
the ability to shape
what is, what will be
and transcend our plane
just in time to realize
we should have known
enough to stop?

Hubble Ultra Deep Field Image

There, against the ultimate gloom
of what we do not know, is
the splattering of everything we do.

The whole place is littered
with tiny disks of whirling stars,
galaxies of millions of suns

and planets and moons
and every color of light in pinpoints
farther off than those

and then farther. All on black satin
or maybe it's nothing, appearing
as space, with the same consistency

as rooms at night, but darker.
We fumble through the threshold
thinking to find with a foot

or an outstretched hand
the thing that will bruise us
or trip us up, not imagining

that we are in it, swimming
in a consciousness beyond fathoms
beyond what we could have conjured

even as children, cautiously
entering the ocean at night
for the first time.

Kindness

From the deck of the beach house
it appeared an orange light
and then a row boat on fire
then a fishing boat and finally
an ocean liner, a catastrophe
of floating fire casting a crooked
flickering finger across the dark-waved ocean,

and then it was the moon, emerging
slow and monster-like from the edge
of the world, greater and greater
and the color of the sun already sunk.
I don't remember, but I must have gasped
when that huge moon birthed
from the black sea. I know

I'd said things, with growing alarm,
about burning boats, calling the Coast Guard
while my host was quiet on this, her family's
heirloom porch, where she'd no doubt seen
this spectacle enough times to know
no boat was burning, no lives in danger....

But she did not let on, say "it's only the moon"
preferring to allow me my own burning boats,
my own unforgettable, a half-century later, moonrise.

Summer Night

I am on my way home on a summer night,
the air a velvet sweater on the skin.

I am on my way home full of the good and bad
of the summer night that will last
no longer than the breath on the skin,
soft as the thought of night,

and the good and bad of going home,
knowing it will be so much less
perfect than a summer night when the air
will hold you, take away this knowledge.

I am on my way home when I see a boy and a girl
who I know instantly as a boy and girl

because their bodies have that birdlike quality
of boys and girls, their postures the gawky
innocence that only boys and girls this young
still have, their clothes the kind of effortlessness
only children's clothes are allowed. They are talking
furtively and I know instantly they are furtive

because they look to see if I am looking
and turn away when they see I am
and I know suddenly what they are

talking about and precisely the pressure
it exerts in their bodies and the scraping
impossibility of it also and how they will turn

away from each other and walk home
in the light sliding out of this summer night
and nothing at home will ever
be as good as it was again.

At the Fair

There are lots of things
spinning here, imitations
of galaxies, universes, mental states.
You and I walk the fairway
that tomorrow will be a muddied swath
through a trampled field, otherwise green.

I imagine the whole production
whirling, jangling, ringing, flashing
rising off the ground, slowly at first
then turning deliberately, pivoting
on its highest point, the Ferris wheel
and then suddenly plunging off

into the deep blue-black sky
leaving a trail of calliope notes
glowing like embers twisting
above a bonfire, shrinking to
a single point of light and then
blink—gone.

I turn to tell you this
and you hand me an apple
as if to say you're sorry
there are no bumper cars
and this, sweet serpent,
will have to do. I do not

touch you, but take a bite
watching your eyes all the while
like a gentleman kissing a lady's hand.

With Without

It is hard to tell if it is the snowfield
I face without you

or the swirling night I dream
empty of you

or the path I search for when I think of living
where you are not

or the sound of a song I hear
and you do not

or the distance into which I must continue
regardless of you

or the view from the height I may ascend to
and find you already gone

or the voice I will turn to
that is not yours

or the beat of time dancing on the wing
passing near you

or the breath I will lose at last
without sight of you

or just the sound of the rain
you will feel on your hand without me.

History

Of course there are clouds, and birch trees
bending deer-like, as if drinking the snow.

There are berries as red as a skinned knee
bright as blood beads glimmering
against the scraped-white skin
of the snow-filled sky.

If a dog barks, others howl in a distance made uncertain
by the hair rising on the back of your neck

as if hair is responsible for perception
and there were a way to forget the way my fingers

swept the hair from the back of your neck
or the way your eyes closed slowly or the way I grew wings
just before the treeline or the way there was suddenly
a complete absence of clouds or sound or air.

The Last Weekend in the Country

*following the announcement of the supposed discovery of the
identity of the "Dark Lady" of Shakespeare's sonnets*

It is Saturday night. He stares at the paper,
wondering if the smooth olive skin,
the robust blossoming of beauty's
"successive heir" is worth the time, the lost
characters and forgotten rhymes....

Emelia sits by the fire. She picks at needlepoint—
again they have quarreled because he hates beans—
so that when, reminding her of more
heated exchanges under this thatched roof, he holds up
twenty-five or so sonnets as proof,

she says, "You're a genius." And goes in to bed.
Saying nothing, he blows out his candle and
goes out, walking on the bank by the cool,
dark river, to give new lines to his favorite fool.

Peepers

His truck rattles down the road
like a bag of cans, banging
over the potholes
until a gear grinds and that
straight-six Ford whines down
as he slows against the engine,
rolls to a ticking stop.

The last indigo of day
silhouettes the still-bare trees.
In just enough light, he sees
the bright green shoots spiking out
from the pale stubble of last summer's reeds
jumbled along the edges of the pond.
He leans on the fender,

and listens. Closes his eyes,
lifts his head slightly
as if picking up some fragrance
or recalling something distant. He is still.
Around him, the sound grows
until it is thick as the air
congealed ghostlike above the pond.

Motionless, he rises on the pulses,
the threads and seesaws of sound,
a syncopation so perfect it weaves the carpet he rides
past years and roads and rocks, feet shuffling
over thresholds, birds and children singing,
sunlight crossing water, the warm back
of a wooden chair in winter.

He enters a room without regret, where
a woman stands smiling, lifting her arms.

Cellar Hole

From the foliage-spattered logging road
it is hard to see this, at first a different
rhythm of leaves, then a pattern of stones,
finally a cellar hole

wrapped around a heap of boulders and cracked brick
that held the hearth and orients me now
to see that the front of the house is what seemed,
from the line of the road, to be the side.

Looked at from the moss-strewn clearing
that was this family's yard, it takes shape
and rises before me, a perfect
5-over-4 colonial, attached barn...

and vanishes again in the sunlight of this crystalline
fall day, as another year's yellowed beech leaves
flutter into the remains of a dream, a life-and-death shelter,
and spread across the pastures now studded with trees
and the road filled with brightly clad Sunday hikers.

I wonder where in these woods the abandoned plowshare leans,
where the hayrake rests near a half-buried wall of stones
cleared by man and horse. Or was it all sold at auction,

the father standing off to the side of the crowd,
eyes examining the toe of one boot
as it slowly spreads the dirt, left and right,
while his wife and children wait in the wagon
for the trip down this road they will never come up again.

His youngest girl stares up into the blue
blue of the autumn sky and watches
the yellow twirl of a single beech leaf
as it makes its way to earth.

Three Yellow Balloons

Would have gone unnoticed
but for the ball of fire.

Except we watched the scene unfold
over and over and there, look

there they are, moments before
coming up the street, bobbing

on their invisible strings
above the crowd, above the heads

of the bombers. Who was it held them?
A child, happy for three balloons

bright as the April sun? A parent
unable to overcome the need

to keep this child from the sorrow
of a sunny balloon lost

into the blue, blue sky?
Or were these the gift intended

to greet the runner
crossing that finish line?

No matter. They are history now,
rising out of the soot-gray billow

of the child's sorrow
of the runner's end

of the smoke that punched up
and then tattered and swirled away

into the air above the street
as bomb smoke always does

Diving into the Moon

for M

Down close to the water
where Bennett Road runs tight along the river
is an outcrop of granite colored by all that earth
and wind and water have to offer. It is easy to miss,
darker than the deep tea color of the river
descending into blackness below sunlight.

It used to be invisible from the road before floods
took away roadside alder and other scrub.
Friends and I would skinny-dip there, sleek
young bodies plunging five feet into the cool flow
where the bending river swept against rock
and steep bank, hidden from passersby.

And one night I took you there, surprised at how easily
you escaped the chrysalis of your clothing, emerging
white and lithe in the moonlight. We stood together
staring into darkness, only ripples sparkling briefly below
and you, suddenly grasping my arm, as if forgetting
our nakedness, breathed on my shoulder

"How do we get in?" It was impossible to describe
any arc that would carry you safely to where I knew
the river was deep enough to accept us. But then
it was there, a wavering, pale yellow circle,
the landing place. I slid my arm around your waist
and drew closer, pointing: "Dive into the moon."

And you did, the long paleness of your body
a tracer from rock to an explosion of white water
and then you emerged again, with a whoop and laughing.

I remember how delighted I was you'd trusted me
enough to take that dive into the black water, but perhaps
you did not place your faith in me, but in the moon.

Cathy Wolff

How to Punch
& Other Essays

These wry, self-deprecating essays are the work of a writer who honed her craft as a journalist. Now she feels free to reflect on episodes of her own life and tell us the stories. For male readers, she also opens up windows on the world of women and the different hills they have to climb. We even get an angle on violence and its contradictory elements. Sometimes, the author focuses narrowly on a topic that intrigues her: fingernails, the role a bed plays in our lives, and an excursion into online dating. The journey through the geographical territory of these pieces takes us from a Greek island and back to the Seacoast, where the author sits in a local cafe, wrestling with Wi-Fi passwords. Love and romance feature in these pieces, as does loss and living alone. Cathy's training comes through in every piece; it's the power of details that makes a good story. G.D

How to Punch

We were in a cavernous bar in Iraklion on the Greek island of Crete. The air conditioner and rock music were jacked up high in anticipation of a crowd of sweaty, noisy dancers. The place was almost empty. The room was cold, gray, smoky, echoing, lost.

Bobby and I had left Piraeus by boat early that morning in hopes of finding less noise and less air pollution. Iraklion was not that, but we were too tired to travel farther that day. We met a man on the street who steered us to lodging. In his sister's home. She rented out rooms. In return, he insisted we go to the bar on the edge of town with him.

I wanted to be outside, sitting in the fading sun, a light that felt different in Greece than any place else I'd ever been. We were both exhausted from the traveling, but also from way too much drinking in the past week, including a rather sketchy wine festival at a monastery north of Athens. But we hunched over our ouzos and tried to be, if not exactly polite, at least not ugly Americans.

"Dance with me," our new friend demanded.

"No thanks, I'm too tired," I said.

"Oh, come on, dance with me." There was an edge in his voice.

Bobby leaned over me, lightly touched the man's arm. "Hey. She doesn't want to dance, okay?" His voice wasn't belligerent, just firm. It's good when you travel to have someone who's got your back.

The man ignored Bobby and pulled up his shirtsleeve, revealing to me a long, jagged scar running from his wrist almost to his elbow. "See this? Knife," he said. Then he pulled back his shirt to show another scar on his shoulder. "So, I don't know why your boyfriend wants to cause trouble."

I felt a heat start in my gut and radiate to my head, arms, legs, fingers, and toes. Every detail sharpened—the smoke of our cigarettes, the mirror ball over the dance floor, the exit signs, even the chilly air. I looked the man in the eye. "If you touch him, I'll eat your eyes out," I hissed.

I don't know where those words came from. I had never said anything remotely like that in my life. I'm not even sure how you would eat out somebody's eyes. But I know that I felt a rush, a sharp-edged aliveness—not unlike the vivid clarity that comes right before or during a car wreck. And I knew, if necessary, I'd attack.

The man threw up his hands, shrugged and pushed himself away from the table. He gave me a rat-like grin. "Make sure you are out of my sister's house by 8 a.m.," he warned and left. I was relieved. I knew I'd be inadequate in a fight. My arms flailing. People would say I hit "like a girl."

It was a time, in the 1970s, when a lot of women were learning "guy things." How to change oil or a tire, chug beer, build a shelf, or swear in public. But it wasn't until a couple of years after the Greek trip that I learned how to throw a proper punch.

My teacher was Laurel, my roommate in Chicago. She dropped out of Barnard to be part of the revolution and moved to Chicago to work in the national office of Students for a Democratic Society. For her day job, she worked as an insurance actuary. Once she spent a week trying to put monetary values on the animals in Lincoln Park Zoo, dealing with what became, for her, philosophical questions regarding the relative worth of an elephant and a giraffe. When she wasn't doing political or insurance work, she studied karate.

I once watched her try to break a board with her forehead. She bashed herself with it three times and failed. "Not enough focus," she assessed later while putting ice on the string of nasty welts.

Board-breaking aside, Laurel had the punch down. She would advance across the small living room of our apartment, each step a punch and a huff. She instructed me: never fully extend the arm, at the risk of dislocation of elbow or shoulder; make the punch one fluid motion; and, perhaps most important, have clear, focused intent.

I left Chicago and moved to New Hampshire, eventually settling in the Seacoast. A man I loved broke up with me, but then suggested we still date and invited me to meet him one afternoon to play racquetball. I showed up. He didn't. That night I went to his apartment. When he opened the door I saw a woman lounging on the couch behind him. Without thinking, but with focused intent, I pulled back and let go with a sharp, fluid left to his jaw. He fell to the floor.

The horrible thing was that it felt good. Physically. Emotionally. At least initially. Even though I almost immediately, and deeply, regretted what I'd done, I could not deny a certain visceral satisfaction. He did tell me several years later that the couch woman's only comment was, "She must really love you."

Despite the bar incident in Crete, the lover punch, and a hesitancy to engage in nonviolent civil disobedience for fear I'd hit a cop if he tried to drag me to a police wagon, I've always seen myself as a pacifist. I still do. At least a pacifist who likes Quentin Tarantino movies. What I have realized, though, is that we are all capable of doing things we want to believe only other people—people not like us—would do.

What is this appalling appeal of violence? Yes, it's a response to feelings of fear, anger, hopelessness, despair, frustration, jealousy; it's a desire for revenge or a demand for justice. But there's something else. Maybe it's the clarity of physical action. The second thoughts, the nuanced world, the endless rational options, the burden of civilization, even the consequences, slide away. And there you are, with everything, at least in that moment, reduced to knowing how to punch.

The Great Christmas Concert Piñata Riot

What I miss most about my ex-husband is our shared sense of humor.

We often laughed at things other people did not—such as the newspaper clipping with the headline, "General Speaks at Breakfast," under a grainy photo of a man in uniform. "I bet his wife appreciates that," noted my husband. For years, it was held by a magnet to our—later just my—refrigerator. It was the kind of "funny" you couldn't explain to anyone else. And we never had to explain it to each other. That's how it was with what we fondly called the Great Piñata Riot.

The Christmas holiday concert was in the gym of our son's elementary school. The basketball hoops dripped tinsel and crepe paper. The chorus, each member wearing a cloth poinsettia, stood on risers in front of the low stage at one end of the room.

Every number—including "The Twelve Days of Christmas," with its interminable stand-sing-sit audience participation— received sustained foot-stomping applause, whoops, and volleys of piercing whistles. This wild enthusiasm struck Ken and me as funny, so we were already in a giggly mood by the middle of the concert.

Just as toddlers began to fidget and fathers glance at watches, the stage curtains jerked opened to reveal a dangling, homemade donkey piñata, surrounded by kids corralled at a safe distance by teachers. A trumpet trio in black sombreros off to one side energetically played "La Cucaracha."

The audience shouted, "Olé!" as a series of blindfolded children failed to connect bat to donkey. Finally, with a war cry, a sixth grader sent the donkey's red-and-green head flying off the stage. Subsequent batters knocked off the legs. But the beast's belly held.

By now, audience "olés!" had turned to a nonstop, rumbling, "Go! Go! Go!" And by now, Ken and I had given up trying not to laugh, despite the disapproving glances of a woman sitting near us. We couldn't stop. It was delightful.

"Give Jason the bat! He can do it!" some woman screamed at least four times.

"Kill it, Mary!" shouted a man as a girl, not much taller than the bat, was blindfolded.

And then, a large boy lumbered up to bat. He rubbed his hands on his pants, tapped the bat on the stage floor and furtively pushed up one small corner of the blindfold before taking a Babe Ruth-worthy swing across the donkey's middle. It cracked. A trickle of candy fell out.

The teachers on stage were waving their arms up and down, trying to keep the kids back. The big boy swung again and the candy poured out. There was no holding back the mob. They dove at the treats. One teacher stumbled and disappeared among the children. Arms and legs shot out of the squealing pile. Dust rose. It looked like a cartoon. The curtains snapped shut, but we could still hear: "It's mine!" "Get off!" "Let go!"

Despite the ongoing commotion behind the curtain, the show went on as a recorder ensemble valiantly played "Little Drummer Boy." The audience quieted down. Everyone, that is, except us. We really did try, but even a glance at each other set us off.

We would have felt terrible if anyone had been hurt. But they weren't. Children began to emerge from behind the curtain. Hair messed, ties askew, shirts pulled out of trousers. But no blood was visible. Most, including our own son, were grinning and victoriously clutching a handful of candy.

We managed—by tightly squeezing each other's hand—to ignore the irony and participate sincerely in the closing song, with its repeated line: "peace on earth, goodwill to men."

Geese

A gaggle of Canada geese gather on Waddlebury Island in Kittery's Back Channel every morning around sunrise. They swim toward the island in pairs, offering scattered honking to each other, their necks gentle gray question marks against the gray sky. Sometimes a few head up the hill, to the other side of the island.

But this morning, they are all together on the rocky edge of the island, all honking at once, like football fans. Or a lynch mob. Their necks stiffen into exclamation points, their beaks point to the sky. They form a loose semicircle around two geese—one on top of the other, pecking at its back, its wings, its head. None waddle forward to help, but none leave.

The attacked goose manages to break away and slip into the water. Its attacker follows and the other geese, still honking, turn to watch. The pursuing goose pushes or drags its victim back onto land and continues to peck, pull, and punish. The honking mob continues to cheer until the goose on top begins to tear at the other's limp body. The honking suddenly ceases and the mob looks away. Their necks relax again into question marks. They stand quietly, not looking at the dead goose, at its attacker, or at each other.

Fingernails Are Not for Everybody

I love long flashy fingernails. But I have a lifelong nail-biting habit I can't seem to break, despite redundant New Year's resolutions. So—on the advice of a young woman who rode the same commuter van as me to Boston every day and who had fingernails to die for—I went to Nail Heaven in Boston's Downtown Crossing, a third-floor walk-up over a sock store.

I had tried fake nails once before. They were the drugstore kind you paste on yourself. They made me feel sexy and I wore them for a one-night stand with my estranged husband, waking the next morning to find one of them stuck between his shoulder blades. Neither the nails nor the night really counted.

Nail Heaven was filled with ten small women with black satin hair, bent over the toes and fingers of their much larger non-Vietnamese customers. I had a quick flash of white liberal guilt, especially after being introduced to my technician, My Lai. I swear that was her name.

Before My Lai could start, I had to choose a color. It had taken a month of angst to decide on a hue for my living room walls and I don't have nearly the intimacy with them that I do with my hands. I used the elimination approach. Blues too Goth. Reds too bold. Pinks too feminine. That left orange. I chose Tangerine Sunset.

Working with tremendous speed (My Lai must have been paid by the finger), she soaked, prodded, and roughed up my nails. Then she fitted, glued, trimmed, and filed a set of plastic nails. At that point she started motioning toward my purse, chattering in increasingly shrill Vietnamese. It took me awhile to figure out the pay-before-paint protocol—and even longer to realize the rationale was to avoid disturbing the nails before the polish "set."

My new nails made me feel transformed, feminized. I started thinking maybe I'd try a facial, a pedicure, liposuction. Go for a total transformation. But I soon had the first hint that transformations are not duty-free. Thoughtlessly brushing away a strand of hair from my face I nearly gouged out an eye. It wouldn't be the last nail-inflicted scratch. And I found the nails slowed down my typing. A small price to pay, I thought.

I started biting the new nails in about a week—just to get the garden dirt out. Then one chipped as I was throwing a broken chair off the back of my truck at the dump, another when I was carrying a small boulder from the beach.

I went to a nail shop in my own town for emergency repair. The Vietnamese proprietor suggested some people were not suitable for nails. I begged him. I promised to be more careful, more responsible. He continued to scold but installed a new set. This time I chose Rusty Rose—calmer than Tangerine Sunset, I thought. Soon there was more breakage. Each time I sought out another Vietnamese nail house. There was no shortage.

I finally had to agree with the salon owner. Not everybody is a candidate for nails. Or for transformation. When the fake nails were taken off for the last time, my poor real nails were pathetic—rough, scarred, pale, and weak. I had to wait a month before I could start biting them again.

More Than a Bed

During most of my marriage, the refrigerator door boasted a full-color ad featuring a young couple sitting happily in the middle of a giant bed. The headline: "More than a bed—a way of life."

Whenever bed came up in conversation, either my husband or I would repeat that line and laugh. Years later, when we separated, he took our bed. I used the futon couch/bed until my back rebelled.

The young salesman in the bed store asked if I liked a soft or hard mattress. "Firm," I answered. "Twin, double, queen, or king?" he wanted to know. I paused and the whole void of my future enveloped me. "That's the problem," I said. "I don't know if I will ever share a bed again." The clerk backed away, saying he couldn't help me with that.

I bought a queen-size bed. In the first weeks I had it, I would lie down in the middle and stretch my arms and legs to the edges, snow-angel style. Somehow, this was comforting. Making myself fit the bed—the whole bed. Convincing myself I didn't need another body present to justify the purchase. Soon there was a permanent dip on the left side of that bed. Sometimes I tried to sleep on the other side to even things out, but I always retreated to the comfort of the familiar contour.

Beds span our lives—from rocker to crib to bunk beds at summer camp to narrow college dorm beds to a Murphy bed in the first apartment. And, finally, perhaps, a death bed. And we let each bed hold us—comfortably or not—while we give, or try to give, ourselves over to oblivion, perhaps even to dreams.

When I was a kid, that was never my take on bed. Sleep was the enemy. After the lights went out, my sister would leave her twin bed and get into mine. She'd scratch my back in exchange for hearing stories about my uncle from Mars (I conferred with him under the covers), or the twelve little pigs (more pigs meant more back scratching). Long after she was asleep, I would stare at the shadows of burglars and ghosts I thought were across the hall in the bathroom. Eventually, I'd seek safety in my parents' double bed. My mother always made room.

At ninety-five, she still makes room for me. She slept on the far east side of a king-size bed, a desert of sheet stretching out to the west. When I visited, I would occupy some of that territory.

It used to take more than half an hour for my mother to make her bed those days, moving from side to side at least ten times, using the bed as support instead of her walker.

She made beds the way her mother taught her to; the way she taught me. There's the unspoken message, handed down from mother to daughter: an unmade or badly made bed bodes poorly for the rest of your day, if not your life.

"It's the only exercise I get some days," she told me of the bed-making ritual, which expanded like High Mass the days she laundered the sheets. She always rebuffed any suggestion of downsizing. Maybe because change is hard. Or because it is the last bed she shared with my father who died twenty-seven years before my mother. Or maybe it was her belief that things should not be discarded if they aren't broken.

But perhaps it's the intimacy. A bed is the most intimate, the most private, of furniture. We bring to it tears, dreams, passion, fresh starts, and regrets. We heal in bed in big and small ways. It is a place that asks no more of us than just to be. It's the place we end each day and begin another.

Bones (1998)

Most days now, when I awake, I reach my arms toward the ceiling and say good morning to my hands. In the predawn light, they dance slowly in silhouette above my head and I marvel at their boney grace and thank them for being.

My body and I have a new, intimate relationship. It's different than the kind of intimacy that let me safely climb to the tops of trees as a child and execute backflips as a teenager. It's closer, but still not the same, as the relation we had when pregnant. Instead, it's a deeply felt partnership—maybe a little like the intimacy some graced couples manage to rediscover after years of dulling familiarity.

This new relationship began dramatically as I was emerging from surgery. In that twilight zone, I watched my skeleton behind my closed eyes. It was a reversed X-ray, with the bones a shiny, dark steel gray and the surrounding flesh translucent white. I could see light through the joints of my elbows, knees, hips, fingers. I could see the fissures on my skull, the depth of my eye sockets, the spaces between my vertebrae. I was in awe of the gentle curves of bone and how cleverly everything fit together.

When I finally opened my eyes, I was told I had ovarian cancer.

For about a day, I was angry, accusing my body of betraying me. Then, looking at the long incision on my stomach and the needle in my arm, I felt sorry for it. But, perhaps because of that anesthetized vision, I soon adopted an attitude of partnership, a we're-in-this-together-and-need-each-other-very-much approach. This division of myself and my body might sound psychologically suspect, but it's working. I never abandoned my body; I just didn't see myself as being the same as it.

Not that I couldn't identify. Losing twenty-five pounds in the two weeks after surgery gave me a rush of silly vanity, for instance. But the hard work soon began. Chemotherapy.

I tried the imaging techniques widely shared in workshops, books, and tapes, such as imagining the toxins rushing into your bloodstream as sharks eating the bad cancer cells. But I soon opted for a more direct approach.

"Okay," I bargain with my digestive tract. "I won't eat dairy products and I will drink gallons of carrot juice, if you will just keep doing your job."

"Listen," I earnestly tell my liver, "I'm counting on you. Cleanse those toxins; hang in there." I actually have found myself offering out-loud praise and thanks to my colon during very private moments.

My bone marrow wasn't as open to negotiation, repeatedly failing to renew its white blood cell production after chemo. But in the end, it always pulled through and I tried not to be too hard on it, knowing we probably have a long haul ahead of us.

So, along with the pep talks, the deals, and the demands, I also take time each day to thank my body for just being what it is and for the times we've shared.

"Love your hands," urges the preacher woman in the movie *Beloved*. And I love my hands, my skeleton, my whole body in a way I never have before.

What's the Password?

The decaf is watery and she's feeling the need for the real thing as she watches the password box on her laptop screen jiggle its rejection for the fifth time. *PortsmouthBookandBar*. That's what the woman behind the counter said when she asked. *Porstmouthbook&bar?* Jiggle. *Porstmouthbook'nbar?* Jiggle.

Ask again? No. It would only underline her gross technical ignorance. For instance, she has no idea why her cell phone isn't ringing. It's not on mute and it was in her back pocket the last two hours. Yet when she looks at it there are two voice messages. Can some people go directly to voicemail so it just looks as if they called? Is there an app for that?

The room has church ceilings. Once a custom house—or was it a bank? Very impressive. Half a dozen couples, all talking quietly. None of the buzz of a bar. Maybe it's the books. Or maybe it's because the background music is turned down low, so no one has to shout to be heard. Tim Buckley's son (what is his first name—so sad when you can't remember the name of the dead son of the dead singer you admired so much in college) is singing Leonard Cohen's "Hallelujah." She wishes they would turn up the sound. She loves that song.

The skinny bald fellow at the next table is playing with his phone, waiting for the woman to return. She does, speaking to him in Italian—or is it Spanish? Not loud enough to decide. Maybe she does need a hearing aid. He answers her in English.

But she didn't come here to eavesdrop on these young couples, although she wonders if any of them met online. That's why she's sitting here—to write a profile for Match.com. With wine-strengthened determination, she joined last night at the minimal rate for the least amount of time possible. But she joined. Now she's wondering why. Does she really want to date after all these years?

She came to Book & Bar because if she went home she would find herself cleaning the pantry, once again marveling at how many jars of jam she has and how she still has no idea how to use the pressed mango she got in Puerto Rico two years ago on her last (forever?) vacation. Would it still be any good to use? They don't have expiration dates in Puerto Rico. Maybe that's why she felt so comfortable there.

And if she started cleaning out the pantry and found signs of mice, she'd have to deal with it. D-CON already is on the floor—under the counter and behind the dryer. She checks them daily, but no more than eight pellets appear to have disappeared and those, perhaps, were just pushed around by a mouse dancing spitefully in the box. Then again, maybe there aren't any mice.

Cleaning the pantry would lead to cleaning the kitchen—or at least thinking about cleaning the kitchen. Or bathroom. And painting both of them. And the stairwell. She would consider the need to rearrange things so money wasn't flying out the door and ancestors and relationships weren't in the backyard as her recent feng shui analysis indicated.

She would take on, at least mentally, one of these unending domestic or spiritual-balancing tasks. And she would feel, if she moved from mind to action, the slightly embarrassing sense of satisfaction when any of them were finally, although always temporarily, addressed.

So here she is, on a rainy night, in Book & Bar, or *bookandbar*, a few miles from house distractions, secure in the anonymity of age. Time to write her Match.com profile. But first the ladies' room. Should she pack everything up and take it with her? She doesn't want to ask the Italian-Spanish couple to watch it. She'll just risk it, walking quickly past poetry, essays, fiction, and reference, through three doors.

The water faucet won't shut off. The sink is filling. She returns and reports this to the woman behind the counter, not the same one who first gave her the password and watery decaf. "By the way, what's the password for Wi-Fi?" she asks, almost as an afterthought, casually, actually stepping away and turning back.

"*Portsmouthbookandbar,*" the woman says, "a-n-d, all lowercase."

Great. It works. She is on. No messages from Match.com even though she's sent—or thinks she sent—two emails suggesting a meetup for coffee, or beer. Must be the picture. She shouldn't have posted those rosy-faced pictures she took with her phone. Especially without an accompanying profile. The depth of the wrinkles, the size of her nose, the grimace of her smile, the sadness of her eyes. Photos of herself have been an issue for a while now. She'll have to get better ones done—a more flattering angle, maybe with make-up. She'll wait until she feels thinner. Or at least more settled with her hair.

The multiple choice Match.com questions are bothersome enough. For religion, it seems eight percent of people choose "spiritual, but not religious." Why don't they offer "religious, but not spiritual" for all the people who go to church for the music, the windows, the coffee, the rituals? Political-leaning choices should include capitalist, fascist, socialist, anarchist, and monarchist.

The pet section invites a person to expand. She thinks of her two wonderful dogs, both now dead for many years, which, of course, leads to her thinking once again about getting a dog. Probably the same urge as Match.com, but a lot easier. When she tries to explain her affection for the four goldfish in the backyard pond (actually more like a sunken kitchen sink), she finds the invitation to explain has limits and she has exceeded her allotted characters.

But before any of this, last night, she had to choose a username. That was hard and finally she just wrote: Notreadytoknit. At least it wasn't already taken. Also, a request for a statement about yourself, your philosophy, what you are looking for. "Growing a bit tired of saying good night to myself," she typed. Rereading it now, she decides it needs to be changed—sounds so self-pitying.

But right now, the profile. Emphasize the positive, she tells herself.

"My only debt is a small mortgage," she types. She pauses and moves the cursor back over the sentence, clicks, and inserts "relatively" before "small." *And you think that will interest men?* she asks herself. She erases it.

"I consider myself an upbeat person with a good sense of humor, especially when I'm taking the Paxil," she types. Erases.

Finally, the coffee is long gone, and something is committed to writing. She'll give it a day before she posts. She saves what she's written, packs up, deposits the cold paper cup in the proper recycling barrel, and goes out into the rain.

Later, at home, she writes:

In style, I lean toward comfortable (but who of our generation doesn't?). In humor, my leanings are black. I loved *Django Unchained* and *Pulp Fiction*, but *Poetry* (Korean film) was the best movie I've seen in years.

I believe society is a collective and should act like one. I hate the scam of bottled water and oil/gas fracking. I don't believe corporations are people. Socially, I like small or one-on-one, but usually have fun at parties. I'd like to be a vegetarian, but I'm not. I like fish, chocolate, ice cream, a good beer, and, infrequently, a good hamburger.

I've made a living writing— for newspapers, AP, magazines, universities. Never a book (too many books already in this world).

The past couple of years I've split my life between an endearing but headache-provoking home in southern Maine and a rented room in Central Square. I love the city. I love the ocean. I love the woods but worry about ticks. In general, though, I don't worry. Except about ticks. And mice. And global warming. And nuclear war, although not nearly as often as when I was little.

I was a gymnast in college (so long ago) and grieve that I can no longer do handsprings in the spring or headstands in the winter. But I bike, practice yoga, and try to remember to breathe.

I'd love to be fluent in Spanish and learn the names of things, especially birds and plants (especially those in my garden). And someday, I'd love to learn to knit.

So who am I looking for? Not sure, except that he can't be a Republican.

She posts. She waits. She connects and has maybe two dates, neither worth writing about. She returns to Book & Bar, but without her laptop. She orders real coffee, not decaf, and eavesdrops with pleasure.

Clark Knowles

Emporium

The stories collected here work individually and *they tell a larger story when read together. I was immediately drawn in by the first person narrator—irreverent, observant, wickedly funny. He takes chances. He makes edgy decisions. He rolls! These stories live in the details—so many details so breathlessly delivered there's barely time to end one sentence and start a new one. Same with paragraphs. They are long and rich and revealing. The details build and build and…then the bottom drops out. It's rollercoaster writing. The tone—often light—makes the emotional depth even more dazzling.*

Clark Knowles teaches writing at UNH. His fiction has appeared in many journals. These stories take place in Portsmouth, Hampton, and Rye—places he knows well. R.R.

Entanglement

When I left home, I got a job working at a seafood restaurant in the city. The manager was called Harold. He smoked filterless Pall Malls. He interviewed me at a table in the front of the restaurant. He told me that he didn't have time for workers who weren't as serious about seafood as he was. I told him I was dead serious about seafood. All day I carried trays of crab legs and lobsters out to the steam tables. When I wasn't carrying trays of crab and lobster, I cut fish. When I wasn't cutting fish, I peeled shrimp.

When I wasn't peeling shrimp, I shucked oysters. There was a man there who only shucked oysters. That was his entire job. That's all he did, all day. It was nothing for him to get the oyster knife into the oyster. He'd shuck twenty oysters for every one I shucked. I don't think he ever said a word to me. When I wasn't shucking oysters, I was out back by the dumpsters smoking weed with the dishwashers. One of the dishwashers rolled the joints. When he didn't roll joints, we smoked out of a pipe made from an apple or tinfoil. When I wasn't smoking weed with the dishwashers, I was drinking beer with a waiter named Gerald, who had spent the previous year in jail for aggravated DUI. He said he didn't know why it was aggravated. He said the cop who arrested him was actually pretty nice. We stole the beers out of the big walk-in cooler and drank them between the first dinner rush and the second dinner rush. Most of the time, while he was talking, I watched the insects swarm in the streetlight above the dumpster. There were always bats swooping in and out of the light. A bat's front claws are far out on their wings. To catch their prey, they pull in their wings, capture the insect, somersault through the air, stuff the food into their mouths, and then open their wings to recapture flight. The bat does this so fast that you can't see it. If you want to see it, you have to watch slow-motion video. I wonder about the people who take video of bats. Do they know that's what they want to do? Is it a calling? Do they just wake one morning and think, I need to take slow-motion video of bats so that people will know how amazing they are? Or is it something that develops over years? Like maybe they go to college and take courses in photography and animal science to fill up their sched-ule once they finish the coursework for their marketing degree, and all of a sudden their life purpose becomes clear? I mean, taking pictures of bats seems like it's a thing that would require a great deal of focus, dedication, and equipment. I don't think you just fall into a job like that. When I wasn't working at the seafood restaurant, I spent most of my time in the room I rented. I didn't really go too many places. Where would I have gone?

What would I have done? When I moved, I brought with me a milk crate of books, a duffle bag of clothes, one pair of sneakers, and a sleeping bag. I washed my work shirt in the bathroom sink when I got home and hung it to dry over the closet door. I didn't have anything in the closet, not even hangers, but someone had installed a shelf in there for shoes. Since I didn't have a chair, I sometimes sat in the closet on the shelf and looked out the window at a woman who lived in the apartment across the street. I didn't sit in the closet with the intent of spying on the woman, but what else was there for me to look at? She had lots of things in her apartment. By that, I mean it looked like she had a full life. By full life, I mean a life different from the life I had. Whatever she had going on in her apartment was about as different from my life as I could imagine. It was almost like I was observing a different species, or maybe a type of highly evolved, intelligent plant. In the part of the apartment I could see, she had a table against the window, two chairs, a shelf where she stacked plates and cups, a cabinet where she kept wine, and a radio. There were also stacks of books and magazines on the table. She had posters of paintings on the wall. The only one I recognized was The Kiss by Gustav Klimt, which looked like two people being swallowed by a gold jellyfish. She wasn't pretty, but as soon as I saw her, I knew that I never wanted to not see her. For a few months, I was convinced that I would live in that room for the rest of my life and that she would live in her room in the apartment across the street for the rest of her life, and that even if we never met, our lives would entangle, and we'd die within moments of each other. By entangle, I don't mean that I ever expected to meet her, or even wanted to. I mean that our respective journeys would intersect in different ways. Like maybe I'd miss her by moments in the grocery store, and that perhaps she picked up a package of Oreos in the cookie aisle, but by the time she got to the produce section had decided that she didn't want them and set them down near the pears. Then I'd come in to buy my groceries, and get all the way to the produce aisle before remembering that I wanted Oreos, and

I'd see the package sitting near the pears just a moment before the produce clerk returned them to their proper shelf. When I wasn't thinking about our entangled lives, I was reading *The Adventures of Augie March* by Saul Bellow. Augie March is a long book, and it's the only book I remember reading in that room, even though I lived there six months, so I must have pulled more than one book from the milk crate. I can't even remember what other books I thought were important enough to bring with me. The only light I had came from the ceiling fixture, and sometimes it seemed far too bright, like I was interrogating the book, and on some nights, it seems like I couldn't even see the words on the page, like no matter how I held the book, it was in shadow. When I woke in the morning, the woman's curtains were always closed. I never saw her during the day. I barely even saw her at night. I saw a hip, an arm, the small of her back, the side of her face. I doubt I ever saw her entire body at once. I had no curtains in my room. I had nothing worth hiding. On my days off, I must have gone someplace, or done something, but for the life of me, I can't recall anything worth recalling. I don't remember the last time I saw the woman. I don't remember when I moved out of that apartment. I don't remember what happened to the milk crate of books. I didn't think about that room, or that woman, or that seafood restaurant until recently, when I went to a Frida Kahlo exhibit at the MFA. In the gift shop, I was looking at the postcards of famous paintings. There were a handful of Edward Hopper postcards, one of which was a painting called Night Windows. In it, a woman is seen through open windows. Her apartment is bright and spare. She's wearing a red dress and bending over for some reason. The apartment looks nothing like my memory. There's no reason why seeing a postcard of Night Windows should have reminded me of anything. There's no reason why this painting by Hopper, who died the year after I was born, should feel like a memory. There's no reason why seeing it should have reminded me of those bats under that streetlight. There was no reason to remember the woman I watched move about her apartment doing normal apartment things. When I looked away from the postcard rack, however, I saw the woman from my memory working the counter in the gift shop. I imagined our entangled lives. Things were happening that were bigger than me, bigger than anything I could explain. By bigger, I mean guided by forces that are beyond my comprehension. But the woman behind the counter was far too young to be the woman I'd watched all those years before. The woman behind the counter really didn't look like the woman in my memory any more than the woman in the painting. She was adjusting the rack of key rings next to the register. She smiled at a young girl who was buying a puzzle of Monet's Water Lilies and Japanese Bridge. She said, Oh, I love that painting. Every time I look at it, I see something different.

Hunger and Thirst

1.

After I quit the seafood restaurant, I rented a room on Dirk Street. The people who already lived there called the place the Dirk St. Emporium. The coffee table was an old lobster trap. There were three couches and probably two thousand LPs in the living room. They were in stacks, on shelves, under the chairs, everywhere. They weren't pristine records, either. They were listened to, hard. The guy whose records they were was named Ford. He said he got most of the records pretty cheap because he bought them in bulk when a record store called Penguin Feathers went out of business. He didn't seem to care what record was on, as long as there was music playing. If you wanted to hear, for instance, Al Green, or Judy Collins, or the 13th Floor Elevators, you just put it on. He had music I had never heard of at the time. He had Nina Simone, CAN, Richard Hell and the Voidoids, EPMD, Kraftwerk, The Monks, Betty Carter, Sonny Rollins, and countless others. If you didn't feel like putting the record back in the sleeve, that was okay. Just set it on the pile of vinyl on the lobster trap. There must have been two hundred unsleeved records in that living room at any given time. I didn't make much money then. I was often hungry. One of my roommates had a job at a local restaurant. I lived on the scraps she brought home. Once, she brought home fresh pasta. I'd never had fresh pasta. I ate it with ketchup. The first time she gave me a loaf of bread, I almost cried.

2.

I had quit working as a cook and found a job in an old theater. I don't know why I was hired. I had no experience. I learned about stage lighting: Lekos, Fresnels, PAR64s. I polished lenses. I sorted lighting gels. I learned how to coil cables, use a trim block, hang a boom. I learned how to run a follow spot. I learned about three-phase power. I learned about dimmer load. I learned a lot of things. It kept me busy. The first show I ever worked was the

Alvin Ailey Dance Company. They performed a dance called Hunger and Thirst. A man wearing only briefs danced toward a glass of water, but he couldn't get close enough to drink. He was repelled by invisible forces. I'd never seen modern dance before. I'd never seen any kind of dance outside American Bandstand or Soul Train. I was still too inexperienced to do any key technical jobs, but they let me operate the curtain. I stood in the wing, downstage right. A woman joined the thirsty man onstage. She was hunger. The man and the woman were kept from each other by a host of other dancers. These new dancers wore suits and dresses. They were formal, rigid. By rigid, I mean they made obstacles of themselves. In one climactic scene, the dancers crossed the stage in slow motion, a dozen taut black bodies bathed in diffuse amber light, chasing something only they could see. The woman disentangled from the group, her arm outstretched toward me, palm open, fingers slightly curled toward her face. She was maybe five feet away. I could see her fully and completely. By completely, I mean she was granting access to me, to all of us. I stood in darkness, behind three 750-watt Leko stage lights mounted on a boom. One light was at shin level, one waist high, and one at my head. All three lights would have appeared to her as a single luminescence. She rotated her arm from the shoulder, turning her palm toward the floor. She wasn't looking at me. She was interacting with the invisible.

3.

I've never been fully inside my body. You see a dancer, you think, how beautiful, how powerful, how graceful. All of that comes from the inside. They pull from the inside to understand and manipulate the outside. I don't think they have a choice. They do this to live. They invoke the necessary focus and fortitude to engage the physical body. This process takes years. I struggle with the most basic questions. I don't know what light is. Music is some sort of aural alchemy. I have a ringing in my ears. I can't even hear silence. If I'm in a room, I might be somewhere else. By somewhere else, I mean my ass and mind are not in the same place. I get overwhelmed by simple things. Bread, for instance. Or a dancer's palm. Sometimes, I'll be listening to a song, and it will be too much, like I've been permeated and if I hear one more measure, I'll dissolve. Musicians call up this internal focus, too. Years after I worked the Alvin Ailey show, a bluesman named Pinetop Perkins came to the theater to play a concert. We had his piano center-stage. He lifted the fallboard and ran his fingers across the keys. He must have been nearly eighty-five. He sat down at the bench and put his feet on the pedals. His manager said, Pinetop won't need the music desk. All the songs are in his head. Pinetop said, My name's Pinetop. That's the top of the pine.

4.

When I lived at the Emporium, I was dating a woman named Marissa off and on. By off and on, I mean she would move suddenly, and I would follow her. That's how I ended up there, in the Emporium. After I'd been renting the room for a few months, Marissa took a job in Albany. I didn't move, but I drove to Albany quite often. I'd leave on Friday night and come back on Sunday. I can't remember much about Albany. I can't remember much about the drive except that the car stereo was intermittent. A lot of the drive was done in silence. I don't remember traffic or road conditions or how I mapped the drive. I don't remember arriving at her apartment. I don't remember leaving. I don't remember our bodies. I can almost remember having sex with Marissa on her flat futon, and watching the flat gray Albany sky outside her window, but even those memories are mostly made up. I can't remember the me that remembered those things. When I wasn't driving to Albany on the weekends, I was working. The best days were days when I was working. One day, John Prine played our theater. I drove him from the hotel to the stage door. He smoked Marlboro Reds. He was drinking an Orange Crush. We didn't talk the entire ride to the theater. He sat with one foot on the van's dashboard and whistled. Later, when I asked him to sign my copy of Sweet Revenge, he wrote, Thanks for the ride.

5.

The last thing we did at night before leaving the theater was set out the ghost light. Our ghost light was a single 60-watt bare bulb on a small boom stand that we set downstage center to keep the ghosts company. It did a remarkable job lighting the inside of the theater. It didn't flicker like a candle, but it injected motion into the darkness nonetheless. There were always shadowy movements in my peripheral vision. I wasn't frightened. I wanted to see a ghost. I took a photo of the theater lit only by ghost light. You can see a bluish blob in the center of an aisle. I call it my ghost photo, but most likely it's the reflection of light on a speck of dust, or a flare of light from an unknown source. It's hard to tell. I showed the photo to my roommates at the Emporium. Nancy was toasting bread for us. Ford had just put on More Songs About Buildings and Food. He was holding the record sleeve in his hand. It was in the late afternoon, and sunlight filled the kitchen. Ford's orange cat was lying in the open window. Nancy set our toast onto the table. I said, Look at this photo. I set the photo next to the butter. We all leaned forward to see what we could see.

Emporium, Commune, Commissary, Grotto

Right after I moved into the Emporium, Ford and I used the Xerox machine at the theater and printed out a hundred flyers for a party we wanted to have. Ford said we had to get the flyers to the right people. I didn't know anyone, not yet. We walked through town with the flyers and Ford handed one to nearly everyone he saw, whether he knew them or not. We walked up Congress past Federal Tobacco and down Daniel Street past Golden Memories. The door was open there, but the bar was mostly quiet and dark. We walked down past the Rosa and down to the park, where we stood and watched the boats coming and going. The memorial bridge went up, and a red tugboat guided a large Cabletron ship through the channel under the raised platform. In one of the waiting cars, someone was playing "Magic Carpet Ride" by Steppenwolf. On the opposite side of the harbor, the shipyard buildings caught the late afternoon sun in a way that made the warehouses and industrial structures seem shimmery and fragile.

We watched it all for a while, and then Ford said we needed to go to the Commune. He said the people in the Commune would come to our party. We went down by Prescott Park and then up South Street and cut through the cemetery until we got to a big yellow house on Sagamore. I don't remember who was living there that we knew. There were several people in the kitchen. They were making spaghetti. They said, Come in, eat. Ford and I went in and told them we were having a party and that they were invited. One of the women there had been in a bad car accident and wore an apparatus on her leg that was fusing her bones. It looked like a medieval torture device. It looked like a cage. I didn't know her name. I didn't know anyone's name. I still don't know their names. If my life depended on it, I couldn't tell you anyone's name in that house. After we ate spaghetti with them, we drank two bottles of wine. We were all sitting around the table smoking. No one was bothered by the smoke. The smoke hung heavy in the room, a landscape below the light fixture, a mountain range. The light fixture hung down from the ceiling on a wire, like someone had pulled on the globe and the entire thing came away from the ceiling. We stayed until dusk. The people there said they would come to the Emporium the following night. When we left, Ford said we needed to drop some flyers off at the Commissary. Ford had a name for all the houses that we went to.

The Commissary was an apartment above Richardson's Market. No one had done maintenance on the building in decades. The plaster was crumbling in some places, and the floor was covered in its dust. In other places, the ceiling was water-stained and bowing inward, malformed by years of leaks. The place was either too damp, or too dry, and sometimes it was both. Three to six people lived at the Commissary at any given time, but when Ford and I arrived, there were twelve people sitting on and around the couch and watching Koyaanisqatsi. No one seemed to notice when we came in. Ford and I sat down at a table behind the couch. I wasn't sure what I was watching, but I was quickly engrossed. It seemed to be a movie about everything, but I didn't have those words then. Someone handed me a beer. I took out a small pipe and filled the bowl and passed it around. No one asked where it came from, but eventually it made it back to me, so I filled it again and sent it on its way. Everything had a life of its own. Everyone was just watching the movie. It was nearly dark outside, but the street seemed brighter than the room we were in. The television volume was very loud; I could hear motorcycles ripping down State Street and parking in front of Wally's. I could hear the chatter of the bikers mixing in with the Phillip Glass soundtrack. I never really liked Wally's, but Ford often drank there. It was mostly bikers and shipyard workers. The pool table in the back room had two decent-sized gouges in the felt. It was mostly dark, and dank. Most of the buildings on this end of the town were dark and dank, the windows small, the walls settled beyond level, the floors uneven, ceilings low. One of the guys at the theater had lived here his whole life, and he said the town had gone soft, spoiled by tourist money. His name was Walter, and he seemed to know everything about rigging, lighting, and stagecraft. Walter said that with the shipyard, the port, and the Air Force base, the town used to have a real working-class vibe. He said the town used to be flooded with Navy guys. He said you'd have Navy guys on one side of town, and the civilian shipyard workers on the other, and the Air Force guys in another. He said it was wall-to-wall drunks, drunks as far as the eye could see. He said he didn't understand how any submarine made it past the Isles of Shoals without sinking, or any plane managed to take off from the air-patch, considering how drunk all the people who worked on those machines were night after night. He said it used to be that if you went downtown on a weekend, it would be wall-to-wall crewcuts. He said the town wasn't anything like it used to be. Another time, he said that the town changing wasn't necessarily a bad thing. He said that if he could get from one end of the town to the other without some drunk puking on his shoes, he'd have to consider that a positive. Still, he said, the good old days.

At some point, Koyaanisqasti ended and the meaning of the word appeared on the screen. It was a word from the Hopi language. It meant life in turmoil. It meant crazy life. It meant life out of balance, life disintegrating, or a way of life that called for a new way of living. When the screen went dark, no one moved for a while. We continued to sit together. People were yelling on the street down below, and it was like they were yelling from the moon, just sounds, not words. The air was hot and damp. The ceiling in the living room bowed inward.

It was well dark by the time Ford and I got out to the Village, which wasn't a house, but a neighborhood. It was a long walk, and we walked on the tracks past the salt piles and the scrap pile down by the old pier built for a shipyard that no longer existed. We walked under the 95 Bridge and up into the Heights, a group of brick buildings that were built to house workers of another defunct shipyard. Ford said that when he moved here, he lived in the Heights. The houses were tiny, but nice. He said his landlord never once came to his house. He said one year the furnace stopped working and he called the landlord seven times before anyone came to fix it. It had belched black smoke up into the house. They had to hire a cleaning company to come in and steam-clean the place. He said the landlord had been angry about it all, stopping short of accusing Ford of sabotaging the furnace. He said he wished Ford had called him before the furnace malfunctioned. Ford asked him how he was supposed to do that. Was he supposed to see the future?

The Village was also built for shipyard workers, but the shipyard still existed. Ford said they were supposed to be nice brick buildings, but the Navy shipped all the bricks to a different Navy housing project down south, and sent all the materials for the southern housing project up north, so that's why they looked like they were falling down. He said they just couldn't handle the northern winters. All the houses looked the same. All the houses looked drafty. Some houses still had the plastic on their windows from the winter. We walked to the clear edge of the development, where we went to a house Ford called the Grotto, mostly because it was always damp. We went around the back of the house and knocked at the sliding doors. Behind the property, there was a steep hill covered in beach roses and brambles and short, nearly leafless trees that seemed exhausted from the sheer act of growing. At the bottom of the hill were some rarely used tracks that led to the power station further up the river. The smokestacks towered in the distance. Billowing clouds rose from them into the night sky. We'd been walking around for hours delivering our flyers. I was tired, and still consumed with whatever happened while we were watching Koyaanisqatsi.

After a while, a young girl came to the door. She was maybe twelve. She looked as if she'd been sleeping. Ford knew her, and she seemed happy to see him. She slid open the door and Ford went inside, but I stayed outside and went over to the hill. I could hear the girl's mother saying hello to Ford. I had the sudden urge to leave and go down the hill to the tracks and just walk. I couldn't tell why I was thinking this. I didn't feel like I was really there. I wasn't sure where I was. I could have been anywhere. I don't know how long I waited outside for Ford to return. It was probably only a few moments, but when I turned around, the axis of everything had shifted. I didn't recognize where I was. I wasn't sure of anything. Ford and I didn't talk much on the long walk back to the Emporium. He said that he expected a lot of people to show up to our party. He said that people sounded excited about it. He said that his band was going to play. Ford's band was called Gandhi's Lunchbox. He said he was trying to get another band to play too, but he wouldn't tell me which band. I figured that it was a band called the Queers, because Ford's cousin played bass. But the Queers had already been mentioned on the cover of Rolling Stone, so it might be difficult to persuade them to play in our basement. He said that no matter what happened, he was getting drunk.

Winter Rental

When I left the Emporium, I moved into a winter rental at the beach. The owner met me at the house. He drove a gleaming white Mercedes sedan. I was leaning against the fence when he arrived. He started talking to me as soon as he opened the car door. He said he bought the place as an investment property, but it was a money pit. He was trying to sell it before it ruined him. He said he'd had trouble with the appraisal, but he thought he might sell it before the winter was up, even if he had to take a loss, and if that was the case he'd try to make sure that whoever bought it understood that there was a tenant in place, but that they might not care, and I might have to move in the middle of the winter. He said the rules were sort of murky. He said he could do very little about it, but he would try. He said it was out of his hands. He held up his hands and sort of shrugged. When he was showing me the house, he pointed out all the flaws. He said he was sorry that he had to charge as much as he did considering the place had so many problems, but he had to make his taxes, at least, or what was the point. He said of all the properties he owned, this one gave him the most headaches. He said it was the only property that he owned that was more trouble than it was worth. This was early October. He had long pants on, but he was still wearing sandals. He looked like a beach, if a beach was human. He looked like sand. He even had a shell on a leather cord around his neck. He wore a watch that was four times as large as it actually needed to be to do its job. His watch was so big that it weighed down his arm. When he showed me the bedroom, he said, This is where the magic will happen. Magic? I said. With the girls, he said. Oh right, I said, magic. Then he showed me the bathroom, and the place where I had to make sure I kept a space heater in the winter or the pipes would freeze. I don't have a space heater, I said. You should get one, he said. You can get a good one for fifty bucks. If you don't, the pipes will freeze, and that's going to be expensive. He said that the roof was good at least, and that I wouldn't have to worry about any leaks. He said the only problem I'd have with water was when it froze in the pipes. He said that the houses weren't really designed for the winter, so he had to make allowances. Allowances? I said. The space heater and such, he said. Then he walked me out into the backyard, which was only about fifteen feet deep, but someone had crammed a shed back there and the shed was packed floor to ceiling with cardboard boxes. The owner said they were there when he bought the place. He said he wasn't sure what was in the boxes, that it could be anything, really. He bought the property at auction, he said, and it came as is. The guy who owned it, he said, was sort of a whack job and never paid his taxes. He said that he meant to come over and clear out the boxes, but he never had a chance. He said part of him thought the guy who lost the house would come by and want whatever was in there, but so far, that hadn't happened. Some boxes obviously had paper in them, and a few seemed to be stuffed with clothes. But it was hard to tell. The top boxes had sunken into the bottom boxes. I was afraid that if I touched them, they'd disintegrate. The owner kept looking at his large watch. We went around to the gate and back out to the front of the house where his big Mercedes was parked. To my left, I could just see the strip and the sky opening up over the water. The owner saw me looking, and he said, You can't see the water, but you know it's there, right? Yes, I said, I know the ocean is there. The clouds that day were low and flat, and it felt like I was nowhere. The owner was still talking to me, but he wasn't saying anything important. The breeze was cool, and all of his words got caught in the wind and disappeared before finding my ears. I already had an envelope of rent and security money in my pocket, almost all the money I had. The owner kept talking and looking at his watch. He put his hand on his Mercedes. A few gulls were floating high above us. I offered him the envelope. I said, Is cash okay? And he said, Cash is king. Then he was gone, like he couldn't get out of there fast enough. I never saw him in person again. I had mostly moved in before he'd even turned off the street. I walked around the house and looked at the different problems. Only two of the windows had screens. The refrigerator buzzed unless you kept a hand pressed on the door. The freezer was so iced over that it was impossible to put new items inside. There was only one working outlet in the kitchen. I didn't have a bed. There was a card table in the closet and a folding lawn chair in the hall. There wasn't much to look at except a big crack in the plaster running up one wall and across the living room ceiling. I pinned a magazine photo of Keith Richards next to the crack. He was wearing a top hat decorated with feathers. The caption said, String us up, we still won't die. This was back when the beach was still a rough place. I could hear yelling on the strip just up the street where there was a bar called the Pearl. Something was happening there, either a party or a fight or both. For the five months I lived there, there was always a fight or a party at the Pearl, sometimes both at the same time. Just past the Pearl was a bar called Willies. And just past Willies was a bar called Majors. There was another bar past Majors, but I couldn't tell you the name. To this day, I couldn't tell you the difference between any of them. I walked down toward the water and even though it was a warm autumn day, there was hardly anyone around. It was low tide and I went along the hard-packed sand and then climbed back up to the seawall and sat for a while watching the gray sky and the silver water. There were several massive tankers far out near the horizon. I stayed on the wall until the wind picked up, and then I walked back to the bungalow. I went out to the shed and wondered what was in the boxes. That's where I was when Ford came by with a bag full of Indian food from Shalimar. He was sorry to have lost the house on Dirk Street. We had packed up all his albums and loaded them into a van he borrowed. He found a room in another house close to town, but they didn't want his albums all over the place, so he had to put the albums in storage. They have a CD player, Ford said with a sour look. We sat on the back stoop and ate from the cartons. The shed door was open. Neither of us wanted to look in the boxes. Ford said,

No matter where I've moved, there's always been boxes already there when I moved in. I told him about the owner of the bungalow and his giant watch. I told him about the space heater. Ford tore off a piece of naan bread. That guy's a dick, he said, let his fucking pipes freeze.

The Storm They Call Perfect

On my days off, I'd walk through town and down Route 1A toward the nearly empty parking lots and shuttered public restrooms of the state park. Just west of the harbor inlet, the Seabrook Nuclear Power Plant loomed beyond the marshes. Mostly people envision the reactor dome, but really it's a huge facility with mostly square or squarish buildings. After the first few times I saw it, I stopped noticing it. I didn't even think about it when I walked across the inlet bridge into Seabrook. It just wasn't as shocking as you'd imagine.

I didn't walk with any purpose. This was before smartphones, so I wasn't looking for a good place to take Instagram pictures. I was just walking. I don't remember thinking about anything in particular. On a warmish day a few weeks after I settled in, I walked all the way through Seabrook and down into Salisbury, where big stone jetties reach out into the Atlantic where the Merrimack River meets the ocean. I walked out just a bit onto the jetty, but the granite was slippery, and a decent breeze had picked up. It took most of the morning to walk that far and on the way back, I stopped and had lunch at a place in Salisbury. I hadn't talked to anyone all morning. I couldn't remember the last time I'd talked to someone when I wasn't at work. I suppose I'd talked to people in the store. I wasn't avoiding conversation on purpose. I wasn't a recluse, I mean. That's just what was happening.

The place I went into was mostly empty, except for three older men sitting at the bar nursing short beers. I think it was called the Star Café, but it reminded me of Martini's bar in It's a Wonderful Life after Jimmy Stewart wished away his existence. It looked like the sort of place that would kick you out if you ordered mulled wine. It was the sort of place that served hard drinks for men that wanted to get drunk fast. But the sign also advertised hotdogs. The three men at the bar kept their heads down. The bartender didn't look terribly friendly, but I asked him for a hotdog and a beer, and he gestured to a table and said he'd bring them right over. The hotdog and chips were on an oval plate that was big enough to hold an entire Christmas ham. There wasn't any mustard, and I couldn't drum up the energy to ask for any. I don't think I would have thought about this place ever again if there wasn't a girl sitting two tables away with a pile of books. She appeared to be doing homework. She was maybe nine or ten years old, and she didn't seem to belong to anyone. No one mentioned her at all. Every once in a while, one of the men at the bar would mumble something to one of the other men, but no one turned to talk to her. I wondered if I was the only one who saw her. But when she went to the bathroom, one of the men turned slightly, acknowledging a disturbance to the tableau. When she came back from the bathroom, she stared at me for a little while. I gave her a little wave. She didn't say anything. She didn't wave back. Eventually, she sat down and returned her attention to her books. When the bartender turned on the Weather Channel, the girl put all of her books into a knapsack and said, I'm going home. She didn't really address anyone in particular. It was like she was talking to the building. When she opened the front door, I could tell that the wind had picked up. The clouds were coming in quickly over the water. I left money on the table and stood up and left the bar, too.

When I got outside, I walked back two blocks toward the beach. The wind was strong and whipped around me. The ocean was stirred up too, like it had lost its focus. The waves seemed to be fighting against each other. I'd find out later that this was the beginnings of a nor'easter that would later become known as the Perfect Storm, and even have a bestselling book written about it, and a blockbuster movie starring George Clooney based on the book. I didn't have a television, and I rarely listened to the radio, and I'd been caught unawares that a storm of considerable force was bearing down. There were actually two storms, and when the nor'easter swallowed up Hurricane Grace, then it became the storm they call Perfect. Hurricane Bob had landed hard two months earlier, but I was living at the Emporium then, and we lit candles and drank wine and listened to some Weather Report tapes until the batteries in Ford's boombox ran down.

I saw the girl one more time before I turned toward home. She was down on the sand, just above the high tide line, looking at the water. Every once in a while, I caught what sounded like snippets of her voice. I thought maybe she was talking to herself. Or talking to the water. Or maybe the wind. I told myself that she must have certainly been related to one of the men at the Star Café. She couldn't be alone. I looked up and down the beach. There were a few more people out now, people interested in watching the storm develop. I thought someone must be looking for her. Someone must have been keeping track of her. I turned around to see if maybe it might be obvious which house the girl lived in. Down near the jetties, there was a nearly empty RV camp. There were some trailers there that looked as though they might have permanent residents. Most of the ocean view houses were empty and boarded for the season, but maybe the girl's family lived in a winter rental like me. Several cars with surfboards strapped to their luggage racks pulled up and parked. The surfers were giddy. The water was ragged and unpredictable. One of them kept saying, Look at it, look at it, oh man look at it. I watched them take down their boards and gather their gear, and when I turned back to the beach, the girl was gone.

By the time I made it home, the winds made walking difficult. I had to steady myself on guardrails and utility poles. By the time I crossed over the harbor inlet bridge, the power plant was a nebulous silhouette in the gloom. The beach had a party atmosphere despite the wind and rain and barbarous skies. There were more storm watchers gathered at the seawall than I'd seen at the beach since I moved in. There must have been several hundred people standing above me on the wall, standing sideways, braced against the wind. I could hear them talking, but their words sounded as foreign to me as Arabic. It didn't occur to me to ask them what was happening. It didn't occur to me that I might talk with them.

They seemed friendly enough, dressed in brightly colored Gore-Tex raincoats and Patriots ponchos. Dozens of surfers were riding the large waves. It was early afternoon, but it felt like night. The light was thick. The surfers all wore wetsuits. Years later, I got to know a winter surfer. He said, There's no surf like a hurricane surf. He said anyone surfing in New Hampshire is hardcore. He said you just really have to love the water. He said it was all about love, really, and even though he knew that was too vague and mushy to mean much, it was the truest way to describe his need to surf. I didn't know that then, that it was all about love. To me, they seemed equal amounts silly and daring. I was soaked and cold so I didn't watch long.

Of all the bars on the strip, only the Pearl was open. "I Love Rock 'n' Roll" by Joan Jett and the Blackhearts was blasting inside, but the wind dampened the song's energy. I had only been in the Pearl a couple of times, but the regulars did not seem like the sort of drinkers to let a little weather dictate their regularly scheduled plans. I still didn't have much in the way of furniture at the bungalow. I dried off and lay down on my mattress and covered myself with my sleeping bag. The bungalow was surrounded by houses and duplexes that shielded it from much of the wind, but even so, the house vibrated with the force of each gust. There were long sustained moments where the walls seemed to expand and contract, and the air all around felt compressed, and my body compressed too, and then the wind would shift, or gust in a different direction, and I would almost float from my mattress. It was as though I was being pulled up by invisible strings, like I was a part of the structure of the storm, as though my presence in the bungalow was of some vital importance in a complex schematic. I felt the rising and falling pressure in the room. I could feel my pulse in my ears. I pressed my tongue against my teeth. I didn't need words to understand any of this. During the long night, I forgot all of the words I would need to describe the moment. Later, when I was asked what it was like to be sleeping so close to the perfect storm, I had no idea what to say.

Paradise

Once, my boss at the theater took me to the Boston Opera House, which was dark at the time. By dark, I mean boarded up, abandoned. Terry knew a guy who knew a guy who agreed to let us remove the old lighting equipment that was sitting unused. They'd probably agreed on some price. Terry had a few work trucks that he'd had since he owned a lighting company in the late 60s. The truck we were in when we went to the Opera House was the truck that Terry used to haul equipment to Woodstock. He hadn't wanted to go to Woodstock. He thought there was going to be a lot of violence. He had worked the Newport Jazz Festival just a few weeks before, and saw someone throw a rock at Sly and the Family Stone's tour bus. The bus driver was spooked and climbed back into the bus and drove off with all of Sly's wardrobe. When Sly performed, he had to wear whatever he was wearing when he was on the bus. I can't imagine Sly was pleased about that. Terry said he never felt safe at the Newport Jazz Festival. People were pushing against the barrier fences, he said, and something bigger was brewing the whole time. He said the whole country felt like that. He said it was only about a month later that the Tate-LaBianca murders happened in LA, although no one knew about Manson yet. He said the whole summer felt like coals smoldering in the dense duff of a forest floor. So when he was asked to come to Woodstock, he originally said no. But then someone begged him to bring spotlights. They didn't have any spotlights lined up, and if his company didn't bring some, the festival was screwed. He thought he could get in and get out quickly. The spotlights he brought were carbon-arc Super Troupers, probably the best spotlight ever made. They were big and heavy, and were hauled in boxes that were also big and heavy. Terry loaded six Super Troupers onto the back of his truck and drove to Woodstock. He said that by the time he unloaded, he knew there was no way out. He said his truck was surrounded by a sea of long hair, road cases, and yellow scaffolding; the chaotic infrastructure of the Summer of Love. It was a good thing, too, that Terry went to Woodstock because most of the stage lighting sat in the mud behind the stage for the entire festival. If you watch footage of Woodstock, the light for the performers came from Terry's Super Troupers. Anyway, that's the truck we were in when we went down to the Opera House. It was a loud, yellow, heavy-duty Ford F-250 with work boxes on the side. If you saw him, you probably wouldn't think that Terry was a guy with a lot of money. After he sold his company, he sailed around the world on the QE2 twice, but then he'd show up to work in a jacket he bought secondhand twenty years earlier.

The Opera House has since been restored to its full grandeur, but on the day that I was there, we went in the back door and straight down into a dank storage room. There was lighting equipment piled everywhere. To me, it looked like garbage, but Terry saw something beautiful in salvage. There was a ten-foot-high pile of black cabling in the corner that Terry inspected. He looked at the boxes of lenses and templates. He flipped out when he saw a Century spotlight from the 1930s. The housing was nearly rusted through, and the hinges on the doors were frozen, but he thought it was perfect. It came from an era of theater that preceded him by about thirty years. Then the guy that Terry knew took us on a tour of the rest of the Opera House underground. It was a maze of dressing rooms with broken mirrors, storage rooms with empty shelves, and evidence all around that someone, or something, had lived or was living in the catacombs. Someone had dragged a twin-sized mattress and sleeping bag into one of the dressing rooms. It didn't look all that different from the mattress and sleeping bag on the floor of the room I was renting. There were numerous padlocked exit doors, but the guy that Terry knew said that sometimes he encountered a homeless person or two. He said they found a way in. He said he used to make them leave, but after a while, he stopped trying. He said they come and go. He said the theater was basically the most insecure building he'd ever seen. In the vaudeville days, he said, the place would have been packed with actors, dancers, musicians, comedians, stagehands, clerks, assistants, electricians, reporters, messengers, trainers—you name it. He said the wardrobe department alone would have employed ten people. He pointed out the tracks in the floor that were used by equipment wagons and supply carts and costume racks. It would have been like a train station, he said, carts and racks and people shouting, the hallways filled with smoke from an endless stream of cigarettes. He said if he closed his eyes, he could sometimes see what it would have been like. He said it wasn't difficult to conjure the ghosts. Both Terry and me stood in the corridor while he closed his eyes. Neither of us interrupted him until he came back on his own. The last room he showed us had three big tubs. When I say tubs, I mean gigantic, tiled pools, each one bigger than any bedroom I'd ever slept in. This is where the seals would have been, he said. Seals? I said. Seals, he said, for the animal acts. They would've had seals, dogs, rabbits, birds, you name it. Even horses, he said. Even an elephant from time to time.

Terry and I spent a few hours picking the best stuff out of the storage room and loading it into his truck. He said the truck would haul a lot of weight. He said he'd just have to check the tires on the way home to make sure they weren't getting too hot. He said if they got too hot, they'd explode. After we got the first batch of lights loaded, we went to Burger King for lunch. While we ate our Whoppers, he told me more about Woodstock. He said he wouldn't trade his experience there for anything. He said it wasn't all fun and games, of course. A couple of times, he had to climb the scaffolding to help someone who went up to get a better look, but then got scared. He said he was never much for drugs, but that he imagined climbing fifty feet of scaffolding might seem like a good idea if you were tripping, but the reality was a different story. He said that one thing he didn't expect at Woodstock was the Army. He said that when he saw the Army helicopters arriving, he thought the peace-and-love crowd would clash with the death-from-above soldiers, but the helicopters were just bringing food. He said when the helicopters took off, the soldiers threw flowers down to the hippies. He said it was one of the most incongruous images he'd ever seen, and that even though he'd seen it with his own eyes, he was never quite sure that it had actually happened. It was only mid-afternoon, but the Burger King was shadowy and nearly empty. Terry said he wouldn't describe Woodstock as a paradise or anything, but what is paradise anyway? He swirled his soda in his cup and reached for his fries.

We loaded the truck with as much as it could carry, but we hadn't even made a dent in the pile of equipment at the Opera House. Terry said we'd be coming back the next day. It was pouring when we left the theater district and drove down Tremont, but by the time we crossed the Tobin Bridge, the sun started to break over Chelsea. By the time we got to Revere, there wasn't a cloud in the sky. You could tell it had rained hard though because the road was steaming, and the water was still pooled in the gutters and parking lots with lousy drainage. Because of the weight, the truck rode high in the front. Maybe it was the angle, or the size of the truck's windshield, but I couldn't tell what time of day it was. The sunlight seemed to be coming from inside the truck. There was a moment when the light was too amber, too purple, too pretty. By too pretty, I mean I didn't have the capacity to explain its beauty. I looked over at Terry to see if I was going crazy, but he was in the light too. Or maybe the light was coming from him. Even though he was two feet away from me at most, it seemed like a different world.

Clawfoot

My wife saw the clawfoot tub sitting in front of a house in an older section of town. There was a bunch of construction material all around the tub. We knocked on the door and the owner said he'd sell it to us for three-fifty. He said after his wife had a stroke, she could no longer climb over the lip. He said it was the communication between her brain and her legs that wasn't working properly. He said it had been a difficult time for them because both of their sons lived in North Carolina now, and they had no one to help with the little things. By little things, he meant getting in and out of the tub, dressing, feeding his wife, and the like. He said both of his sons worked for the University of North Carolina at Chapel Hill. He said they both were in finance and they both married sweet gals and had two great kids each. Symmetry, I said. Pardon? the man said. Don't mind him, my wife said. The man told us that he'd hired a company to renovate the bathroom and install a stand-up bathtub. He said that's the price you pay for getting old. He said he didn't have much good to say about getting old. He said each year, things got five percent more difficult. He said he wasn't sure how long he could even stay in his house.

The tub was extremely difficult to move. It's cast iron, and it weighs three hundred fifty pounds. We had to bring it upstairs using the only staircase, which has a ninety-degree angle in the middle. It took three of us nearly an hour. We succeeded in moving the tub, but we were all defeated by the process. My neighbor leaned against the wall with his hands on his knees. Another friend joined me lying on the floor. Later, that same friend would help us tear down one of the house's crumbling chimneys. I bought a couple of small sledgehammers for the project, but the chimney was in such bad shape that we barely needed them. We just lifted the bricks off and threw them into the side yard. We worked our way from the roof to the second floor, first floor, and then basement. We looked like we'd been down in the coal mines. The chimney had been filled with a century of soot, bird bones, insects, and spiders. We found trowels and brushes dropped inside during some repair, decades ago. Later, that same friend helped me pour a foundation where the old farmhouse summer kitchen once was. One hundred thirty bags of concrete in a single day. That's ten thousand four hundred pounds of concrete mixed and poured. So, in hindsight, moving the tub was difficult, but nothing is easy here. When I think about the difficult days of renovating our house, the tub barely registers.

The man who sold us the tub said that his two boys would sit on the lip and slide into the basin. He said they had to put towels around on the floor to soak up all the water. He told us this when we went back to pick up the tub. My wife gave him three hundred fifty dollars. One dollar for every pound. The time in the man's life when his sons were enjoying the tub sounded like some of the best for him, before the sad truth of aging, the sad truth of children living far away, and the sad truth of a younger couple driving away with the tub sticking out of the back of a minivan. But we didn't have time to worry about the tub's previous owner. My wife worked diligently to scrape away the many layers of paint on the outside. She used some caustic chemical peels to vanquish the paint buildup in the ridges of the claw feet. She wore a mask in case the old paint was leaded. It took her weeks to prep the tub. And still another year before we were finished with the house. All of that seems like a long time ago, the memories of the difficult work swept away by newer memories. We have our tub memories in addition to the memories that it came with. We brought those memories into our memories. Perhaps those memories help shape ours. My daughter, for instance, also liked to slide from the lip down into the basin. Now she's grown, too. Now she has moved away. Now my wife has a hip that makes it difficult to get in and out of the tub. Now I look at the tub and I see our final tub. When I fill the tub, I think, how many more tubs of water do I have? How many more times will I bathe? If I take a shower in this tub every single day for the rest of my life, how many showers? Eight thousand? Is that enough? When the previous owner remembered his boys sliding, how many memories was he accessing? A hundred? No, too many. Three? Maybe not enough. Let's say ten. He was thinking about ten baths that his sons took before growing and moving and having families. How much time are we talking about? Ten baths, maybe a half hour each. Five hours that are fixed as memories worth remembering. Five hours that mean something. Enough for him to want to relate the story to us. Enough for me to remember his memories.

Evie painted the tub and claws glossy black. She scrubbed the tub and scoured away any stains, any evidence of use. The shower curtain was white cotton. It was made in Vietnam. I'm thinking about the man who made the curtain. I'm thinking about his home and memories he has of his children. I'm thinking about the container ship that carried the curtain over the ocean. I'm thinking about the crane operator that pulled the shipping container off the ship. The apparatus for making things is a spider web. The man who opened the container. The person who drove the forklift. The person who drove the truck. The person who cut the box. The person who stocked the shelves. The person who scanned the barcode. My wife, who carried the curtains to the bathroom, who clipped them to the rods with silver clips. The tub itself, Lord, the tub, and all the fingers, bodies, soaps, unguents, salts, scrubs, skin, hair, blood, tears, particles, molecules, electrons, energy, heat. How about the systems that allowed the tub to become a basin, a playground, a receptacle of memory? What of the designing, shaping, smelting, pouring, painting, shipping, connecting? What of the water cycle, the vast system of reservoirs, the public utilities, the miracle of indoor plumbing, the weight of the tub as we hauled it up the stairs, the muscles in my legs, back, shoulders, the sweat on the floor, my pounding heart, our ablutions? Is there any way to contain or codify the absurdity of these nearly infinite connections?

Yesterday, I walked past the house where we got the tub. The house had new owners. Perhaps the man and his wife could no longer bear the emptiness of their home. Perhaps they had died.

The house had been completely renovated. If I hadn't been sure that we'd bought the tub there, I never would have recognized it. The new owners had added a wraparound porch. They added a garage. There were three girls playing on a swing set in the backyard. They were yelling, or laughing, or singing. Someone had planted tall grasses along the back fence. Just above the treetops, I could see the giant Toyota sign at the dealer's on the bypass. I didn't pause long. There wasn't much I wanted to look at there. I kept moving down Boyd Street and turned onto Dennett. I followed Dennett until I hit Maplewood. I stayed on Maplewood until I could cut behind the Sheraton and down toward Ceres. There, I stood at the docks and watched the tugboats jostling against their moorings. From there, I walked over to Four Tree Island and over the bridge by the fish co-op. I cut down through the park and out past the pool to where there are picnic tables. I climbed down onto the rocks and watched the boats in the channel move past the old Navy prison. There was a flat-bottomed gundalow moving slowly through the difficult currents, probably with a group of students on board. The gundalows were traditionally used for the rivers and estuaries and harbors. This boat gave historical and educational tours. My friend who helped move the tub and tear down the chimney volunteered as a deckhand. He said he loved being on the boat and watching the shifting landscape from the deck. He said he particularly liked the moment when the boat left the harbor and went further inland, toward Great Bay. He said it was like moving from one world into another, where river current and channel current collided. He said understanding wind was important, of course because it was a sailboat, but the currents in our river were fast-moving, and understanding them was para-mount. He said people always complained about the treacherous currents, but he found them meditative. He said the two currents are endlessly pushing against each other. He said the water just does what it does, and all he had to do was pay attention.

S Stephanie

What We Brought on the Journey: 16 Poems

In her poems, S Stephanie provides the reader with a compassionate view of human existence observed from a deeply empathic standpoint. In local scenes, this poet observes her community and herself with the eye of someone whose personal experience has made her an advocate for justice. As the best poems do, these show glimpses of us as characters in our various myths, fighting heartbreaking loneliness after loss, and expressing fears of a world that seems to keep stampeding over the most vulnerable of us. In the final words of her collection: "Grief–this was the song every plant along the way, sang/as those we started out with dropped behind/dropped away." J.P.

I don't often dream of Johnny Depp

but images of the instinctual work of crows
building a nest each year, only to have it
stolen by the cuckoo or another
brood parasite, these are what woke me
this morning. These and images of all
those idiosyncratic personalities
Depp must become for each new
blockbuster season.
I think I woke because, well

who among us hasn't fallen
into our own Cheshire smile
or sunk into an ocean of ghosts
of our own making. In the dream
I think we were hurling sticks
at ourselves. Nothing was really
stolen. I think the clips of identity
we were caught up in, and the ones
we took of ourselves, were reeling
frame by frame in the slowest of motion
back there in the dark, while
we were the transfixed audience
watching. Yes, there we are
that's us! The ones in the last row
with our hands over our eyes.

Ghazal For the Man at the Next
Table Who Looks Like He's Praying

The sad trees miss the color-filled feathers of parrots
The green moss beneath mourns the real wisdom of parrots

Oil is tugged at, pulled up, out of earth, tossed to the sky
It saturates all, smells like the tongues of dead parrots

At night border refugees huddle against wire, pray
But their prayers land on the invisible ears of parrots

Our sick trade their medicines for food, a little light
When our sick die, no one wins, not even rich parrots

The man at the next table looks like he's praying, as if
Our country has fallen into the beaks of dead birds

While waiting for the Italian Omelet Special

which comes with a side of "Phil's Red Hash", an elderly couple next to me eats in silence. I am struck by how peaceful they seem with no need for conversation. No need for eye contact or cues. She finishes her coffee while he finishes reading the news. When it comes time to pay the check, he reaches smoothly into his worn back pocket. She doesn't watch him, instead I do. And I remember my friend's grandmother, how when her husband died, we discovered she did not know how to pay the bills or drive the car. At first it seemed as though we were forever helping her. But then we realized how short a time it was, just three months between his death and hers.

Family History

Years ago or yesterday
earlier than that, once
upon a time

all those details
led through a forest
or was it a cabin

she had a wart
no he had a cane
they died or divorced

her shoes were lost
no his acorns were stolen
they threw the baby out

it returned
forgave them
with a vengeance

he climbed a tower of hair
she danced dishes around dwarfs
but they kissed

everybody always kisses

Widow's Fugue

(Inspired by Sylvia Plath's "Little Fugue")

What do I know of fugues
or yew trees for that matter?
I live East, in a house of brick

and watch the solid maples
drop red leaves without spilling
blood year after year in this place

I call home. I watch clouds
from the kitchen sink and read
their daily messages about water

and dry hours. I talk to my dead.
Yes, I remember their fingers
that tap to no song now.

But sometimes I catch their voices
talking to another woman
who must have at some point been me.

After High Tide

(after Sylvia Plath's "Berck-Plage")

Swells of memory roll in, and again
just as relentless seas flush cove
loosen rock, they leave so much salt
in their wake, leave stringlike weeds
in my throat. Long strands
of a marriage, of love, change color
change texture before my eyes:
now brown, now brittle, now dry.

Seagulls screech at tossed heaps
knowing the work it will take here
to find a morsel of substance

something, anything that won't
wriggle its way under or out
of grasp. Gulls believe in
something that died a good death.
That is what is respected here.
That is what is considered holy

what is safe for the stomach.
But I know better; I know the gulls
are misinformed, the gulls are worse
than lemmings. Let the gulls swoop
to others' conclusions. Memory is
only one part nature, the other walks
a line in the imagination—trudges
through its thick stretch of griefs.
Shell shards and all, hidden
beneath the pretty sea roses.

My Fear

(Inspired by Zbigniew Herbert)

My fear sleeps with its clothes on
raises its head every hour or two
glances at the clock, checks the stove
is off and jumps at the echo
of the latest neighborhood shooting.

My fear can barely fix its hair
with the dull comb of news some mornings
or brush its teeth with rust-bristled stories.
It hears my Irish grandfather turn in his grave
at how ill-kept and pathetic my tools.

But some days my fear walks
along the banks of this town's river
watching for the children in cages
those slouching in heat at the borders
and women missing from everywhere.

It either buries them carefully in gentle graves
of memory, or presses them softly
between pages. And yes, it saves them all.

Different Views

There are those who have seen
The inside of thirteen foster homes
Thirteen ways to store your toothbrush
Thirteen bruises from a belt, a switch, a hairbrush
The sandpaper stubble up close
of one who kissed you but shouldn't have
The importance of those who didn't

Those who have seen
The wrong words on the side of a building
The right words in a book
The many shapes the sky takes on
depending on the angle of daydream
The talk of trees when you sit beneath them
The crazy zigzag maps of bumblebees
traveling the flowers and favorite poems

The sentence handed to the poor each election
The exact keys to all locks
The courage it takes to turn them
And there are those who certainly have seen
None of this
Who for whatever their reason
have chosen a different version

About Our Silence

They've squeezed our..., wait
I am searching for the right word here.
What is it they squeeze? What
is it they are trying to wring out of us
our own neighbors and classmates
those we think are like us?
They have squeezed our...but
it is now such a crisp fall morning
we begin the season with sweaters
and with each sweater we put on
we are trying to protect that...
they squeezed when they began
locking children in cages.

*No one can take our...*we yell.
We will not let it roll down the street
like a loose apple!
We will not let it disappear
like those young Indian Women
from the reservation.
But we won't hold our...either
can't let them shoot it
full of holes at the next mass shooting.
We can't let them shoot us!
So under each layer of sweater
we hide our..., muffle it a little more
until we ourselves can't hear it
or until we ourselves forget it.

Come Back

(After Kate Knox's "Moving to Canada")

Staggering on sea legs, the horizon singing
       out

our wild wind-touched dreams
      just ahead

But how we drag our salt-soaked childhood
       behind

Will the next spindly step
      bring us

to the sky-saturated window
        the bird's eye view

Years later
    barnacle drenched and leaning

all our holes and history
      creaking

under those magnificent clouds
       dreams come to

At Dorrs Pond I see,

I will not be drowning myself today.
Not because I am happy, I am not.
But because the wind has turned
the water a menacing grayish blue.
Because the closed yellow pond lilies
those floating, flashing suns
and moons are all the planets
I cannot reach. And I can't go under
while trees stand idly by, drinking
in whatever the sky offers.
True, the lady's slippers in their pink
breathy fullness might have a word
locked inside them that any poet
would wait another spring for
but I think the real reason is
that lone blue heron out there.
How she stands stick-still
impervious to the shallow cold
swirling about her. How
her lidless eye seems to accuse me
seems to say: *Go Back.*
You do not belong here.

February's Question

for W.E.B.

Stepping out onto the ice-thick Massabesic Reservoir, its sheer expanse of white overwhelming me—and didn't I know it would? I must have known—those miles of snow and that sky with no gull crossing, and those scattered flakes falling through full sun, falling absurdly. Absurdly! Yes, I am sure I knew how memories could be called out to fly up into such silence. Abstract bits and pieces of past, how they can blow about with no place to land but on themselves, no way to rise in such heavy oblivion. Was I tempted? Yes, I believe I was. I believe I could have sat down right there, filled that frozen lake with our years together. But no, I walked back, nearly two miles to the shore—why? Somewhere in me, did I really think I'd find more solid ground to bury them in, a more meaningful grave to honor us?

All that work we have done,

cutting the lifeline in our palms shorter, carving those mysterious creases and crevices that only Madame X at the carnival can read. She keeps things from us, we know. Perhaps she thinks we are better off not seeing, so she tells it vague: *Yes, you are headed for a change. It will involve strangers.* But we walk away feeling she has just exposed our Soul, and we are wondering what the lifeline etched on its opaque hand looks like, how stooped are its transparent shoulders, and is that its left leg dragging a little? Yes, she has probably seen thirty or forty of us today, our gray, slumping souls tagging behind us for the rides, the sideshows, and the cotton candy. Yet she offers no clues as to how we should proceed, has no comments on the Grand Finale under the Big Top tonight, or which games we should try our luck at next.

The American Elm's Sonnet

Before the ugly rain of bark beetles
when the 20s were done roaring and my
fate was sealed to become this Platonic
theory of tree art, become this shadow

of a shadow of myself, I too sang
in winds with the voice of adolescent
invincibility! How my green hands shook
with other's hands instead of fear! How I'd

never heard the words: plague, immunity
disease, distance. Watching my family fall
was a little like watching this town as
it tries to remember itself, before

its streets started collecting ghosts and hours
its closed library, the dirge its books sing.

The Elephant in the Pandemic

In '83, when Carlos de Andrade died, they said
his Elephant died with him. We knew it would.
I mean, it being made of nothing
more than Carlos' big love, crooked smile, and salt
from one of Carlos' eyes. It was August 17th
and they say the streets were windswept
and colder than they had ever been in Rio that day.
But the Elephant wouldn't have described it as such
since every day for years he had walked out
greeting those streets, saddened at what lay under them
while wind and emotion tore right through him.
So much so, that poor Carlos spent a lifetime of nights
putting him back together with spit, pen, and glue
only to have him torn apart again the next day.
Such labor, such patience, and in hours of such silence.

On my own walk today through this pandemic
riddled town, I thought I saw the Elephant
hobbling along up Main Street. The street
was so empty! Wide enough to really think in.
And I thought I saw him pause, as if he might
reach out, pat the dog being walked in the shadows
by a stranger. Instead, he kept the rules of social distance
and took a left down Foundry Street. Poor Elephant, I thought.
Such times and such walks with no one to tell a private joke
a secret or story to. All day walking, only to find
its own ragged self at the end of its own frayed tail.

What We Brought on the Journey

a little bit of Blood—but mostly water
Salt—carried tightly behind our eyes
Anger—bulging in four-letter words
Lovemaking—we could not leave love behind
        any more than we could leave our bodies
Joy—we let it fly before us
        most of the time for no good reason
Persistence—each swung a hammer of sweat
Persistence Against Tyrants—each drank gallons
        of the sweat that went before them
        each remembered its taste
Wine, Dark Beer, Spirits—instinctively we knew
no one goes anywhere without these
Astonishment—at the capacity for human cruelty
        around each century's corner
Creativity—this is what we swirled in the bottom
of our cups on those dark nights we sat around asking:
        Where are we? Where are we going?
Grief—this was the song every plant along the way
sang as those we started out with dropped behind
        dropped away

Mary Ann Cappiello

Searching for Dinah Tuck

Sometimes a story insists on being told but has to wait for its writer to come along. Dinah Tuck—a young African American woman enslaved in the New Hampshire seacoast and nearabouts during the late eighteenth century—waited several hundred years until Mary Ann Cappiello writes of her existence. The author recalls the shock of seeing a human being included in a list of possessions and she felt compelled to tell this unknown story. The author delves into the historical records to piece together as much of Dinah's life as she can. With only so much factual material available, the author wonders aloud how life must have been for this young woman. Mary Ann does so with curiosity, a fine writer's sensibility, and enormous compassion. As a result, Dinah Tuck comes alive on the page and can now inhabit our imaginations—a fine accomplishment of research, faithful writing, and fellow feeling. G.D.

Imagine it's midmorning, January 5, 1776. Perhaps the sky is a brilliant blue, in sharp contrast to the snow and ice that coat Star Island. The unceasing winter wind blows hard.

Fourteen-year-old Dinah Tuck stands near Fort Star, along the western edge of the island. Born into slavery, Dinah gazes across the frigid waters that stretch between Gosport Harbor and the mainland, stealing a moment of solitude.

She walks along the fish flakes. Rows and rows of wooden racks line the granite, holding hundreds of split cod fish until they are dry enough to be sold to merchants on the mainland or to passing British warships.

Perhaps she finds herself in the burial area, strolling among the unmarked graves, wrapped in her shawl and her memories of her mother.

Likely, Dinah fetches water from the communal well and carefully carries it back to the cottage in which she works and sleeps, trying not to slip. Water surrounds the island. Water offers isolation. Privacy. But on the granite rocks that comprise the island, well water levels are carefully watched. There is never enough. Fire always threatens.

Dinah walks over thousands of buried animal bones: pigs, cows, and cod. Mingled among the bones are broken bottles, ceramics, and clay pipes from across Europe. Deeper still lie prehistoric stone tools, pottery, and spear points.

Back at the cottage, Dinah spends much of the morning preparing dinner. To maintain heat, all the windows are shuttered against the winter wind. The burning sod in the fireplace—there are no trees to cut down for firewood—is the only source of warmth and cooking fuel.

Later in the day, Dinah may make her way up the hill to the wooden chapel, built from the remains of a Spanish shipwreck. As she walks along the rocky path, icy stones slippery beneath her feet, a herring gull might watch from a rooftop. Maybe a snowy owl strikes at a mouse or vole. Always, she hears the music of the surf swirling around her. Always, she smells the salt water on the wind.

Perhaps Dinah steps inside the chapel, taking refuge from the wind and snow. The school day, if it happened at all, is over. She is alone. As she sits in the fading light of late afternoon, what does Dinah wonder about?

Does she pray? Maybe.

If you stood at the center of Star Island on a beautiful summer day, as I have many times, you'd marvel at the glorious ocean views, the quiet lap of water against granite, the gulls squawking overhead. Blue envelops the island as ocean and sky meet on the horizon, and the mainland feels even farther than the ten miles that separate the island from the rest of New Hampshire. Despite the ever-present forces of nature that abound, you might also smell fresh bread baking in the oven of the great nineteenth-century Oceanic Hotel.

But if you stood on Star Island in the midst of January, as I once did in my search for Dinah Tuck, the yeasty smell of bread would not permeate the air—only the icy water and winds of the Atlantic that pummel the island day in and day out. As I slipped along the snow and ice, shivering despite several layers of twenty-first-century winter gear, I marveled that anyone ever lived here year-round, ever raised children on this small spot of granite sticking out of the ocean.

While the severity of Star Island in January is a challenge, a sensory overload, the severity of circumstances that young Dinah Tuck endured is unimaginable. Born into slavery over 250 years ago on the eve of the American Revolution, Dinah remains mostly a mystery. The written historical record offers us precious little about her, mere glimpses captured through the lives of others. I've spent countless hours trying to honor the young girl who survived enslavement and isolation, to reconstruct her life so that others can remember her, too.

The Shoals—Star Island, Smuttynose, Appledore, and six others—were once the bottom of a mountain. Millions of years of erosion and several hundred thousand years of glacial activity during the last ice age gave the islands their jagged edges and granite base. For another approximately 15,000 years, the islands were connected to the mainland. As the receding glaciers melted, sea levels rose, and for the last approximately 7,000 years, the islands as we know them have sat in the waters of the Gulf of Maine.

The physical islands speak to us, revealing their hidden histories. Over the last decade, archeological digs on Smuttynose have revealed hundreds of thousands of artifacts confirming that Indigenous Americans lived on the Shoals for longer seasonal periods than previously thought. Smuttynose has offered thousands of years of marine life, plant life, and Indigenous culture, and revealed the range of people and ships that sailed through the Shoals in the early modern era.

For thousands of years, the islands endured. Each spring, Indigenous First Nations, the Abenaki—"People of the Dawnland"—came to the Shoals, likely the Newichawannock, Piscataqua, and Winnacunnet that lived along the coast. They fished and hunted seals, cultivated crops, carved tools, and crafted pots along the shore. When summer faded, they returned to the mainland. Seals and snowy owls arrived to overwinter. In spring, migrating birds returned to nest, as did humans, only to leave again when the days grew shorter. Supplies were abundant.

Then, the cycle was interrupted.

Europeans arrived at the Isles of Shoals.

The process of drying and salting codfish played a vital role in globalization. During the early medieval period, the Vikings in northern Europe had learned how to dry cod in the cold air, which gave them the opportunity to stay at sea for longer voyages. In the later medieval period, Basque fishermen, who lived in the coastal border regions between France and Spain and had access to salt stores, learned how to salt cod at sea. When cod is salted and dried, the loss of water causes it to shrink, making it hard and stiff, easy to store in an era without refrigeration. This enabled the Basques to stay at sea longer and bring back larger amounts of salted cod to Europe.

Why would people in Europe clamor to eat hard, dry, overly salted white fish? In medieval Catholic Europe, there were many days on the calendar, including every Friday, when Catholics did not eat meat, but they did eat fish. Unlike fresh fish, salted cod could be stored and transported inland, making it highly marketable. When mixed with some water, the cod reconstitutes into soft flesh, ready to be boiled or fried. People could get rich off this demand for cod. This made the French, Spanish, and British jealous of the Basques.

Where were they finding all of this cod?

Eventually, by the late 1500s, western Europe figured out that Basque fishermen had been secretly fishing in northern New England. Giovanni Caboto, an Italian explorer sailing for England under the name John Cabot, claimed Newfoundland for England, and Jacques Cartier, sailing for France, claimed North America for France, and according to a contemporary source, "also noted the presence of 1,000 Basque fishing vessels." Soon after, French, Spanish, and English fishermen started to sail regularly to New England.

Captain John Smith, Jamestown settler and explorer, liked the Shoals so much when sailing past in 1614 that he named them "Smyth's Isles," and wrote that they were "a heap together, none neere them." The abundance of codfish available drew British and French fishermen to the islands. Some men stayed on land to watch the cod, turning the fish regularly and covering them up during damp weather. At some point, British sailors discovered that an even better quality of cod could be caught in the winter; when dried, it was called dunfish. Unlike the Abenaki, the British decided to stay on the islands year-round.

By the early seventeenth century, colonists were invading what is now Maine, New Hampshire, and Massachusetts in quest of cod and lumber. The coastal Abenaki from Cape Cod to Downeast Maine were assaulted by the diseases spread by European traders, and their population dropped by three-quarters, from 12,000 to 3,000. While the Pilgrims of Plymouth and the many myths that surround them can make for an appealing tale of white America's origins, much of the story of European settlement in America begins with the Shoals. And the story of the Shoals is one of money, and the lack thereof, power, and the lack thereof, and small islands, small boats, and small houses that some say could float across the water. For over 150 years, the global price of cod was determined on the Isles of Shoals. Codfish made New England rich. And codfish loved the waters off the Shoals.

In 1621, the King of England gave two men, John Mason and Ferdinando Gorges, a land grant that included all that now comprises the states of New Hampshire and Maine, despite the fact that the Abenaki people had made the land their home for thousands of years. The purpose of the land grant? Money, not religious freedom. Around the same time, in 1620, the Pilgrims sailed from England and landed in Massachusetts. While some were seeking religious freedom, others were hoping to make some money by catching cod. But those wishful entrepreneurs did not have any experience in cod fishing. In 1623, cod fishermen from Strawbery Banke, now Portsmouth, New Hampshire, saved the residents of Plymouth from starvation.

By 1634, the Mason and Gorges land grant was split. Mason's land became New Hampshire, Gorges' New Somerset (now Maine). Because they were considered so valuable, the islands that make up the Isles of Shoals were split down the middle. Even today, half the islands are in Maine, half in New Hampshire.

For a long time, only men were allowed on the Shoals, and the islands enjoyed or endured, depending on how you view it, a reputation for crudeness and lawlessness. Certainly, life there was difficult. At ten miles out to sea, the islands were mostly granite, with little topsoil. There were virtually no trees, and the residents supported themselves through the bounty of the sea. Originally, the men settled on Hog Island. By the mid-1600s, there were upwards of 600 people living on Hog Island. By 1652, women were permitted to live there as well, and by 1661, the town of Appledore, Maine was incorporated on the island. It had a fort, meetinghouse, and even a school for boys.

Through another series of shifts in leadership, both New Hampshire and New Somerset became part of the Massachusetts Bay Colony in 1641, but in 1679, New Hampshire was made a Royal Province while Maine remained part of Massachusetts. Star Island was part of New Hampshire, while Hog Island, with the town of Appledore on it, was in what is now Maine, but was then considered Massachusetts. In perhaps the first commitment to a tax-free New Hampshire, the forty or so families of Hog Island moved to Star Island to avoid paying Massachusetts Bay taxes. This certainly established a precedent for the residents of the Shoals, who resisted paying taxes and obeying most other mandates from the mainland.

By the late 1600s, the shipbuilding industry began to flourish in what is now Portsmouth, New Hampshire, and the growth of the fishing industry followed. Those who made huge profits now lived on the mainland. Those who remained on the Shoals were largely poor. Physical survival required constant resolve against the elements.

By the mid-eighteenth century, more changes impacted the islands. Archeological research on Appledore revealed that the further archeologists dug, the older and larger the codfish bones; those from the 1600s were the largest, and those from the 1800s were the smallest. As the codfish size and supply shrunk, so too did the number of families living on the Shoals. The changing cod stock, the intermarriage of families, the geographical isolation, and the abuse of alcohol had all taken their toll on the town of Gosport, on Star Island, by the third quarter of the eighteenth century.

So where does this leave Dinah Tuck in January 1776?

The baptismal records for Gosport reveal that on September 5, 1742, "Candace, a Negro Child belonging to Mr. John Tucke was baptized." Twenty years later, Candace's daughter Dinah was also born into slavery and baptized by Reverend John Tuck on April 18, 1762. There were only two other enslaved Black people baptized on the island, according to church records: Peter, baptized on July 11, 1742, and Dolly, on January 3, 1748. In 1733 and 1734, a "Black Charles" was paid to ring the bell at the meeting house, but he then disappeared from the records.

Was Peter Dinah's father or was it Reverend Tuck? Someone else? Was Candace in a loving relationship, or is Dinah the result of rape?

Tuck, a Harvard-educated Hampton native, was ordained as minister of Gosport on July 26, 1732. His arrival brought order and structure to the Star Island community. For the first time, Gosport acted like other New England towns, holding annual elections for town officials such as clerk and moderator, and keeping records of town meetings. Within a year, residents approved the support of an on-island school. By 1755, records indicate approval of a new fine for those that left fish heads above the water line. Money was tight and the island was small; such a fine suggests the smell was putrid enough to prompt such action. For many years, Reverend Tuck was one of the best-paid ministers in New England, despite the pervasive poverty on Star Island. For he was paid by the barrel—in codfish.

Dinah's circumstances were cruel. She was owned by another. I try to imagine her childhood. In 1767, when Dinah was five or six, there were 284 residents of Gosport. As likely the only Black girl, surrounded by whites without economic, political, or social power, Dinah would have had to steel herself against rampant racism. I wonder if she ever felt safe. If she ever was safe.

I assume that she was not permitted to attend school. Perhaps she taught herself how to read anyway. Perhaps she found the arrival of ships in Gosport Harbor exciting. Some of the sailors were likely free Black people who sailed the coast of New England and beyond. Maybe it was a comfort to see and talk with them. They could have told her of life beyond the island. But my mind takes another tack: perhaps the arrival of ships prompted terror. If white male strangers, deprived of social interactions and female companionship for lengthy periods of time, arrived on the island and laid eyes on her, she would have had reason to be afraid.

Most likely the Tucks did not protect Dinah's childhood. Rather, I imagine that they ignored her age and expected her to do the work of a woman. We can guess at some of her skills: sewing, laundering, planting, cooking, and cleaning. From an early age, she might have carried water from the well to the cottage, regardless of weather. I can see her doing the laundry, her hands chapped and raw. And there

A Record of Baptisms by

Jan. 13th 1760. Mary, Daughter of Jr. Beekman & of Mary His Wife, was Baptiz'd.

Feb. 3d 1760. Betty, Daughter of Jno. Tate & of Esther His Wife, was Baptiz'd.

Feb. 24th 1760. Nanny, Daughter of Jno. Newton & of Sarah His Wife, was Baptiz'd.

April 27th 1760. Samuel, Son of Saml. Haly & of Mary His Wife, was Baptiz'd.

June 1st 1760. Margaret, Daughter of Jeremy Lord & of Elizth. His Wife,
Abigail, Daughter of Elisha Horn & of James in His Wife, } were Baptiz'd.
Sarah, Daughter of Thos. Chapel & of Abigail His Wife.

June 15th 1760. Joanna, Daughter of Jno. Brag & of Joanna His Wife, was Baptiz'd.

July 6th 1760. Molly, Daughter of Ambrose Perkins & of Sarah His Wife, was Baptiz'd.

July 13th 1760. Edward, Son of Rich. Currier Junr. & of Mary His Wife, was Baptiz'd.

Septr. 7th 1760. Jno. Son of Saml. Downe Junr. & of Marjory His Wife, was Baptiz'd.

Septr. 24th 1760. Jno. Son of Roth. Randal Junr. & of Ruth His Wife, was Baptiz'd

Decr. 28th 1760. David, Son of Reuben Bachelor & of Miriam His Wife, was Baptized at Hawk

Jany. 11th 1761. Jno. Son of Wm. Holbrook & of Eliz. His Wife, was Baptized.

Jany. 18th 1761. Henry, Son of Henry Carter & of Deborah His Wife, was Baptized

Feby. 15th 1761. Joseph, Son of Nat. Downe & of Molly His Wife, was Baptized

Feby. 22d 1761. Wm. Son of Robt. Kearswell Junr. & of Eliz. His Wife, was Baptized

March 1st 1761. Rebecca, Daughter of Amos Horn & of Abigail His Wife was Baptized.

April 26th 1761. Mary Saunders, Daughter of Henry Shapley & of Elizth. His Wife, was Baptized.

July 12th 1761. Robert Saunders, Son of Luke Power & of Sarah His Wife, was Baptized

Augt. 23d 1761. Joanna, Daughter of James Allard & of Sarah His Wife, was Baptized

Octr. 4th 1761. Abigail, Daughter of Sam. Eliot & of Abigail His Wife, was Baptized

Octr. 25th 1761. Susannah, Daughter of Chr. Ellenwood & of Anne His Wife,
Wm. Son of Henry Walker Andrass & of Rachel His Wife, } were Baptized

Novr. 1st 1761. Margaret, Daughter of Sam. Haley & of Mary His Wife, was Baptized

Novr. 8th 1761. Molly, Daughter of Edw. Houdy & of Sarah His Wife, was Baptized

Jany. 17th 1762. Jno. Son of Thos. Horn & of Elizth. His Wife,
Benjamin, Son of Arthur Randall & of Lydia His Wife, } were Baptized

Feby. 14th 1762. Sarah, Daughter of Arthur Randall Junr. & of Ruth His Wife, was Baptized

April 18th 1762. Dinah, Daughter of Candace, a Negro, was Baptized.

Dinah Tuck's Baptismal Record from the Church of Gosport. Photo Credit: Courtesy of the New Hampshire Historical Society.

she is, hanging clothes out to dry in warmer months—the shifts and skirts, at least, dancing in the sea breeze. In colder months, perhaps she hung the laundry within the cottage itself, the cloth soon taking on the smell of ash, fire, and codfish. I can picture her making candles. It wouldn't surprise me if she took care of the private needs of Mary Tuck, Reverend Tuck's wife, throughout her various ailments. I see her dropping into bed exhausted every night.

It's also possible Dinah had a working knowledge of herbal remedies and tonics, an understanding of the contents of the green, brown, and clear glass bottles that lined a shelf in the parsonage for Reverend Tuck to minister to the physical ailments of his congregation. Perhaps she learned some of these skills from her mother, Candace. Perhaps she learned some of these skills from Tuck, his wife Mary, or one of their daughters, Love and Mary. Perhaps she wasn't taught, but thanks to her own agency, she watched and learned.

Imagining her living in such close quarters; I wonder, did she have privacy, or any time to play, alone or with others? When, if ever, did Dinah steal joy? I like to think of her as a girl, skipping along the snippets of sandy shore of Gosport Harbor, splashing her feet in the cool water. Perhaps she liked to play with a rag doll. I see her resisting the Tucks' control by making the most of any free time she had—climbing the rocky shoreline of the eastern side of the island, dancing amongst Mrs. Pusley's cows grazing in the pasture, stealing fleeting moments of escape.

After Dinah's baptism, her mother Candace disappears from the historical record. So too does Peter. Funeral records were not commonly kept. Candace may have been a refuge for Dinah throughout her childhood, a source of strength and resilience, a role model. Or she may have been a ghost.

By the summer of 1773, when Dinah was approximately twelve, both Mary and John Tuck were dead, Mary on May 24, John on August 10. Perhaps Candace labored to take care of Mary only to fall ill herself. It could be that Candace was long gone and Dinah had been alone for years, laboring to take care of both John and Mary Tuck through their illnesses. Likely, Dinah also took care of their daughter Love Muchamore, who lost her four-year-old son that

Reverend John Tuck's Probate Inventory, 1773. Photo Credit: Estate of Rev. John Tuck, Rockingham County Probate Old Series 4039, at the NH State Archives very same year, and gave birth to another in October, just weeks after losing her parents.

When Reverend Tuck's probate inventory listing of all his possessions was completed, sandwiched between "sundry apparel" worth 8.10 pounds and "4 pairs of sheets" and other linens worth 1.10 pounds, the inventory reads: "Diana, a Negro Girl of about 12 Years of age," worth 20 pounds. After the house, barn, and land, which was listed at 70 pounds, Dinah was the most valuable property, just another possession to be counted and appraised between a pile of sheets and a bunch of clothes. There was no mention of Candace among Tuck's possessions.

With Candace, Reverend Tuck and Mary gone, Dinah's life must have changed. The record suggests that Dinah stayed on at the parsonage with Love and her husband Jeffrey. Married on June 4, 1766, both Love and Jeffrey had been born and raised on Star Island, a year apart. Jeffrey had recently been elected a selectman. Love's sister Mary Walton and her husband Mark likely resided with them, along with their sons Mark and baby John.

By January 1774, Jeremiah Shaw, a minister from Hampton, was appointed to serve the congregation, but he came over intermittently and did not live on Star permanently. By 1775, there were even fewer people living in Gosport. Dinah would have seen the British navy ships patrolling the Gulf of Maine, stopping at the Shoals to trade, causing great consternation on the mainland. In December of 1775, Dinah would have seen British soldiers arrive on the island and slaughter her neighbor Mrs. Pusley's cows.

History books don't pay too much attention to New Hampshire during the American Revolution. It was the only colony of the original thirteen that never had a battle fought within its borders. But it was nevertheless a center for communication within the New England colonies and an active participant in the Continental Congress. It has its own stories.

On January 5, 1776, the Provincial Congress in Exeter declared itself a state congress, signed the nation's first Declaration of

Independence, and established a state constitution. Amidst this significant step towards statehood, the Congress did something else that day—It voted to remove the residents of the Isles of Shoals to the mainland. The historical record gives us some clues why Congress wanted the Shoalers relocated:

> Voted, That Captain Titus Salter, and Captain Eliphalet Daniels, be appointed to go over to the Isle of Shoals, and inform all the inhabitants there, that it is the opinion of this Congress that the situation of the said islands is such, that the inhabitants are exposed to our enemies in the present unhappy controversy, and may be obliged by their weak, defenceless circumstances, and inability to defend themselves, to assist our enemies; and that, for said reasons, it is absolutely necessary that they should, immediately, remove themselves, with their effects, to the main land, (to tarry during the present dispute,) to such place, or places, as they may choose; and, provided they neglect to comply herewith for the term of ten days after this notice, that they be informed that they must be brought off by authority.

The congress was quite clever in how it framed this vote for the written record. Reading it in the present day, without the context of events of the period, it might appear it was out of concern for the Shoalers and their safety that the congress wanted them off the islands. But there's another possibility.

Two British warships, the *Canceaux* and the *Scarborough*, patrolled Portsmouth Harbor for much of 1775. While the ships were present, fishermen could not leave the harbor to fish. But those out on the Shoals could. Some have suggested that the congress knew Shoalers were selling fish to the British—they weren't to be trusted.

Bad weather prevented the committee from getting out to the Shoals immediately after the vote on January 5 to become a state congress. But on January 16, 1776, five men representing the state congress in Exeter sailed to Star Island and disembarked in Gosport Harbor.

Dinah was a witness to events on that winter day. *I see her near the shore when the men arrived, watching as people from the other islands got off on Star to hear what the officials had to say. Likely they met at the chapel. Probably only the men were allowed inside—the town selectmen, such as Mark, Mary Tuck Walton's husband. Love's husband Jeffrey Muchmore, no longer a selectman, was a Private in Captain Samuel McIntyre's Company, based in Kittery.*

At some point during the day, a census was taken. There were only two hundred and twenty-seven people remaining across the various islands of the Shoals, the majority of them children. Star Island, where fourteen-year-old Dinah lived, had 159 people in all, with thirty-one men, thirty-four women, and ninety-four children. Dinah was alone and enslaved. She could have counted as a girl or a woman.

The residents of the Shoals were probably shocked by the idea of removal. Most had lived their whole lives on the islands, and their families went back generations. All made their living from the sea. They must have wondered where they would go, where they *could* go. They would have to make a living, pay for their own relocation.

How did Dinah react to the news? Did this feel like a chance at liberation? In Portsmouth and Exeter, other Black people lived in community, some free, some enslaved. Perhaps Dinah knew that. Perhaps she hoped to move to Portsmouth, where Nero Wheelwright, an expert cooper, made barrels and buckets, Primus Fowle operated a printing press, and free and enslaved Black residents held elections each year for their king, drawing upon West African models of leadership.

Before the committee departed, they may have found refuge from the cold in the parsonage. Dinah may have fed them dinner, brewed them coffee or herbal tea. When they left, she may have followed them down to the harbor, full of uncertainty.

Something shifted that afternoon on Star Island, and ultimately the Shoalers were not forced to relocate. On January 18, the committee returned to Exeter and submitted their census numbers from the Shoals. On the 19th, the House met and voted to choose a committee of five people to consult with the Committee of Safety from Portsmouth and report back "what they think best to be done respecting removing the People from Gosport." That very same day, the appointed committee submitted a report, stating:

> That it is our opinion that the inhabitants of Gosport, on the Isle of Shoals, remain there until further orders from this House; and that they be allowed to purchase any necessaries of life, sufficient for their own families, at Rye Harbor, or Little Boar's Head in North Hampton, on making pay for the same in cash, or good fish...and that said inhabitants be forbid going to, or trading in, any other harbor or harbours.

The House then voted that "the Inhabitants of Gosport remain on that Island till further orders from this House." No other conversation regarding the Shoalers took place during this time. The Shoalers were being watched—they were being told where they could and could not purchase "necessaries of life," but they could stay in their homes, however small, however primitive.

Over the next few months, the focus on the American Revolution shifted southward. On the morning of March 17, 1776, George Washington surprised the British forces in Boston, having lined Dorchester Heights with weapons and cannons under the cover of night. The British evacuated Boston, never to return.

Despite their freedom to stay on the Shoals, over the next few years, families continued to leave. By 1779, Dinah likely moved with Love and Jeffrey, Mary and Mark, and their children to York, Maine, still part of Massachusetts. Local lore has it that those leaving the Shoals floated their houses across the water. While moving houses on land was done with some frequency in the eighteenth century, floating houses across the water would have been impossible. At some point between 1777 and 1780, the thirteen-by-seventeen-foot parsonage on Star was disassembled, and the pieces floated over to York Harbor, serving as an addition to a house at the bottom of Sentry Hill that the family occupied with Dinah. More babies arrived. Dinah was likely cooking, cleaning, and laundering for the household.

I wonder if Dinah had the opportunity to get to know other Black members of the York community, free or enslaved, or others in nearby Kittery and Portsmouth. I hope that seventeen-year-old Dinah heard—perhaps in hushed voices on market day or after church—that on November 12, 1779, a group of twenty enslaved men in Portsmouth—including Nero Brewster, Peter Warner, Windsor Moffatt, Samuel Wentworth, and Prince Whipple—petitioned the state government for their freedom, using the political discourse of the Enlightenment to make their case. I'm curious how long it took for twenty-one-year-old Dinah to find out that the state of Massachusetts ended slavery on July 8, 1783.

On December 27, 1782, Love Tuck Muchamore died. Within a year, Jeffrey Muchamore married Lucy Milberry, and his family continued to grow. There are no marriage records for Dinah. Throughout this time, she likely continued cooking, cleaning, and laundering for the household.

By 1790, Jeffrey Muchamore and his family were living in Newburyport, Massachusetts. That year, the federal census offered columns to document any free non-white men and women living within households. Jeffrey Muchamore had one free non-white woman living in his household, likely twenty-eight-year-old Dinah. For another nine years, Dinah likely lived in Newburyport. It is unclear what Jeffrey did for a living or where the household resided. Nothing tells us where Dinah lived after 1790. There are no marriage records or birth records for a Dinah Tuck in Newburyport.

I consider Dinah's freedom and autonomy during this time. I hope she experienced some of the good things in life: joy, friendship, and companionship within the Black community of Newburyport, love. I wonder if she ever learned to read and write. I imagine her making a living delivering babies and tending to the sick. But I suspect that she cooked, cleaned, and laundered for all of her years.

Dinah Tuck's name appears in print precisely three times: when she was baptized as an infant on April 18, 1762, when she

Dinah Tuck's Death Record, 1801. Photo Credit: courtesy of the Newburyport Public Library Archival Center

was listed on Reverend Tuck's probate inventory after his death in 1773, and when she died in Newburyport on June 30, 1801 at the age of thirty-nine. From infancy, Dinah's life was likely filled with back-breaking labor, isolation, and oppression. Because her whereabouts parallel those of the people who legally owned her for the first twenty-eight years of her life, there is no way to know if she was ever truly free.

Back in 2003, on my first trip out to the Shoals after moving to New Hampshire, our guide on the M/V *Thomas Laighton* shared the story of Shoalers floating their houses across the water. I was transfixed, and set out to write about the relocation in a historical novel for young people. A few years later, when I began my research, I discovered Dinah in John Tuck's inventory. It was a shock to stumble upon a twelve-year-old girl—a human being—listed with possessions in probate such as sheets, a candlestick, six cane chairs, and three feather beds. As I combed through the various families of Gosport to trace their relocation to the mainland, I could not get Dinah out of my mind, my heart, or my imagination. I was determined to find out as much as I could about her.

Initially, I tried to follow her through Tuck's son, whom I assumed inherited much of his father's estate. But he passed away in 1777, while serving as a chaplain in the Continental Army. It was only when I began to follow Tuck's daughters, and their husbands after their deaths, that I was able to ultimately find Dinah through her death record—or what I presume to be her death record—in Newburyport. The day I learned that Dinah died in Newburyport was both triumphant and devastating. I had an end to Dinah's story. But it wasn't the end that I was hoping for. I wanted so much more for her.

I soon realized that I couldn't write Dinah as a fictional character for young people. It wasn't my story to tell—not via fiction, not for young people. For years, I kept Dinah's story to myself. But that didn't feel right, either.

On a clear day, it is possible to stand at Jenness Beach in Rye and see the outline of the Tuck Monument, a forty-five-and-a-half-foot stone obelisk erected on Star Island in 1914 in tribute to Reverend John Tuck. The tallest tombstone in the state of New Hampshire keeps his memory alive. Summer visitors on Star see it from all directions.

Dinah was not a member of John Tuck's family, but she carried his name until her death. There is no record of where she was buried. There is no grave to visit, no headstone upon which to leave a remembrance.

Ultimately, all that I can say definitely about Dinah Tuck is that she was born and baptized, she labored, and she died.

Dinah Tuck lived.

Now, we can remember her.

Selective Bibliography

1790 United States Census, Newburyport, Essex County, Massachu-setts. Ancestry.com.

Bardwell, John. *The Isles of Shoals: A Visual History.* Portsmouth Marine Society/Peter E. Randall, 1989.

Bolster, W. Jeffrey, editor. *Cross-Grained & Wily Waters: A Guide to the Piscataqua Maritime Region.* Peter E. Randall, 2002.

Bouton, Nathaniel., editor. *Provincial Papers, Documents and Records Relating to the Province of New Hampshire.* Volume 8. Concord, NH, George E. Jenks, State Printer, 1867.

Dishman, Robert. B. "'Natives of Africa, now forcibly detained': The Slave Petitioners of Revolutionary Portsmouth." *Historical New Hampshire,* Vol. 61, No. 1, pp. 7-27.

Isles of Shoals Collection, Portsmouth Athenaeum, Portsmouth, NH.

Jenness, John Scribner. *The Isles of Shoals: An Historical Sketch.* Michigan Historical Reprint Series, New York, Hurd and Houghton, 1873.

John Langdon Papers, Portsmouth Athenaeum, Portsmouth, NH.

Knowlton, Deborah. *Color Me Included: The African Americans of Hampton's First Church and Its Descendant Parishes, 1670-1826.* Peter E. Randall, 2016.

Kurlansky, Mark. *Cod: A Biography of the Fish That Changed the World.* Penguin, 1997.

Lawson, Russell M. *The Isles of Shoals in the Age of Sail: A Brief History.* The History Press, 2007.

Minutes of the Executive Council, 1767-1991. New Hampshire State Archives, Concord, NH.

The New England Historical and Genealogical Register, Volume LXVI. The New England Historical and Genealogical Register, 1912.

New Hampshire Gazette. Manuscript collection, New Hampshire Historical Society, Concord, NH.

New Hampshire Provincial and State Papers, New Hampshire State Archives, Concord, NH.

Newburyport, Essex County, Massachusetts Death Records to 1850. Ancestry.com.

Petitions to the Governor and the Executive Council of New Hampshire. New Hampshire State Archives, Concord, NH.

Randall, Peter and Burke, Maryellen. *Gosport Remembered: The Last Village at the Isles of Shoals.* Portsmouth Marine Society/Peter E. Randall, 1997.

Robinson, J. Dennis. *Under the Isles of Shoals: Archeology & Discovery on Smuttynose Island.* Illustrated by Bill Paarlberg. Portsmouth Marine Society, 2012.

Rutledge, Lyman. *The Isles of Shoals in Lore and Legend.* Star Island Corporation, 1971.

Rutledge, Lyman. *Ten Miles Out: Guidebook to the Isles of Shoals, Portsmouth, New Hampshire.* 7th Edition. Revised by Edward Rutledge. Isles of Shoals Association, 1997.

Saamons, Mark, and Valerie Cunningham. *Black Portsmouth: Three Centuries of African-American Heritage.* University of New Hampshire Press, 2004.

Tallman, Louise. *Some of the Families of Gosport at the Isles of Shoals, 1715-1876, Compiled from Church and Town Records of Gosport.* Photocopy, Louise Tallman, 1969.

Vaughn Cottage Manuscript Collection, Unitarian-Universalist Association, Star Island, NH

Wall, Patricia Q. *Lives of Consequence: Blacks in Early Kittery & Berwick in the Massachusetts Province of Maine.* Portsmouth Marine Society, 2017.

Whipple Traill Spence Collection, Portsmouth Athenaeum, Portsmouth, NH.

Whittaker, Robert. *Land of Lost Content: The Piscataqua River Basin and the Isles of Shoals: The People, Their Dreams, Their History.* Alan Sutton Publishing, Inc., 1994.

Wills and Probate Records, New Hampshire, 1643-1982. Ancestry.com.

The York Necrology, York Historical Society, York, ME.

James Patrick Kelly

Grandma +5ºC

"The crowd whooped as a robotic leg made a spectacular leap over Willow's racing arm." That first line grabbed my attention. But then, in the second line, when "the leg stuck the landing," I laughed out loud. I was hooked. I stayed hooked. How wonderful to trust the sure hand of highly skilled writer and enjoy a story as it unfurls—naturally, inevitably, yet full of surprises.

James Patrick Kelly is a Nebula and Hugo award winner. In his cover letter, he says, "'Grandma +5ºC' is recent work. It appeared in the 2021 March/April issue of Asimov's Science Fiction *and is probably my most political science fiction story. Because it's set in a small town in western NH, writing it felt very, very real to me. It takes place during what some call the slow apocalypse, where society has eroded but has not completely collapsed. In this story I've extrapolated the trends of climate change and pandemic that we all know but that too many of us fail to accept. I wrote it because I'm scared."* R.R.

The crowd whooped as a robotic leg made a spectacular leap over Willow's racing arm. When the leg stuck the landing, she covered her eyes in frustration. She'd worked so hard to modify the arm, swiped from Grandma's illegal stash, for the April Fools' bot showdown. Practically new, the arm was way more reliable than the junk robotics in Willow's workshop. She'd even added an elbow-twitch routine to the standard finger crawl. The arm had taken the lead in the race right from the gun, writhing and scuttling out of the start circle of the bullseye course, and had reached the three-quarters ring well ahead of the rest of the pack. Meanwhile the leg, which belonged to Zoya, Willow's childhood nemesis, had begun the race with a stumble and fall, wasting precious minutes as it thrashed into position to kick itself upright again. Now all it needed were a few modest hops to the finish ring. Zoya would win again.

But no. The leg had stalled, blocking the arm's path. More bad luck since Willow couldn't instruct the arm to go around. Nobody had direct control of their racing limbs once the robotics showdown started.

"What's happening?" Frack pressed close to Willow in the chilly gym, his breath warm in her ear. "Why doesn't it go again?" The kid had romantic aspirations that Willow wasn't necessarily encouraging. She nudged him away on the wooden bench.

"Dunno," she said. It was hard to see since half the ancient gym's lights had failed and had been left dark to save electricity. "Battery drain?"

"Could be." He scooted closer again. Frack was persistent, but what else could she expect from a horny seventeen-year-old? "Between kicking back up after that start and making the last jump. Serious power suck."

Willow noticed the arm that girl from Marlow had entered—Alejandra Something—had cleared the halfway ring on the opposite side of the course. In third place, it was crawling steadily on finger power alone.

"Uh-oh." Frack pointed. The leg's control cabinet was missing its door, and now everyone could see function lights blink from green to yellow and then flash red. He gasped. "Over-discharge?"

"Shit." Willow worried that it might be worse. "Hope that last move didn't puff her batteries."

As if in answer, the poly skin beneath the leg's controls bulged, then peeled open, emitting a wisp of dirty green smoke. Even from the contestants' row, she could smell the terrifying stink of catastrophic LiPo battery failure. It was like snorting steel wool. Shouts and a scream rose behind her. Spectators came clattering down the gym's rickety folding stands.

Willow fought her own panic; this could be the kind of disaster that would bring serious trouble. She had to grab her arm and get out of there. The rangers were hunting for Grandma. If anyone guessed that she'd come home to the Hollow....

"Willow, no." Frack clutched at her but she hurtled onto the course, dancing over the other limbs still scrabbling toward the finish ring. She scooped up the arm in stride just as twin jets of fire burst from the stricken leg. Something slapped at her. A scab of molten plastic stuck to the back of her hand. With a shriek, she tried to shake it loose, then scraped it off against her leg, scorching her jeans.

"Ow, ow, ow, *fuck!*" She stared at the angry red blotch in disbelief.

Frack was by her side. "Come here, you." He put an arm around her waist.

She sagged into him and let him take Grandma's arm. He led her back to their seats. The stands were almost empty now. Her hand hurt and she'd lost the race and all that barter credit, but the arm was safe. She'd been crazy to risk showing Grandma's arm, but she was sick of all the hiding.

"You all right?" Frack reached for her burned hand. "Let me see that."

"Fine." She yanked it away from him. "It's fine." The burn was turning the color of pale toast. She blew on it to cool it down.

Zoya burst into the gym the carrying a fire extinguisher. Willow had no idea where she'd found one; she hadn't thought any were left in the defunct school. The flames had guttered out but Zoya aimed the nozzle at the still-standing leg and pulled the trigger. A sick cough, a thin fizzle of monoammonium phosphate spray, then nothing.

Zoya howled in frustration. "Does anything in this brokedown dump work anymore?" She flung the useless thing away and it bounced with a metallic clang and rolled to a stop near Alejandra, the girl from Marlow. All the other competitors had picked up their limbs but she'd waited for her arm to cross the finish ring, still hoping to claim the win.

Good luck collecting.

Zoya stalked toward Willow and Frack, fuming. "Where did you get that arm?"

Willow felt a sandpaper itch of annoyance. Zoya had no right to be asking rude questions. Her sketchy batteries could've burned the whole gym down.

"Found it," she said.

"Found it where?"

She could feel Frack gather himself next to her and she knew he was about to do something careless and loud and Frack-like. "Storage unit," she said, restraining him. "Out near the industrial park in Nashua. Lots of working Waytronics stuff." Willow had her cover story ready.

"When was this?"

"Couple of weeks ago."

Zoya scowled. "Bullshit."

"Three," said Frack. "Three weeks ago, during the heat wave. Melting hot for March, it was. And the next day was that blizzard."

Willow struggled not to show either her surprise or appreciation. Without any prompting, Frack had corroborated a story that he knew was a lie. She hadn't thought him to be so quick-witted. Maybe she'd underestimated the kid, just because he was four years younger than her.

"You were with her?" Zoya looked as if she needed to punch something.

He smirked. "She's my girlfriend."

"Lucky you," Zoya sneered. "Here, let me see that." She reached for Grandma's arm.

"Piss off." Frack swiveled it away and stuck a foot out, as if to trip her. "What are you, some kind of ranger wannabe?"

She considered, then thought better of trying to take it from him. "People been all through Nashua." She turned back to Willow. "Town is picked clean. Especially the storage."

"Lucky thing nobody looked where I looked." Willow needed to escape.

"Okay," Zoya said, although clearly it wasn't. "Okay, but I never saw no arm do that before." She rubbed her own elbow. "Not sure that's fair."

"Why?" Willow had grown up with this bully and was sick of her arrogance. Besting her had been one reason she'd taken this stupid risk. "Because it means your leg doesn't get to win the damn showdown every year?"

Frack laughed. Zoya's stare was hot enough to start her second fire of the day.

Willow stood. "I'm done here." She took Grandma's arm from Frack. "You coming, *boyfriend*?"

He followed her out, still chuckling.

◆

In 1900, New Hampshire had been 90 percent farmland and 10 percent woodland. By 2000, environmentalism and rural flight had reversed those percentages. When the hordes of post +5°C climate refugees stampeded north in the 2040s, fleeing the desiccated southern wastelands where summer was a death sentence, few chose to stop in the stony and unforgiving forests of the western Granite State. Most crowded east along the coast, clinging to the fragile economy of the Northeast megalopolis. Then the Marburg-null pandemic of 2046-7 swept up the East Coast from Norfolk, Virginia to Portland, Maine. The economy crashed, properties were abandoned, government floundered and services became erratic. About the only thing that united the fragmented country was hatred of the greedy generation responsible for all their problems. Rangers still tracked boomers trying to evade incarceration in the protective detention camps, fugitives like Willow's criminally healthy Grandma who had been able to afford the Life-x longevity treatments.

In the dismal spring of 2065, folks in the Hollow survived the slow apocalypse of power outages and fuel shortages and ongoing digital crashes by relying on the traditional New England talents. Scavenging and making do.

For her part, Willow was making do with Frack. If she stayed in the Hollow, he might be her best option. Not much boyfriend talent around. Or she could leave home, but the world beyond the Hollow was scary for a woman alone. Willow had planned to head to Canada with Jake Standtall a year before, but then he'd taken off without her. Furious both with him and herself, she'd fallen into a funk that Frack had just recently coaxed her out of. Then Grandma had arrived last week, one step ahead of the rangers. Leaving the Hollow would solve Willow's Grandma problem, but then she could never come back to this dreary-but-safe place again.

The crowd had thinned by the time they left the gym. Some of those from away headed home. The rest trooped into the school cafeteria for the traditional potluck, despite the fire scare. Theirs was a community used to sudden failure and ruined plans, but a meal was a meal. And the April Fools' celebration was a matter of pride, a sign that Cheshire County hadn't lost its sense of humor like the rest of their blighted state.

Frack stood astride the mountain bike she'd traded to him and watched her bungee the arm to the Trek that she'd looted from Keene. He was expecting her to say something about what he'd done. She thought about showing some gratitude. Maybe she wasn't ready to be his girlfriend, but he'd stuck up for her and been quick about it. He'd obviously been hoping for an invite home, especially after all the time they'd spent flirting in her workshop. But since Grandma had shown up she'd had to shut Frack down. Having anyone over to Lakeside House was too dangerous with her unwanted visitor there.

She swung a leg onto the bike. "You want to go to the library?"

He was disappointed. "What's there?"

"Books, kid." She wriggled her butt on the seat. "And me."

The Gilman Memorial Library had closed in 2050 but Helen the librarian had left the keys when she'd gone to live with her brother in Maine. A couple of dozen readers passed duplicate keys around and cared for the place. They met for book club when they could agree on a choice and called themselves the library trustees. There were neither lights nor heat in the old brick building, but Willow kept a portable LED work light in her down vest.

She tried the door but it was locked. Which wasn't a problem, only she'd been hoping one of the other trustees might be about to keep Frack from getting ideas. But of course, they'd still be at the potluck.

"So when was the last time you were here?" she asked as they wheeled their bikes into the entryway.

He glared at her. Something in her voice must have annoyed him. Or maybe he'd been hoping for more than a visit to the library. "Just because I don't like books doesn't mean I'm dumb."

"Whoa, where did that come from?" Willow pressed a hand to his chest to calm him, spread her fingers in a brief caress and stepped back. "Just asking, Frack." She had to remind herself that he was just a kid. "Didn't mean anything by it." She gave him a contrite smile.

"Okay." He searched her face, as if afraid of what he'd find there, then his shoulders softened. "Sure." He shivered and then peered at the shadowy shelves, as if listening to his memory. "My mom used make me read stupid kid books. Out loud. Right over there." He nodded toward the children's stacks. "I wasn't good at it. Sucked, actually. People would stare. I mean, we're supposed to not talk in the library."

"My rules now." She steered him toward one of the round tables by the circulation desk. "Talk all you want." She set her work light on it. This was her favorite place in the Hollow other than Lakeview House. The Formica on the tables was chipped and the foam upholstery on the chairs had shriveled with age but Tiny Costello had braided round chair pads to cover them for book club. Willow settled Frack and then went around the desk to raid the communal snack drawer.

"Since we're skipping the potluck." She poured homemade trail mix into a bowl, unwrapped half a dozen slices of venison jerky, set them in front of him and pulled up a chair.

"Private party, I get it." He smirked, unsnapped the thigh pocket of his cargo pants and offered her a silver flask. "My own mash recipe." He beamed with pride. "I'm calling it Pure White Evil."

"You cut this, right?" She unscrewed the top but then hesitated before tasting the moonshine. "Don't want to go blind."

"Three passes through the still," he said. "All hearts and just a squirt of the tails for that corn flavor."

She sniffed, then sipped. "Sweet." The back of her eyes burned as she passed it back.

He watched her watch him drink. "So now what?" He set the flask down next to the trail mix.

She grinned. This wasn't a question that Jake, her old boyfriend, would've asked. She'd be fighting him off by now. Frack's inexperience was a plus. Made him manageable.

"I'm not your girlfriend," she said. "I'm not anyone's girlfriend. But I'm going to kiss you anyway. Get ready."

He stared right at her as she leaned in and brushed her lips against his. A tongue flick—just out of habit—but he started from it as if shocked. His eyes were the size of eggs and then he was laughing.

"Sorry, sorry, sorry," he said.

"Okay, that's okay." She backed away, concerned but amused. "But what the fuck, kid?"

"I couldn't stop thinking...." He was shaking his head. "It's just, I...never had a wish come true before."

His astonishment was so cute that she was tempted to kiss him for real then. "Maybe you should try wishing harder."

That was the wrong thing to say. He practically leapt off his chair at her but now she was the one laughing. "One and done, mister." She fended him off and he sank back into his chair, deflated and confused. Fine by her.

Willow reached for the flask and pretended to take a big swallow. "Let's just say we made a good start." She waggled it at him. "Drink to that?"

"Really?" He gaped at the flask as if it held his future, and then at her. "A start?"

"Sure. I like you, kid, but after that asshole Standtall...let's just say I'm not in the mood yet." She arched an eyebrow. "But hey, moods change."

"Okay." He drank. "But maybe you should stop calling me kid."

After another round, she made him put the hooch away. They split some jerky and replayed the showdown disaster. Frack guessed they'd roll the big prize over to the Fourth of July race, scheduled for the Grange in Marlow, where that Alejandra girl would be on home ground. Willow said they should ban Zoya, or at least suspend her. Frack doubted that would ever happen. There was a pause and she expected him to ask about Grandma's arm but he didn't. She liked that. Showed discretion. He must be curious about the real story.

Willow felt herself relax as they chatted and felt comfortable enough to tease him about his haircut. He was the only man in town who didn't look like he slept standing on his head. Frack admitted that he let his mom trim his hair once a month. She told him that he was lucky to have a mom since she'd lost hers. Of course, everybody knew that her mom had bled to death at home after giving birth to Willow's stillborn sister. But she wanted to remind him why she would always be cautious about sex, what with the nearest hospital sixty miles of bad roads away in Dartmouth.

To break the awkward silence, Frack asked why there were stacks of books on the floor and Willow explained that the trustees had been raiding abandoned libraries for the Hollow's collection. Frack wondered if anyone was still making new books. She said she hoped they were, maybe in Minneapolis or Milwaukee or Canada.

"Then we'll never see them." He sighed. "The world is so fucked up."

"Yeah, but we aren't the ones who fucked it up."

"But it's on us to put it right again." He scooped a handful of trail mix. "That's why I'm going to be a ranger."

"Really? I didn't know that." Despite her down vest, she shivered. "You do know there's school for that now? They're not just gangs and you don't get to appoint yourself. You'll have to move to Concord and enroll."

"Better than rotting in this dump."

She grimaced at the insult to her little library. "What good is being a ranger anyway?" she said. "You looking for revenge?"

"That for sure. Either bury those boomer fucks or ship them to the camps where they belong. But to get things working right, we got to go back to the old ways. You know, where people don't take stuff that isn't theirs." Seeing her reaction, he held up both hands. "Don't get me wrong, I like to scavenge just like everyone else."

"Looting," said Willow. "That's what the boomers called it. We're looters."

He snorted. "Call it whatever. But in a better world, it won't matter whether stuff belongs to friends or strangers. We'll have to leave it be. What people own belongs to them."

Willow thought that Frack's idea of a better world was equal parts moonshine and naiveté. "I looted that bike you're riding." How could she even consider being with this kid? "I have no idea who it belonged to."

"Probably nobody alive." He nodded. "That's part of the general fucked-upness. But when you found it and cleaned it and gave it a tune, it became yours. And then you traded it to me, so now it's mine. And I don't want no one stealing it. When we fix things, there'll be laws to protect bikes and houses and everything. Robot parts, like your arm. And us rangers will make sure that the laws get obeyed."

Us rangers. The library felt cold and airless in the gathering dusk. Willow was in no mood to debate the rangers with this kid. Or to think what he'd do if he found out about Grandma. She couldn't be with him now. Maybe not ever. "Hey, I was just thinking…" she said, feeling miserable and just mean enough to drive him away. "When you were here with your mom, what books did she make you read?"

"I don't know." Suspicion shadowed his face. "Just books."

"They're probably still here." She carried the work light to the children's stacks, leaving him in the dark. "Some of the trustees wanted to move the kids' books so we can shelve our new loot." She babbled to keep from thinking what she was about to do. "But there might be more kids here someday and they might want to read, no?" She could hear Frack bumping past the circulation desk after her. She stooped by the C-D shelf, calling out titles. "Let's see. Something by Carol Chang? Beverly Cleary? Here's the whole Land of Stories series."

"Why are you...?" His voice was thick, but it wasn't from the moonshine. "What's this about, Willow?"

"Everyone loves Roald Dahl!" She pulled books off the shelf. *"Charlie and the Chocolate Factory*? *James and the Giant Peach*? *Fantastic Mr. Fox*? Come on, kid! Which one?"

"That one." He pointed but his voice would've fit into a thimble. "The fox."

"A classic." She flipped it open to a random page and thrust it at him. "Did you know they made a movie of it?"

"Yeah." He recoiled as if it might give him a rash, but then took it. "Saw it on Mom's laptop."

"Read, read it." She angled the work light until the pages shone. "I want to hear you read."

Even in the gloom, she could see his distress and confusion. "There was no f-food for the foxes that night and soon the children dozed off." He read as if each word were a hurdle. "Then Mrs. F-Fox dozed off. But Mr. Fox couldn't sleep because...because of the pain in his tail."

He glanced up to see if he could stop. She waved for more.

"'Well,' he thought, 'I suppose I'm lucky to be alive at all. And now that they've f-found our hole, we're going to have to move out as soon as possible.'" Frack let the book sag out of the light.

"Keep going," she said, hating her fake enthusiasm. "You're doing great."

"No," he said. "This sucks." Sorrow twisted his face. "I think I should go." He tossed the book onto the pile at their feet.

Now that she'd embarrassed him, Willow was sick with regret. She should have found some other way to escape him, one that didn't hurt them both. She'd been so rattled ever since Grandma had forced her way into Willow's life. She didn't know who she was anymore. She wished she could snap the light out and creep into the darkest corner of the library where no one could see her. Instead she aimed it at their bikes in the entryway.

"Fine with me," she said, hiding in plain sight. Her life was all about hiding these days.

◆

Willow skidded to a stop when she spotted the trike parked by the town beach. Nobody would be swimming on April Fools' with ice still on the lake. No rider in sight and Willow's driveway was just around the corner. She hid her Trek and approached the trike. It had started life as an electric Harley but its owner had stripped off the fiberglass trunk and fenders and replaced them with an upright metal cargo box that rose high behind the rider. Probably as much for protection as extra cargo space. Locked, of course. She circled the trike without touching it, wary of alarms and booby traps. Dual battery packs serving as running boards, oversized tires with a nasty off-road tread, although the knobs were worn from use, high-rise polycarb windshield that could shrug off bullets and yes, an empty gun rack behind the cockpit. For an assault rifle?

A ranger, or a wannabe.

She had the same sick feeling she'd had when Zoya's leg had caught fire, only this time it might be her life in the Hollow that burned down. She bushwhacked up the flank of Windmill Hill, circling toward home. At the edge of the north hayfield, she crouched, listening to the pulse and whine of the Hollow's wind farm above her, and tried to think of what to do.

Lakeview House was a classic New England farm building—big house, little house, back house, barn—all attached to each other in a shabby sprawl just a stone's throw from the lake. Willow had rented the upslope hayfields behind the rambling house to Luke Garbesian, who'd just moved his tractor up to her barn in anticipation of the season's first cut. The two bays of the back house garage were where Willow ran the electronics repair business. She'd inherited it from Nana Beth who'd worked at Waytronics in Nashua before it closed. The little house was filled with musty old family furniture, which Grandma had moved so she could open the bunker she'd built back before +5°C happened. If the ranger had found the hatch in the floor of the little house, no longer hidden by the Shaker sideboard and Uncle Seth's piano, then Grandma was probably arrested. Or on the run again. Or dead. And what would he do to Willow for harboring a runaway boomer? Except there was a chance Grandma had pulled off her disguise. Even though she was over a hundred, she'd been gorging on the Life-x rejuvenation drugs she'd brought up from her bunker. She could pass for sixty, couldn't she?

But as Willow watched, someone yanked the curtains of the back parlor open. A shadow moved across the dark window. Now she realized that the shades in the kitchen were up too. Ever since Grandma had staggered home and offered to swap some of her bunker treasures for safe refuge, Willow had kept the house buttoned tight against nosy neighbors—and intruders.

The ranger must already be in there.

"Shit, shit, *shit!*" Willow sprinted across the field to the shelter of the barn. She slipped into the gloom through the side door, breathing hard. What next? Maybe she could surprise them? The sour brown smell of old hay made her nose wrinkle and the futility of this reckless plan made her wince. But what choice did she have?

She tapped the control she'd rigged on Grandma's arm and set a five-minute delay. Then she crept through her workshop and cracked the connecting door to the little house open. Eased the door open enough to push the arm through and aimed it at the entry to the big house. Back outside, she skirted around the foundation of the big house, hunkering low around to the front porch. What the hell was she thinking? Even if the ranger heard the crawling arm and went to investigate, even if she got through the front door and made it upstairs and got her Ruger 45, did she really want to bring a handgun to a shootout with an assault rifle?

"What the fuck?" said a bristly voice, muffled by the bay window.

Willow was onto the porch and through the door in an instant, but skidded to a stop in the entryway. Grandma leaned back on the bentwood rocking chair in the front parlor, eating a bowl of dry Cap'n Crunch cereal from her stash.

"Hello, honey," she said, her skin flushed with the Life-x drugs. "We have a guest." She gave Willow a distracted smile. "Better have a seat."

Even as Willow hesitated, the ranger stomped back into the parlor, carrying the still twitching arm and a SCAR assault rifle. An angry, sour man with shoulders hunched against the troubles of the world, he wore a cracked leather jacket and a grubby blue-jeans uniform that dated from the rangers' vigilante days. His muddy boots left prints on Willow's scavenged Zuni rug.

"This your granddaughter?" he said.

Actually, Grandma was Willow's *great*-grandmother. Nana Beth, her grandmother, had died of the flu in '46. But Willow wasn't about to confirm or deny anything about Grandma just then.

"I'm Willow Jenness," she said. "Where did you find my arm?"

"Yours?"

Grandma was rocking now. Slow and easy, shoulders flat against the spindles of the chair back.

"Sure, I left it in the shop," Willow said. "I fix things here in the Hollow. I was recharging the batteries. Raced it this morning in the April Fools' showdown."

"Saw you there." He offered her the arm and she reluctantly accepted. The damn thing would be a nuisance if she had to make a run for it. "That leg could've burned your school down."

"I know." The arm twisted as Willow groped for the kill switch.

Grandma watched and rocked.

Willow's struggle to control the arm amused him. "Printed that, did you?"

"No way. I've got some old printers but no thermoplastic." She finally flipped the switch. "My business is all salvage and refurb."

"Seems like a lot of robot shit in these parts," he growled as he shifted the gun to his right arm.

The rocker creaked back and forth, back and forth, like something counting down.

"Because of the Waytronics plant over in Nashua," Willow said. "My Nana Jenness worked there. I found this one in an abandoned storage."

"Found, Willow?" He made her name sound like a threat.

"Well, you know. Nobody else was using it." She had the crazy feeling that they were just saying lines, as if they were rehearsing a play. "Place was burned and picked over. Had to wrestle some collapsed roof to get at it." Any minute now they'd throw their scripts away. And then what?

Shit would get very, very real.

"You know what I miss?" Grandma caught herself on a forward rock and paused, as if trying to remember what she had been about to say. "Bananas," she said. "That's when I knew we were well and truly lost. I was just a kid when mom told me that all the bananas got sick and died. I cried." She snorted. "That was long before everything happened. Mom said it wasn't anyone's fault, but I blamed her. I did. Because I loved bananas on my cereal. I told her it was her fault."

"Fuckers fucked us over," said the ranger. Righteousness stood him up so straight that he seemed to fill the room.

"Language, son." She glanced up at him, shocked, as if she had forgotten he was there. Then, seeming to notice the bowl of cereal in her lap for the first time, she offered him some.

"Where did you get that shit?"

Grandma looked puzzled. "The box in the kitchen cupboard?" She said it like a question. "Kind of stale."

Willow wondered whether Grandma's feverish cheeks and flattened affect were side effects of the rejuvenation drugs. And now she was slumping to one side in the chair, spilling her cereal. "Are you okay, Grandma?"

"No, honey." She considered. "Is the room really tilted?" She chuckled as if she'd made a joke.

"What's wrong with her?" said the ranger. The barrel of his gun nudged up.

"I don't know." Willow dropped the robot arm on the couch and helped her up. "Maybe you should go to your room and rest, Grandma?"

"Sure." The ranger's voice was a purr. "Let's all go for a nice rest." His grin filled Willow with dread. He pointed the gun toward the stairs.

She thought about pushing Grandma at him and sprinting for the door. Whatever was about to happen, this wasn't Willow's problem. Grandma was no family to her, gone these nineteen years. Willow and her mom had barely scraped by after Nana died. And her bunker filled with pre+5°C treasures? Locked until Grandma showed up with the only key.

But Grandma's other robot arm, the everyday prosthesis she was now wearing, closed around Willow's waist, locking her in a cruel and unwelcome embrace. They headed for the stairs, but as they wobbled past the ranger, she stepped on Willow's toe.

"Oww, *shit.*"

Willow stumbled and Grandma released her and spun away, swinging her now-free everyday arm across her body. The back of its wrist struck the ranger's neck. "April Fools', asshole!"

Willow heard an angry snap as a blue spark forked into his flesh. Then the ranger was on his back, his rifle clattering to Grandma's feet. He twitched, once, twice and went still. The smell of sizzled meat and the gray scar that bloomed where the arm had struck him made Willow's own burn from that morning throb again.

Grandma was doubled over, panting as if she'd just run in from town. Then she straightened up, giggling.

"What?" said Willow. It wasn't funny. Nothing about this was funny.

"Million volts," she gasped. "Makes military tasers seem like static electricity." She was still grinning. "This arm is armed, honey." It flopped uselessly from her shoulder. "Although it's going to need a serious recharge after that."

"Is he dead?" She wanted to check the body but was afraid the ranger might snap out of it and grab her.

"Usually, they are. If not, you'll have to finish him off. Haven't got the strength; that last dance took it out of me." She picked up the rifle but then sagged back onto the rocker. "No rush, though. Even if he survives, his brain is pretty much barbequed." She must have seen Willow's horror but misinterpreted it. "Don't worry, honey. You did good."

"I did nothing." Willow forced herself to stop gulping air.

"Sure surprised me." Grandma tried to eject the magazine, her fingers stiff and clumsy. "Must have snuck in through the back house." Finally she succeeded. "Oops." It skidded across her lap onto the floor. "No idea how he got here but there must be a vehicle somewhere. Or a horse."

Willow picked the magazine up and examined it. "A trike down the road." Looked to be twenty rounds, more than enough for two women.

"Okay." Grandma combed fingers through her hair, considering. "Okay." Willow was still amazed that she could be over a hundred years old and not have a strand of gray. And her skin was already smoother than it had been when she arrived just the week before. "Perfect, actually. Be a good girl and fetch it up to the barn. What say you make some quick mods, or at least splash on some paint? Change the look and I'll take it and go. Tomorrow morning. Unless you want to come with?" She brightened. "I could use the help."

Willow shook her head, trying to slow down. But her life was stuck on fast forward. "Back up a minute," she said. "That arm...." She gestured at the couch. "The one I took from the bunker. I had it apart and never saw anything like a taser electrode."

"The prototype?" She shook her head. "Never had it weaponized. Or skinned. I was keeping it as a spare, just in case. That's why I left it behind here."

Willow swallowed her anger. It went down hard. "And you're just going to go?"

"Always the plan, honey." She started rocking again. "A nice visit to the old homestead, get a Life-x recharge and head right back out. Safer for everybody, you in particular."

"Then tell me the combination to the bunker."

She gave Willow an appraising stare. "It's biometric—eye scan and fingerprints." She cackled again. "I am the combination." Her jokes pleased her.

"Then leave it open for me."

"Oh honey, I'm sorry." She pretended regret that neither of them believed. "I'm going to need what's down there again someday."

This was what they did, Willow realized, the people like Grandma who had smashed their world. They took what they wanted, did what was best for themselves and left messes for other people to clean up. Like this body.

Willow's rage at boomer callousness made her bold. She stepped up to the ranger and nudged him with her foot. No reaction. "What am I supposed to do with him?" she said.

Grandma shrugged. "I'd put him in the lake. Stones in the pockets. If he comes up next fall, he'll be unrecognizable."

"I swim in that lake." Willow's voice was sharp. "My friends drink the water." As she approached the rocker, her boots crunched the spilled cereal from Grandma's stash. "He was right about you." She loomed over the old woman, fists clenched. "You fucked us back then and now you're fucking me."

Grandma gazed up, her face in Willow's shadow. "Don't you be judging, honey. It was a different time, different values. Everybody was dumb and happy. None of us knew it was going to be this bad." She rocked backwards and stayed, as if to put as much distance between them as she could. "Hey, I was better than most. I recycled, drove electric. Who do you think put the windmills on the hill? And I never voted for those assholes." Her tone changed from plea to whine. "But just because I was born in 1955 and made some nice money and took care of myself, bullies like this want to chase me down and drag me off to some camp." Her everyday arm still useless, she fumbled at the stock of the assault rifle with her good hand as she realized her real danger. "You stay away from me, you hear? I got out once and no way I'm going back to sleep on concrete floors and wait in line for outhouses." Her voice rose to a desperate shout.

"No," said Willow, "no, you're not."

♦

"Looks like ice-out could come any day." Frack paused by the parlor's bay window to button his shirt. The golden sunset had ignited the line of hemlocks on the eastern shore of the lake.

"Better last until Wednesday." Willow stepped into her panties, came up behind him and circled arms around his chest. The island of punky ice had been shrinking all week and there was a margin of open water along the shoreline. She rested her chin on his shoulder and told herself that she didn't care that he was shorter and younger than her. She'd feed him. He'd grow. "I pulled April 11th in the betting pool." She grabbed his belt and turned him around. His face was flushed and his smile was as wide as the sky but she could tell he was still stunned by what they had just done.

As she was.

"Don't worry." He kissed her. "You're already a winner."

She'd have to work on his kissing. "Why?" she teased. "Because I have you?"

"You've had me for a long time, girl." He tucked his shirt into his jeans and turned back to the view. "No, you win because you have this awesome place on the lake. And you're book smart and everyday smart. And you've got one rocking body."

She bent over and picked up her green Celtics jersey and shimmied into it beside him. "I've got something to show you." She pointed him at the couch. "Stay, boy."

"*Rawf!*" He barked in agreement.

She returned from the kitchen with a bottle and two glasses. "Check this," she said and poured a centimeter into each. "Not some backcountry mash that was cornmeal last Tuesday." She handed him one of the glasses. "It's valuable, so sip, okay? No need to gulp it before the stink catches up to you."

He sniffed it suspiciously. "Smells like cordwood."

"They used to store it in oak barrels back in the day."

While he considered this dubious claim, she clinked her glass against his. "We both have this place now, Jerome. You and I are going to live here. Happily ever after."

He stared, whether at the use of his real name or her surprise announcement, Willow couldn't be sure. But his astonishment pleased her. "Remember, just a nip." She watched him drink over the rim of her glass. His eyes got wide.

"Holy shit!" His voice seemed to come from far away. "What is this?"

"Scotch."

"Scotch what?"

"Whiskey. It's old. Older than everyone we know."

He licked his lips. "Smooth, all right. I could get used to it." He set his glass on the coffee table and bent to examine the bottle. His lips moved as he read the label. "Where did you get it? And no stories about storage sheds in Nashua."

"I found me a stash."

"I kind of figured when you brought that arm to the show-down. Where?"

She ignored the question. "Must have been some kind of prepper. Amazing boomer shit. I cleaned it out good last week, so no sense in going back." She gave him a sly smile. "I'd show you the haul except you're going off to be a ranger. Don't want to get in trouble with the law."

"What's that supposed to mean?" He straightened in alarm. "We don't care about boomer stuff as long as there're no boom-ers attached to it. And I'm only going away for the summer." She had him confused again. It was easy to do. "Wait, last week? Does this have anything to do with that ranger who went missing in the lake?"

"The one who left his trike at the beach?" She shook her head. "Pretty sure not. At least, I didn't see sign of him. Or any packs of rabid grandpas." In the slant last light of the day, she noticed that there was still the shadow of a stain where the rocker used to be. Maybe she should move the Zuni rug over. "They still talking about dragging for the body?" she said.

"Nah." Frack picked up his drink. "If that's where he is, he'll come up when the lake turns over." He finished the last of it.

"Right," she said, although she knew he wouldn't. The sins of her past were locked in the bunker beneath them, hiding behind a steel door that would never—*could never*—be opened. Which was just where they belonged.

"Scotch," Frack said, rolling the word around in his mouth as if he liked the taste of it. "Those boomers knew how to live." He reached for a refill.

"No," she said, pushing him away. "No, they didn't." Willow screwed the top onto the bottle. "And we can do better."

Todd Hearon

Ensemblings

In these tightly packed poems and an album of songs whose words sing with sonic love, history is questioned, and a dramatic monologue rivets the reader. We hear cadences that rock us with the lilting rhythms of this poet's musical ear. In "Persephone in Half-Light," Persephone speaks: "...I was free./But what they couldn't touch, and didn't get:/the seeds.//I'm not saying that's the strangest thing./I'm not saying anything at all./I am the buzzing at the windowpane,/the frost that claws, the ticker tape that binds/your line of vision to its floundering hook/trawling and tearing in the murk of me." J.P.

Quabbin Bodies

1. The Meeting of the Waters

Sempiternal waters, sing-
ly sing, gush glottal-less & all
onomatopoetical your
triphthong's liquid pluraling
through rock & ruck & rill
purl, pounce, pronounce & preen the sourceless
flourish of your sundry selves, unseamed
anima, antiphonal

Ursprache,
        ensembling in simul-
taneous tumult the babbling
Earth's eternal tongues;
              O airy
Yggdrasil, within whose watery limbs
climbs the burgeoning current
of birdsong indistinguishable—
wren-trickle, thrush's trill,
aria of orioles
dissolved in the dawn chorus
but intimated tributaries
still:
      voicings of a universal
dialect, a will
gone malleable & migratory
raptured in translation, diaspora
becoming at a stroke
diapason; O
Ouroboros, origin-&-end,
in Bacchic spring come thundering
down the escarpment's scree & skim
littering the valley
with erratics, scattered limbs
of a glacial language extant only in
lacunae, contour,
kettle, esker drift,
congregated relics
where a village went; what crook
denotes you truly, what
wandering wand divines
your secular in-saecula-
saeculorum sign:
your mouth's green myth
pressed to the ocean's ear,

your mountain tale in touch
with some ridiculous sublime
that slips like the gopher soul into its hole

surfacing into the world of time:

2. *The Valley of Lost Names*

Think of a time our own names conjure
nothing but a body of unbroken water

(*Moon over Quabbin. Body of bottled light
poured across the body of the water,*

*something far, at the surface—finned or feathered?
rolling in distress—*)

at dawn the sudden, trumpeting eagle
strikes.

The drowned towns, four-square, hymned in stave & stanza,
swallowed walls on walls of song, each stone a tongue

where the salmon canter over the meadow baffle dam
& smallmouth bass hosanna...

Too deeply now for any to remember
so why does it seem important to remember

when we will ourselves, these fluent selves, like water
subsumed in greater water be impossible to remember

to distinguish the veins in the hand that worked the lathe
wove the straw, rippled at morning into a gesture of love or praise

or clipped the dewy lilac from its stem
or turned the fieldstone into the sunken wall

of a cellar hole, the jam jars lined within
the vagrant bittersweet unwinds among

when the shore recedes (*in the twinkling of an eye*)
the tombs stick out like knees.

Deep in a time that is no longer time
but the greater dissolutions of the water

within whose workings ever unspool our names
as it were (as it will be) upon a ghostly bobbin...

3. *Questions for a Disincorporation*

   "*to undo, separate or dissolve from a body*"

   *Dana, MA; Prescott, MA; Greenwich, MA; Enfield, MA: April
   28, 1938*

A solitary grebe
filling itself, in reflection,
into a globe—

Where does the body go?
                              Is it the same

as the wind in the trees
                        the wind in the highest limbs

that sweeps them uniformly like the necks of swans
swimming in consort
                        so they seem in time

with a music it is impossible to hear
from this distance

                    (we are very far)

—as in a silent film, the couples dancing,
the sweeping of light & limbs across the floor
as across the water's surface, in reflection,
when the wind lifts
& the glacier of a cloud pulls over
& the mares' tails fly
like tribes, nomadic tongues, erratic stars?

Winterlong
the bodies of lost deer
lie littering the ice.

The human graves, carved up & carted
to the minted cemetery on the hill.

The summer fields, under the frozen surface...

(*Something of us remains   Something of us shall not suffer
to be changed*)

In spring, when the small birds come
back to the north meadow & the eagle-fretted bones
rise from the ice

                    across the breaking floes

as it were upon another shore

where does the body, through the fields of other bodies,

go?

4. Atlantis

About that country there's not much left to say.
Blue sun, far off, a watery vein
in the cloud belt. The solid earth itself

unremarkable: familiar ruins
littered with standing stones our people
had lost the ability to decipher.

How deeply had we slept? Beneath the jellyfish
umbels of evergreens, each one a dream,
and the effervescent stars, cold currents

tugged at our thoughts like tapestries
unraveling into war. All spring
the nightingale perched on the green volcano's lip.

The rats had abandoned the temples.
My mind was a voyage hungering to happen.

5. Poem with Any End

When all this All doth pass from age to age—

this City on a Hill, its golden dome
and cupolas a quiet sea floor,
the crabbed, neurotic streets still disentangling
obsessive thirst, obsessive westwardness...

what is a city without
water?

Rome, its spidered aqueducts

bearing the bounty of barbaric springs
down mountaining arches, a song in the valley

　　　　　　　　　　　　sempiternal waters
sing

over the sunken ponds & soapstone quarry,
the Dipper rising with inscrutable stars
over the village where they made the bobbins

to slip down dark, infernal aqueducts
(like shades to slake the high, titanic thirst
of Boston)
　　　　　　　　to Boston.

Persephone in Half-Light

The Nude, a young actress of twenty-six, lies in an artist's Boston studio. Around her, the typical trappings: pillows, scarlet fabric, more swatches piled off to the side. She sips red wine from a glass—slowly, in choreographed fashion—perfunctorily refilled as she gets low. Beside her, on a table, a bowl of pomegranates and a pack of cigarettes. Two large fiberglass Greek columns lie over to one side, over which drape her clothes. Clutter of canvasses throughout. Low music—jazz—floats from a stereo, forming a backdrop for her words, which the artist never hears. She has been told, "Lie still. Don't talk." Her reverie is inner monologue.

Time: Night. The present. She thinks:

The train in the subway was a kind of birth.
Or death. A canal at any rate,
far down at the black end a shade of light.

I stood up by the driver, the car was quiet,
bags at my side, staring through the dark
blinking into stations as we passed.

I thought of worms, moles, groundhogs, ants
grazing around us in the burrowed rock,
and once my stop came to a still I stepped

down to the platform and I saw a rat—
a huge black rat with tiny human hands,
pink, its wet fur slimed and spiked

with sewage maybe, sitting on a bench
as if it waited for me.
The terminal was empty. One green light

sputtered as the train wheels groaned and went.
I dropped my bags and, turning to the bench,
the rat was gone, but in its place (and I

never will forget the mark this made)
a girl sat, something smoldering on her lap,
and when she looked at me, her face was mine.

That was, for me, the beginning of the end.
Not that I'd not had visions. Long before
voices in the elm where no birds were,
cornflower angels in a fume of sun,
across the lawn the ghost of gasoline
where white sheets tucked and bellied on the line,
I saw the spider dancing on the wire
that separated bliss from bliss.
But that was Kansas. You expect that in a place
the tornadoes whip up so quick so quick
one minute you're just sitting on the yard,
familiar patch of grass and tall sweet tea,
the next you're in a ditch ten miles away.
This was different. For one thing it was two
thousand miles, in a city where I knew
no one. And I was standing underground
and looking at a girl who has my face?

I'm not saying it's the strangest thing.
I'm not saying stranger things can't hap—
in fact I saw it as a fitting in,
a kind of consummation, in the dark.
Two Acts, a little interval between
(or big: two thousand miles and twenty years)
before the houselights flicker and the draw
reconvenes,
thick in its drowse of wine and nicotine,
the veins surged up with coffee, and the thrust
proceeds, sub specie aeternitatis:
Act Two: "The Meaning of It All." (Act One:
preliminaries, setting up of action,

determined quirks of character and place,
time to praise what tragicomic flaws
there be—all set?—the circus wired to blow,
the cannon propped, leveled at the stars,
the nerves erect, straddling the ball's
homage to the guts' evacuation—
purge!—
where as yet the brooch just glimmers in the eyes,
the revenger's cheeks are ruddy but with rouge,
and Ophelia in a florist nine-to-five
happily arranges poesies.) Sol la mi.
Prepare the beheadings!
Prepare the beheadings! Lop. This wine.
It gets me. Makes me want to dance.
(O surely some evil will befall someone!)
Would you like that, darling? Tell me. Shall I dance?
Or, no, might Madame's movement interrupt
the Maestro's progress? or is it regress? these
exquisite pains with which you undertake
to get the both of us: vis-à-vis
the image of me bedded in your head
warring with the one beneath your brush.
I can be still. ("Lie still," he said. "Don't talk.")
I can lie still and quiet as a moth.
I am not tempted by the claret flame.
Still as a churchmouse. Docile as a frog
splayed on your dissection board, its veins
impassioned with the artificial dye,
pinned, a Prince of Pieces, crucified,
in dread anticipation of your kiss.
I can be that. Quieter than a fish
at the bottom of the moonless pond you cast in.
Still as the frost that claws the windowpane.
As…

  Silence.

Sometimes when I'm on the stage I think
the audience exists for me alone.
They give me being, as I give them breadth
of character, a role to fall into.
A part to die for. Maybe that's the thing
that keeps them coming back. They glimpse in me
the manifest illusion or facade
of some divine fecundity of purpose:
that from these clumsy bodies, sacks of curd,
fodder for frauds and psychotherapists,
an impulse might arise, Athena-like,
step out along the catwalk of a night
and move among us, speaking in blank verse.

That was a way of saying it. A bit abstruse.
(Fecundity? Haven't heard that one in a while.)
Back to prosaic earth. Ho hum. He he.
Where was I? On the stage.
Mostly I think of it along the lines
of sex. It all comes slobbering back to that,
does it not, my darling? like a beaten dog?
Sex: the way there's something going on,
something intimate and highly strung yet
solitary, too, terminally at one
with transience. Not saying it's not fun,
sublimely fun, metaphysical roulette,
nightly little tryst between the hook
and those cold fishes sweating in the dark,
leering at you, searching out your curves
from every angle. But you're in it, too.
You come here every night, do what you do,
the old routine, you take the same way home
regardless of the fact at every turn,
in every alley you can feel their eyes
fixing on you, casting out their nets.
And the weird thing is, you love it. You're the fly

that thrives on its ability to rest
still in the cobweb in the corner of the pane,
up to the instant when it feels the line
tighten, just so slightly, and it bursts
free of the just-forestalled catastrophe,
screwing its head in frenzy on the glass
with a lunatic's abandon—wa la whee!
Although not every time. It comes to pass
(Act Two), the prompter drowsing, unaware,
the celestial timekeeps working to a T,
it thinks the web was ruffled by night air
and nestles down into the spider's care.

Maybe that's not the best analogy.
I could do better if I had my head
free of the buzz of this infernal jazz.
God's balls, my boy, the things that I could tell!
Sprung from the wellhead of a pure idea,
nurtured with earth, partaken of the bowels,
a basket braided with the Bible's belt,
Moses-Minerva, may I so propine,
Sir, this sip in honor of your health,
this blood-red seed where swims the sunken host
of Pharaoh's devils gnashing up my sleeve
(or not), adrift in the throat's captivity:
the dreggish fumes you take if you take me.

Words, words, words, words. Ti-tum, ti-tum, ti-tum.
Nonce sense. To pass the stones of time...
Where are you now, da Vinci? Psst. Leo.
Be wary as you sail into my smile.
O Christopher Columbus, test your map
against that which you least expect to find:
my nothing-nuggets, glaciers of the heart,
the morsels on this continental plate

whose taste would be the final chill of you.
The blankness of the canvas bleeding through
may be the closest that you come. To me,
immensity requires an open mind.
What think you, Galileo? What are those spheres
whose music is the opposite of sound?
These frequent vacancies so tightly crammed
inside my skull you'd think I was the crowned
empress of emptiness (as I am).
What think you, Sigmund? Am I nuts enough to crack?
Or am I (ah, my Guildenstern) your flute?
The open stops, you know, admit the tune
as much as those foreclosed. What stops in me
lie bared beneath the taxi of your hand,
unmanned, unsunken, still to overcome,
your camel hair that waves toward this mirage
with ever-pressing thirst to stake its claim,
your palette that would pluck the very heart
out of my mystery?

The mystery was there, and moved among us
in the first place, although we knew it not.
The mystery was staring at my face
that shuddered on itself and disappeared
like a fume of—. Except that it was dark.
The terminal was empty. One green light.
And whatever it was was smoldering on her lap—
No. I knew exactly what that was.
And as she went up in a plume of smoke
made from my mouth before my very eyes,
that bundle went up also, to find its birth
beneath the playbill of a different night,
under the molehill of a different earth,
when winter would with characterless grace
bequeath my just deserts.

Silence.

My father was an artist. Sculpted things.
(That's the idea, a little conversation.)
Maybe you've heard of—no, you wouldn't have.
Our boondock primitive, all arts and crafts.
What was it they called him in *Time Life*?
The "Junkyard God." A "Rodin of the Sticks."
"Earthshaking—in a mild, midwestern way."
People used to flock from miles around,
miles off the highway (there used to be a sign)
to stand in our front yard, take photographs.
The Minister of Cultural Affairs
(whoa whoa whoa whoa whoa whoa whoa whoa whoa whoa—
The MINiSTER of CULtuRAL aFFAIRS...
Holy baloney, a perfect blank verse line!   *Bells sound, the lights in*
Somebody grab a pencil, write that down!   *the room flash on and off,*
Sure it's not immortal but screw that,   *a game show...*
maybe I'll get a grant.)   *Bells, lights fade.*
Where was I? dum de-dum de-dum...Ah,
the bigwigs in Topeka making plans
to get him in the capital. I mean
his masterwork. The fruit of twenty years.
Twenty years, and close to seven stories tall,
back of the house, sprung against the fields,
Olympic mess of scrap and burnt-out steel,
chicken wire, water heaters, broken-down
tractors, bedsprings, gutters, he didn't care,
engines, axles, radiators, pumps,
two twisted harrows jutting at the sky
like arthritic hands at prayer, the spike
of a tapping drill to represent
the steeple, four old shot-up sides of steel
pulled from the bus that rusted in a ditch
after the wreck that killed some local kids

not long before, became the folding doors
that opened on the haywire, busted-up,
light-crazed and jumble-tumble maze he called
Cathedral.
And people, they would come from miles around
to stand there, in it, ogle at the what-
in-heaven's-name-don't-rightly-know-but-Mister,
it's a marvel. So it was. Beautiful.

Fruit of the years before his child was born—
inheritance? a birthright, can it be?—
and finished it and went up in a fume
out on the highway, underneath the sign,
TEN MILES TO KANSAS ARTIST TURN RIGHT HERE!
while white sheets tucked and bellied on the line
sitting in the yard of my six-years'
familiar patch of grass and tall sweet tea
thinking *tornado* when my mother called…
But it's still there. And bunched with what remains
of the yard and picket fence and bone-white house
caught in the throat of whatsoever child
that was.
I can remember how I used to be
infatuated with his hands.
I remember how they smelled, like gasoline,
and they were very large, and thick, and brown,
with pink flecks at the knuckles where he'd knocked
the flesh away. Oh, they were lovely hands.
All bruised and chipped and knotted with his work.
Hard work. Not like the dainty stuff you do.
Wrenching, stripping, welding, hammering,
beating the metal to submission like
a god might do with us—
                              make it obey,
to break and bend us to the beautiful.

I can remember how I used to sit
on his lap at the table when we used to sing,
and out behind the house I used to hear,
at night, him out there pounding, pounding,
while I watched the spiders dance across the sill
and white heat lightning splashed against the fields
like patches of God's canvas bleeding through.
"He's got the whole world in his hands,
He's got the whole wide world in his..."
But it's still there. I'm going back someday.
I am. I'm going back, and I can see it,
see myself again inside the maze,
that ruin-haunted, *Time*-undaunted, crazed
cornfield Cathedral of my dad. (And oh,
you therapists, if that won't be sublime
transference, I don't know what in hell is.)

Where was I? Boston. Underground.
Lured by the artificial lights.
The train wheels shuddered once and disappeared,
and there it was. The writing on the wall:
THEATRE DISTRICT. Scale of what I knew.
I took my bags that night and walked around
the Garden. The reflecting pool was drained.
Ice in the willows made them lean like grand
dames that cast their pearls to the lights,
and the dark was full of whispers like applause.
But this is exposition. How express
that feeling, not that I was on the verge,
but that I'd actually broken through
to the new form, that it had broken through
on me, in me—that I couldn't be the same;
that all my life had been a preparation,
a close and careful study of a glass
drawn with well water, water I'd divined
and tasted on my tongue the tinge of iron

the core distilled—how can I express
that fleck of cold, that filament of fire
caught from the old earth's veins, a cold
so absolute and sere my throat inflamed,
flamed in my very being as it swept
over the smothered heart and racing lungs
and washed across my belly where the seeds
lay waiting, hushed, with hungry open lips
like a nest of birds.
like a nest of birds. I remember once
I found a nest of meadow larks,
far in the fields, tucked among the green
folded ears of corn. The sun was loitering
down in the next field by the whitewashed barn.
Seven of them. Babies. On the ground beside,
the mutilated body of the mother.
Killed by—what?—whatever kills, the whim
of some boy's gun as she came arcing past
homeward, almost home. It must have been
a while. The eyes. Her body just a sack
of meal the ants grazed in. And from her young,
as I leaned over, from their mouths arose
so thick a silence it was palpable.
Not even any strength to make a sound,
just splayed there, craning, pure with fear,
their jaws like razors, diamonds of flame
so frail that just to touch would be to quench,
so fierce that to touch would be to burn
the edges of your soul from everything
that kept you safe and separate, at home—
so pure a hunger, and so absolute
a lack,
that to lift, to taste, to even tilt that glass
would flush you through at once and make you whole.
And the silence in the fields was so immense
around their open mouths I didn't hear

my mother calling, hours after, when
she found me there, their mother on my lap,
a wisp of smoke, a sack, the seven babes
like votives, candles drawn in homage round
a circle of my cornfield makeshift shrine.
Their hunger was a portion I divined
from a single glass of water from a well.
And since deep-drawn, the seeds it watered burned
and swelled as if engendered by their own.
But that was Kansas. All that I could tell
of depth and distance, of immensity,
when you came down to it, was water from a well.
What would I tell now I could taste the sea?

The sea was somewhere else. But I could smell
its tincture in the mist that swept across
the Garden air and pecked against my lips.
There were the Swan Boats, ready to set sail
across the bubble of a hoodwinked eye,
chained like children. In the spring I'd see
them glide, I'd watch them from the willow leaves
ferry bright tourists with their plastic shades
beneath the droppings of the pigeoned eaves,
baying like beagles at the reverend dead
enshrined in recent stone. I paid my coin
and crossed myself one spring. I lost my own
glasses peering down into that green
obliterating murk. I ducked
my hand and found the sunlight out of reach.
My own face faded. What was I looking for?

I know one thing. The city swallows you.
Loads you in its throat, into its veins,
clamps you to its tracks and drives you down,
a B-line smack to the gangrened heart.

(Red Line to Braintree, Blue an opened vein
to Wonderland—what matter? All the same.)
It's cold as hell in there but you don't freeze.
You don't. You only sit and think and wait
in an empty theater, on a banished throne
midwinter, in the darkness of a day,
while ripples crown and film about your head
in celluloid, the lives you might have led,
peeling like an onion to a core
that never comes. You peel. You peel.
You peel to emptiness, and that is death.
So much is certain, is it not? So much
seems my soul, my being caught between
what passes for truth and what just passes.
And what, whatever else may be, may spring—
the manifest illusion of divine
purpose? Where is purpose in this? Say.
What purpose in these syllables I lay,
Procrustes, on the rack of this blank verse?
Lop. Th'alternative? Well. The mind goes blank,
the field remains untilled, the enemy
advances.
Silence and stillness are the enemy,
your enemy, my dear. For what you said,
in that defining moment when I dropped
my clothes (you loading up the stereo,
as if that could protect us), in the glow
of lamplight on my skin adjusted so,
in that defining moment when you said,
"Lie still. Don't talk." and in that, opted
not for the monstrous music of the spheres,
not for the icy orchard of my heart,
not for the labyrinth of deep and dazzling darkness that the poet says is God,
but for a shell, a surface (through your pride? through fear?),
what you gained was jazz, but lost a world, my dear.

I don't even like jazz. Never have. Not me.
But it will be there. In the portrait, it will make
its notes felt in the squiggling of a curve,
in the smoke that winds up like a clarinet
if I should smoke. (Should I smoke?) It will infect
even the polished purity of fruit—   *She reaches*
Plastic! Leonardo, I'm appalled.   *into the bowl.*
And look, the paint is even chipping off.
Okay, okay, I'll put it back! Jeez.
Not like it's life or death. Or is it? Say,
how big is this? Should I expect someday
to be found hanging in the MFA?
(Maybe even plastered to the T,
a token to your immortality?)
Maybe on a Wednesday (the old routine)
strolling through the vacant lunchtime air
among schoolchildren, ravens in my hair,
the nibble of gentry at lubricious tarts,
Monet on the mouse pads in the Museum Shop,
ching-ching, the bell, ascend the sandstone stair,
down the long corridor to find me there
framed on the far wall of my favorite room
gaping the gulf, lounging on the brink
of all I will remember from this night?
And what will I remember? How the wine
flared like a will-o'-wisp inside my head?
How the fake fruit tempted, how we might have said
anything to keep the rats at bay,
nibbling at the onion of this silence?

Oslo was like that. Oslo. Oh,
just a guy I lived with for a while.
Ha.
More like a pact between the dying and the dead.
Though at first it seemed the opposite of that:

a dying to be alive. At any rate.
Sometimes at night I'd watch him as he lay
smoldering in his rosy opiate dream
of cellphones, celluloid and private jets,
the TV on, but mute, the images
dancing on the walls like hieroglyphs
in our subterranean domestic gloom,
and think that if I took a knife and pressed
its point into his sole and opened him
from toe to tip, peeled hard and pressed inside,
I just might find the thing that made him tick,
beyond the heart, that like a blood-gorged tick
dropped from a limb, brushed from a blade
of grass, climbed leisurely to nurse and suck
upon your softest places—beyond that,
and far beyond his need, his junkie's need
to have me under him at any cost,
and not just that, I'm telling you screwed down,
pinned, like a June bug, iridescent wings
spreading for a flight that never comes,
or if it does, to come in fits and bursts
(his mostly), mine a bursting just to twist
free of the spike he'd drilled into my heart
that kept me there, even as the first,
even as the first was being lost—and then
to hold that over me as if it was my fault,
my choice, indicative of something in
my self that would choose death in any case?
If I could press
past that, I thought that maybe I might find
the chip, the fleck of mica in the soul,
embedded in the shards that made him whole,
a tiny thing, a cameo . . .
And still the whole time thinking that, I knew
this process would go on forever, peel

on peel, an endless stripping back until
nothing remained to tell me who I was,
why I was here, what part in hell I played,
nothing but silent, unrepentant air.
And that was terrifying.
                     So I stayed
beneath him, night by night, until I made
a thing between us. And I kept it. And one day
in the glistening dead of winter, she was born.
I named her May.

The jazz has wound up, the bottle by now is empty. The artist moves to the stereo, fetches another CD (more jazz), opens another bottle of wine. She sits up, stretches. Takes a cigarette from the table, lights it. Sings, like a lullaby, to a broken tune:

         A slumber did my spirit seal.
         I had no human fears.
         She seemed a thing that could not—feel?
         the weight of earthly years.

         No motion has she now. No force.
         She neither hears nor sees.
         Rolled round in earth's diurnal course
         with rocks and stones and trees.

Full of surprises, ain't she? The auld girl.
My mother taught me that.

Recites:
         O joy that in our embers
         is something that still lives,
         that nature yet remembers
         what was so fugit—

         O joy that in our embers
         is something that—dost live?

that nature yet remembers
what was so fugitive.

Dost? Doth. Dost to doth. Ha. Embers. Ash:

A plume of smoke as she exhales.

I don't even smoke.

*New jazz starts up. She puts the cigarette out, takes her former
position. The artist comes forward, adjusts the lights (a flicker),
refills her glass, returns to his easel.*

Back to the drawing board, eh? Curtain, and…
Scene.
Where are we now? Don't tell me, let me guess.
(It's not so easy when there's two of you.)
Deltoids? Clavicle. Croak if I get close.
Lower? Help me now. I see it. Almost…
Oi! Fer feck sake Ma, 'e's on me tits!
Ehem. That's *bosoms* to you, young lady.
O see, see how aloof the Maestro stands
just at the distance discipline demands
(neither too close for the libidinous hooks
to catch, nor so withdrawn to be a clam),
my peerless knight of mediocrity!
Heart's conquistador, thwarted though you be:
Columbus in his crow's nest, Moses damned
to view, cloven beneath him, Canaan's lands,
New Worlds of curds and lamplit honey. How
like a martyr to the limits of his art—
famously resigned—how like a saint he drops
his eye in deference to the suffering lot
of mere humanity. What a load of stink.
Tell me, darling, really what you think.

Am I worth the crossing? (Obviously not.)
Or am I a jewel, hung aloft the night,
dangling from the lobe of Afric's ear,
the unrecovered country which you passed
once in a dream, and then only as near
as the gods of All That Must Not Be allow—
for I know (believe me), how your life depends
upon the thing forever out of reach,
apple or plum, cluster on the vine,
star-cluster, or the brightest star that beat
once at your own breast in its milky way,
I know,
I know it in my motherbones. (My May.)

> *Silence.*

Where was I? So. You getting any of this?
I'll bet you are. I can read it in your squint.
Old Pokerface, stoking me for old flames,
ghost embers, angels' dust of what remains.
It'll take more than jazz. The cards are stacked,
and I've got hands no one is gonna touch.
Flush of diamonds like a nest of glowing seeds.
Ace of hearts, the queen of sunken spades.
Card-house cathedrals and immensities.
Myths, darling. Shall I tell? One goes like this.

Marlborough Street. I'm walking toward the Garden.
Magnolia petals float like boats on air,
swanblossoms, milk-white votives setting out
over the darkness of the waxen green,
that undertow of shadow. It must be spring.
Then it's not. And they're not. I'm not. Nothing is.
The grid that holds that fierce fantastic play
of sun on stone, geometry of glass,
sky-mirroring tower and the Trinity-,

alters, minutely, shifts—as if the mask
you all this time had credited as flesh
and blood, as lover, mother, soulmate, friend,
slipped at your touch (my god) but still the eyes
hold, though offset now, half-right, and dark
withdraws the incandescence, flutter out.
What is the howl of all Hell to that flood
that sweeps across you then? Salt, acerbic,
bile in the wound your own incisors shred,
your own benumbed and famished flesh consumes,
betrayed by life, conscripted by the dead
to sit in abject silence on a throne
at the bottom of a moonless pond you cast in—
No. Not pond. Not well. Nothing but the sea,
while ripples film about your head, the swirl
of tides beyond you; far above, the dome
of sunlight beacons where your sometime-home
lies still in state,
interred in metal husks and brittle springs,
the peapod of a house, the quiltpatch yard,
from the col a still voice calling…
And the silence of that floor was so immense
the sirens couldn't touch it, and the depth-
charges paralleveled at my heart
couldn't sound it.
couldn't sound it. Not till they had pumped
me clean, and seven days I lay in State,
turning and turning on my clammy bed,
strapped like Andromeda as Medusa's head
(my savior) turned their therapists to stone,
did they get the word they wanted. I was free.
But what they couldn't touch, and didn't get:
the seeds.

I'm not saying that's the strangest thing.
I'm not saying anything at all.

I am the buzzing at the windowpane,
the frost that claws, the ticker tape that binds
your line of vision to its floundering hook
trawling and tearing in the murk of me.
Be careful, Sherlock. Elementary:
There are things in here you might not want to see.
Consider our capacity for loss.
Consider that each absence leaves a space
fitted to what filled it, husk or shell,
footprint, tidemark, crater, well,
lacunae of cicadas on the tree,
snakeskin stocking like an evening glove;
consider that these voids are everywhere,
given our propensity to move,
that everything that takes shape takes away,
matter from matter, mirrored, as it moves;
consider, too, my dear, that this is true
for all that insubstantial stuff we call
The Inner Life, imaginative play,
the little Lyric Black Box tucked away
inside an alley of the skull, your Globe,
whose repertory troupe will run the rounds
as long as you sustain them, for you are
both audience and actors, manager and crew,
props, costumes, lights, and literary rep,
dyspeptic in-house critic with a lip
for all outmoded artificial trash,
tinseled pretension, dialogue that smacks
too much of Poetry, of the unReal
(but, oh, with such a soft spot for O'Neill)—
for it's no secret that ideas have form,
as every man will tell you from his bowels
the instant that he hears the marriage vows,
and the figure of a dream exerts upon
a nation, till it equals obsolete
or till some other figure beats it down,

stamps it in the monolithic mud
for eons maybe—tum, ti-tum, ti-tum
goes Time in all its vengeance...
Consider this: that matter, consciousness
meet at the crest of this momentary wave,
swell on their own consumption, have their say
and sweep into obliterating night;
that all life is the blind, usurping spite
of twindling inbreds dying to be born,
bearing each others' heads as up they sway
and crash without a sound upon the deep
that is as deep and silent as the mind
of God, our dark protector and our stay,
reflecting pool and Universal Dad
splayed on the highway as the fume of sun
wriggles like a maggot on the lawn
some six-year's Sunday child sips tea in.
Consider, too, what passes for the shade
of life, a leech strapped to an invalid,
itself grows gorged and falls back on the dark
before, behind, within us, all around;
that vacancy's our nature, and the void
our first inheritance (both throne and cell);
that from the moment of our birth, expelled
from ripeness that clung to us like a glove
we trail, cresting on a wave of blood,
howling to heaven for the fields we fled,
O is it any wonder that we wail,
already mostly dead?

You get that, Leonardo, and you've made
a start. Your fifteen-minutes' burst of fame
veining the shaft you drop down endlessly,
tied to a line of scent, a dim perfume
vaguely at one with the odor of the womb
you half-remember and will pine for always.

It's cold as hell in here but you won't freeze.
You have my surety on that. Proceed,
first through the horns of ivory, my smile,
my dark tongue lapping like a river boat
edged to the shore; look, it takes your weight
beguilingly. (And did I see your coin?)
Godspeed...
Downstream dark angels flit about you now,
attend your thick descent, like baby bats,
their faces remembered out of childhood books,
all that Pandora loosed, the withered Sphinx,
faces far back as preschool you had thought
undone forever, twirl there—your first kiss
stolen over figures in the clay,
companions swimming in the sandbox frame
or housed in the school bus unaware
of the grim twister ripping at their heels—
lift from a ditch light-years away
to linger, twirl to one, disperse
across forgotten lawns like Sibyl's leaves.
By now you are a chambered nautilus
of thought; harpies and sirens hold no sway.
Fast from the shore the river slips
downwinding, willows bending in their strings
brushing the current where reflected, there,
beneath you—what?—a film of memory,
a fleck, a flicker, kernels and gives place,
dissolves. And darkness ravishes the stream.

If you remember when you light upon
that deepest cove that opens on the orchard,
ask for me there. It's where I keep my court,
seven crowns about my head, the blood-red
orbs from my branching memories, the seeds
full-fruited in the orchard of my heart.
And if you feel the chill that passes all

belief, be calm, my dear; as evening falls,
my lord routinely takes the garden air;
it's he you sense beside you, circling there,
it's he, the black moth guttering your flame,
dark ravisher, the frost that claws your pain.
It's he that taught me everything I know
and then some. O vagrant little soul,
I am, I'm almost sorry for your loss,
as much as I, the most of it, can be.
But how impossible to remain (can you not see?)
impartial in these matters that concern us.
Snatching and patching, as if you could contain
in a stroke, a brush, a canvas, in a frame—
no matter. (Did you even ask my name?)

I'll give you something. A little verse I tell
myself at bedtime, which is wedtime, cold
as the frost of fifteen, twenty wild Decembers,
when in disgrace with fortune's seedy eyes,
when the stage ghosts haunt me and I long to take
the artificial light into my veins,
to stand there and be brilliant for a while,
the way I used to stand inside the maze
of light at morning when the six-years' sun
prismed through the steel and broken glass,
and the fields stretched out forever, and the voice
I made was mine and full and free
and endless as it leapt up from the nest
like larks ascending—

                            their mouths like little flames,
candelabrum mirrored in a glass,
chalice of well water that I brought
to the altar as the days pushed past
from May to August in the summer of his going,
summer replacing spring, and autumn then,
a tall, refinèd taper with its flame

of husk, a wisp, a shell of what had been
stamped from creation (how?), the very self
that made the bed of earth I walked on.
And how I'd take that water from the glass,
and the dry nest kept and tucked into the side
pocket of the altar he'd created
from the seats of the bus in which the children died,
and sprinkle it with water from the well,
and sing my darkness to the long-quenched flames,
my six-years' sorrow to those little beings
that lay beyond me, all earth's now, and sing
for all poor creatures born to light their day
under the bower of unbroken stars, the sway
of night behind the golden dome of noon,
my song a steeple, spiring like a stem,
sunflower rising from my native state
all the mute morning, folding like a hymn
at heaven's gate.

Hell:

Hell is a place where everything you've lost
beds down with all you'd ever hoped to gain.
The offspring is a dumb, detestable
poor stunted creature called What Might Have Been.
And it's your destiny to nurse that thing
into Oblivion.
And everything you've left—the bone-white house,
the yard beneath the sun's prismatic ray,
gurgle of well water in a glass,
your mother's voice alighting from above
as you lay drowsing with the breezes at your head,
candescent angels in a field of—May...
Hell is a place where everything you love
lies out of reach. That's what I should have said.

Silence.

Tick-tock. Tick-tock. Tick-tock, tick, tick, oh, words
what words what sounds what syllables for this
what measurement what stanza line what verse
when in the very act the mind goes blank—
which act? Which act of what? Where was I? (tick)
The heart a time bomb ticking out its loss
mured in the muds of winter? (tick) Stand still,
stand still, you ever-moving spheres! O how
to force, to apply the rigors of what craft—
Intention. Think. Think. You have your head.
What's your intention? Ha. To let it be
(or not). Whether 'tis nobler for the mind
to suffer to be happy for a time? (tick tick)
To leap to the streets with artificial joy
or a pure joy passing understanding but
happy? Perhaps? O haply I think on thee
(or not). Tick-tock, tock, tock... *Earth, gape!*
How long have I been here? O Lord my God,
how long how very long have I been here.
"When I survey— "When I in awesome wonder,
consider all the worlds thy hands have made—"
God, the infernal racket of this jazz!
But oh, somebody (Father?) tell me please,
mother of mine, how long have I been here?

Silence.

Spring. In the spring, it must have been. (What year?)
Magnolia blossoms floated out like swans
on air, like votives, candling the air.
Processionals... What I was driven to.
I with my midnight walking. Overhead,
the gas lamps huddled in their little fumes.
Marlborough Street. So quaint. All quiet

but for the baying of a dog, far down
at the Garden end. tock tock, tock tock
my footsteps as I slipped from pool to pool
under the lamps spread out like stepping stones,
stations, spotlights tripping down the dark
infinite proscenium of God,
our heroine
in her one-night-only, searing monologue,
"Now You See Me Now You Don't." tock tock, tock tock
Flash! I am a star, I am a queen,
I am the greatest actress in this town!
Zip: *tock tock, tock tock...* The old routine.
And on and on. It must have been a while.
My veins were rearing but I had my head.
(Oslo, the rat, had left some in the bed
under the mattress where she lay, still sleeping.
I lit the candles and the silver spoon
and hey nonny nonny, went out to jump the moon...)
Near four, it must have been, I started home.
Fairfield to Exeter, Dartmouth, down
the long line angling at the Trinity,
tower behind it like a grid of night,
starless, a dark too daunting for a star;
tock tock, southward, crossing now Columbus
(O my conquistador, where were you then?),
my breast a white moth leaping into flame,
my phoenix heart, the dust inside my veins
opening to a desert where I see,
still I see it, spread before me like
Wonderland: Jerusalem, wriggling like a fume
on the horizon where the streetlamps bleed to sky,
eternal City, transparencies of stone,
prismatic towers, steeples, and the one
sound, within it, pounding, pounding,
hot on the anvil, hammering the heart,

working its darkness to a golden bird,
my father pounds the grace notes as I come
closer, lured on the siren of her call,
my mother standing on the white-framed porch,
inside the white-framed picket fence
framed in the fields and over all, a sky
no longer winter, sere,
but touched, refined with early autumn's tone,
husks of late summer refolding into June
like hands at prayer, suckle on the vine,
land of milk and honey, and I'm there,
I'm really there. My God. I've made it. Home.
And the street erupts, geysering the sky
like fireworks, sparklers whirling on the line,
roman candles that we'd hold and burst
across the yard at fireflies on the Fourth,
red orange blue stars above me, then a blast
like an A-bomb shakes me from my state—
O God. This is my street, and it is burning.
O God. This is my street, and it is burning.

What is the howl of all Hell to that cry
I let, my darling, as I leapt into the flame
to pluck you out, still sleeping? It was I
burst through the brownstone calling out your name,
I who through arms and axes, helmets, took
to the burning walls and corridors and blaze
of the stairwell, down the tunnel clogged with smoke,
not stopping till I lighted on your face,
nested, like an angel in its shrine,
seven flames about you, dancing in my brain,
not stopping till they held me at the door—
I was the one who saved her she is mine!
And they took you. And they hid you (o somewhere here...)

and I never saw my baby's face again.

The jazz has wound up. Silence. She lightly sings:

> A slumber did my spirit seal.
> I had no human fears.
> She seemed a thing that could not feel
> The touch of earthly years.

> No motion has she now. No force—

The artist's finger rises to his mouth, in concentration. She stops. He resumes. She takes a cigarette, lights it, resumes:

> She neither hears nor sees.
> Rolled round in earth's diurnal course
> With rocks and stones and trees.

Poor soul. I could almost pity you.
Stuck on that patch of shade between my legs.
When millions of such shadows in me tend.

No matter.

Strike up another number. For Jesus' sake,
give us a lively one. Come on. *Come on!*
The universe shall live by jazz alone.

from *Border Radio*

(link to full album: https://soundcloud.com/toddhearon)

All My Best Intentions
https://soundcloud.com/toddhearon/03-all-my-best-intentions

All my best intentions always somehow end up working in the graveyard
All my best intentions always somehow end up mopping up the floor
All my best intentions always somehow end up playing second guitar
I'm old enough to know
The things you just let go
Don't get too far

All my best intentions always somehow end up sitting in the dugout
All my best intentions end up starring in somebody else's show
All my best intentions took to Percocet when forty pulled the rug out
I'm old enough to know
The things that just don't show
You don't talk about

I was gonna be King of the Bengals, King of the Buckaroos
King of the Jungle, King of the Jews
But best intentions like messiahs just climb up on their cross and die hard
With the world to lose

And I've grown happy with the wealth of my deficiencies
I'm satisfied to be a sinking star
I've come to terms with my outstanding mediocrity
I've set the bar
So
Low
The dreams I've just let go
Don't hurt too hard

All my best intentions always end up working midnights at the Walmart
All my best intentions hung their hats up in Las Vegas long ago
All my best intentions send their genuine condolences from Hallmark
I'm old enough to know
The dreams you just let go
They don't hurt too hard

I was gonna be King of the Bengals, King of the Buckaroos
King of the Jungle, Jesus, King of the Jews
But best intentions like I mentioned just climb up on their cross and
    die hard
With the world to lose
Like I lost you
Like I lost you

Evangeline

https://soundcloud.com/toddhearon/05-evangeline

Evangeline you don't come 'round here anymore
Your smile's gotten strange to me
All your poetry was an open door in the forest floor
To insanity

Wanna do right by your mama, by your papa too
By their big Impala, 1962
Now come on Evie, grab your Chevy, let's see what she can do
We'll go holy rollin' for a while

Evangeline with the far-off name and the walleye trained
On eternity
In your cutoff jeans you're as long and lean as the poets' dream
Of immortality
Wanna climb into your bearskin, wanna be born again

Eat peyote in the desert with your medicine man
Now come on Evie, grab your Chevy, let's take her for a spin
We'll go holy rollin' for a while

Holy rolling
Holy rolling
Holy rolling
Going out in style
Turning those tricks on the Miracle Mile

Evangeline you're a junkyard queen and a saint's wet dream
Of criminality
All your sweet-sixteen and your submachine, they're reminding me
All is vanity
Save a spot for your grandma, all your Oklahoma kin
Save a spot for the preacherman with his pocketful of gin
Come on Evie, grab your Chevy, let's pile the whole clan in
We'll go holy rollin' for a while

Holy rolling
Holy rolling
Holy rolling
In and out of time
Turning that holy water into gas-o-line

Holy rolling
Holy rolling
Holy rolling
Going out in style
Turning those tricks on the Miracle Mile

You just smile, pretty baby
You just smile like you're crazy
You just smile and I'll be happy for a while
Turning those tricks on the Miracle Mile

You'd just smile, pretty baby
You'd just smile like you're crazy
You'd just smile and I'd be happy for a while
Turning those tricks on the Miracle Mile

But Evangeline you don't come 'round here anymore

Mary Dyer

https://soundcloud.com/toddhearon/06-mary-dyer

I came here with the reckoning done
And I saw the scales sink into the sun
And the fields were heavy with the heresy grain
And a lone tree leaned and chuckled my name

Oh up in Boston
It's a hard falling from grace
Oh up in Boston
It's a dark professing place

Well they welcomed me into the fold
And they bound my arms my hands to hold
They kissed my cheek my tongue to check
And knitted me a pretty noose around my neck

Oh up in Boston
It's a hard falling from grace
Oh up in Boston
Such a dark professing place

They tied my skirts and covered my face
My house of bone and blood to raze
My body you kill, my spirit flies freed
As the big wind taking a dandelion seed

Spin my shroud when I come to die
With a thread too bright for the magistrate's eye
No tongue can tell nor eye can see
That diamond dangling from the gallowman's tree

Oh up in Boston
It's a hard falling from grace
Oh up in Boston
Such a dark professing place

Such a dark professing place

Where the Well Don't Run Dry

https://soundcloud.com/toddhearon/15-where-the-well-dont-run-dry

There oughta be an answer on that highway
There oughta be a mansion in the sky
There oughta be a fat paycheck come Friday
I'll meet you where the well don't run dry

There oughta be some beauty in the desert
A little speck of bluebird by and by
A private little bucketful of pleasure
And I'll meet you where the well don't run dry
Where the well don't run dry

Sunny days and meltaways
Beyond the Great Divide
Fortune-wheeled or far afield
You know I will always be on your side

There oughta be a way to live forever
On Church's chicken wings and cherry pie
Jim Beam and grenadine and Dr. Pepper

Man I'll meet you where the well don't run dry
Where the well don't run dry

There oughta be a better way of leaving
Some way to say farewell without goodbye
There oughta be a heaven worth believing
And I'll meet you where the well don't run dry
Where the well don't run dry

Christina Keim

Two Essays

Christina's writing traces a theme familiar to many: the quest to gather our experiences into something that we feel is our whole person, blemishes and all. The author yearns to feel complete. Bittersweet childhood memories evoke struggles with her mother. She describes experiences that have left her wanting and striving to make sense of them. Years later, when the author is on the other side of the globe, hiking in China, she still finds herself confronting the mystery of painful episodes. Memories of her mother accompany her on steep mountain trails. The stories are delivered with the sure hand of an experienced narrative writer. Centuries ago, Seneca pointed out that, like it or not, we carry our interior burdens wherever we go. I think the author would agree, as she works towards her own personal destination. G.D.

Dispatch from Tiger Leaping Gorge

We near the end of the steepest part of our ascent, the rhythm of my steps remaining steady and strong, even though each stone block is perfectly positioned for one stride of a hiker with legs longer than mine. From here we must cross only a small knoll, where the trail lays in winding, dusty loops before ascending a stone staircase to the trailhead at street level. I tighten my fists around the grip of my hiking poles and focus on the rhythmical *click* of their metal tips striking the blocks, hand-carved from the native lime and sandstone rock that forms Tiger Leaping Gorge.

Suddenly I am reminded of a hallway 10,000 miles and several decades away, when the similar rhythmical *click* of my mother's canes heralded her tentative steps. But her rhythm was labored as she dragged unwilling limbs along the linoleum surface. Her toe caught and she fell, canes landing with a clatter, while she sobbed in frustration and anger.

I shake the memory and return to the present, the pale brown stone, the metallic shine of green poles reflecting the sun slowly descending behind Jade Dragon Snow Mountain, its towering summit perpetually shrouded in cloud. The muscles in my thighs, calves, and back feel the effort but they continue to push and propel my body up each step, one beat closer to triumph. My knees, too, are almost silent despite the stress. My personal kryptonite, my knees have been letting me down for nearly a decade. They have kept me in near-constant pain and limited my life. I am in disbelief that they say nothing now.

We reach the knoll and the striding is easy. The wind has increased. Its strength becomes my strength, the power flowing through my body as easily as the blood that now eases the lactic acid from tired muscles. My poles swing freely through the air and now I am almost floating over the earth. It is as though my whole body is light; movement is effortless. I fairly skip up the stone steps to the trailhead.

For this moment, I am free of worry. I am high on the power of my own body. I have hope.

◆

No one understood why I wanted to visit China. When I announced the destination to my friends six months before my trip, I couldn't fully articulate it either. I just knew that I wanted to be somewhere different. And I couldn't shake the feeling that I was running out of time.

My mother had wanted to travel the world. As a young woman, she made it as far as Europe, touring Italy and the Swiss Alps. But our family rarely ever took vacations beyond visiting my grandparents in Massachusetts and Pennsylvania, traditional journeys taken on typical interstate highways.

"We'll travel when we retire," said my practical, fiscally conscious father.

But instead, my mother was diagnosed with multiple sclerosis at forty-two. I was just thirteen when my childhood ended and her decline commenced. By the time I was twenty-one, she lived in a nursing home full time, her body a shell imprisoning the vestiges of a mind once quick and generous. She left when I was twenty-eight, a soul finally free.

For years I ran from her shadow. I fought any restriction on my wants and desires, certain the world would be snatched away from me like it was for her. But no matter what I did, I was always left with the feeling that there was a missing piece, something I sought but could not identify, that I would never be able to grasp.

Doctors assumed my knee pain was the result of hiking mountains, riding horses and sending tae kwon do kicks through boards. But the usual treatments did nothing more than briefly mute it. The pain increased, until it screamed so loudly I couldn't sleep, couldn't be civil. I only cried when I thought no one was looking. I started to watch life instead of living it.

It was the third specialist who finally made the diagnosis—an incurable inflammatory autoimmune condition, possibly treatable with medication so powerful it carries black box warnings. The specialist oozed confidence, but all I could think about was her. How doctors told my mother the same things about multiple sclerosis, that her body's autoimmune destruction would be slowed by their medications. They were wrong then. I believed they were wrong again now.

It was in this state that I fled with my boyfriend to China and its Tiger Leaping Gorge, one of the world's deepest chasms, plunging over two miles into the earth. The trail along the Upper

Middle Gorge, carved along the edge of Haba Snow Mountain and overlooking the unnavigable rapids of the Jinsha River, is nearly seven miles long with 3,280 feet of elevation gain.

Tiger Leaping Gorge gets its name from local legend—a tiger was pursued by a hunter to the edge of the powerful Jinsha, so the story goes, and leapt from a stone nearly one hundred feet across the river to freedom on the other side.

Perhaps I thought if I went halfway around the world, I could outrun the shadows of my past that now seemed to consume my present. But mostly I ran because of fear and the unrelenting certainty that despite my efforts, I, too, had become trapped.

◆

I am in the front seat of a full bus heading from Shangri-La to a dusty city named Qiatou. The road loops back upon itself over and over, winding through the crags and outcrops of Himalayan foothills. The bus engine whines as the driver downshifts to slow our descent, while in the other lane, overly laden trucks filled with cool gray stone barely creep forward.

Qiatou is little more than a row of half-empty storefronts hanging over the waters of the Jinsha, its only purpose seeming to be providing access to the gorge. The Naxi ethnic minority indigenous to this region eke out an existence growing grain on steep terraces and herding goats. When China first allowed foreign tourists into the region in 1993, enterprising residents opened guesthouses and private trails catering to hikers. Our larger bags continued on the bus without us to Tina's Guesthouse, the nearly universal end point to any hike along Tiger Leaping Gorge.

Tina is a shrewd businesswoman; she owns this bus and another, providing exclusive gorge access to a steady stream of hikers coming from Lijiang and Shangri-La, the nearest cities. Her family's guesthouse provides both lodging and sustenance, stocking plenty of beer to quench a weary hiker's thirst and selling yak cheese dumplings, a sweet, westernized bastardization of the traditional Chinese dish.

We buy our tickets from an unsmiling agent behind a plexiglass wall, who swipes our passports with crisp authority. By 9:30 a.m., we are on the trail; after thirty minutes, we are joined by a Naxi woman and her pony.

She offers to let us ride him part way (for a fee). When we decline, she offers to pack our day bags. Again, we decline, but she solemnly follows us anyway, even as the trail becomes rock scrabble and the going gets harder. I want her to stop, to not subject the pony to a difficult walk for no good reason, and I am relieved when she silently turns back. We will pass locals who spend their days sitting under crudely constructed shelters selling bottled water, candy, and cannabis, or charging a small fee to access trails to lookouts. Hikers are essential to the local economy.

We gain elevation quickly. Far below, the Jinsha River is coffee brown and narrow as a thread. Yet this tributary of the mighty Yangtze sculpted the entire region, patiently eroding rock surfaces once forced from the earth's crust by its own internal fires. It reminds me of the game "rock paper scissors". The mightiest force is not always the most powerful, but instead the most persistent. Western China is one of the most seismically active regions on the planet, and sometimes the trail here is obscured by rock falls and slides. But this danger is more common after the rains come in August. In these late days of June, we instead bear witness to the delicate pink blooms of pitcher plants clinging tenaciously to the edge of the trail.

Soon we have reached the trail's most notorious challenge, the 28 Bends, a nearly vertical segment of grueling switchbacks which starts at 6,500 feet. Each elbow is numbered in painted English and Chinese symbols, until it levels out at 8,500 feet, the highest elevation on the route. I am anxious. I do not trust my own body anymore.

I place my feet carefully on each stone, using my poles to balance and relieve pressure on my knees as I push up and around each bend. The loops lay atop each other like ribbon candy and I stop counting after eight as each turn quickly falls away. Low pine shrub obscures the view upwards and all that exists is the step right before me.

We continue to the Tea Horse Guest House, so named for the ancient trading route connecting Chinese provinces to Tibet and the Middle East. We stop here for the night, and for the first time since arriving in China, there is near silence from the omnipresence of humanity. I sit on a stone patio hoping for a glimpse of Jade Dragon's shy peak. A solitary rooster crows from a terraced landing below, songbirds trill territorial assertions, and swallows swoop and dip in their quest for evening sustenance. The mountain stalls the progress of any clouds making their way across the sky; encountering the mountain, their mists begin to swirl, a summit making its own rules.

◆

Early the next afternoon, our steps disturb the browsing of brown goats that have climbed to the tops of small shrubs, and the grazing of a stocky bay pony tied with a single rope around his throatlatch. All pause only briefly to look up and assess our presence before returning to the important business of survival.

The Upper Middle Gorge trail gently rolls through grasses and low shrub before depositing hikers, without ceremony, onto a concrete driveway directly across the street from Tina's Guesthouse, in a village known as Walnut Grove. It is both the ending and the beginning.

We are encouraged to rest after our two-day hike, but I have learned there is a way to get to the river's edge. From above, the river looks like an artist's innocent doodle. We must see it for ourselves to believe that its power is as impressive as the scenery around it.

The trail to the bottom is privately built and maintained by local families. We pay fifteen yuan each—about two dollars—to descend. And descend it does. The drop is rapid and steep, with a series of punishing switchbacks to rival the 28 Bends. When even switchbacks cannot do the job, a rusted ladder has been fused to rock. I try to not look down and concentrate on the rhythm of my limbs, left foot, right hand, right foot, left hand.

The roar of the water increases in intensity as we drop, filling my eardrums with vibration until there is no room for more. I risk a glance to the bottom where the water tosses and rages through the constricting walls of the gorge. I look up and see what appears to be a sheer rock wall. I wonder how we will ever ascend.

Suddenly we are at the bottom and the swell and thrust of the river makes speech futile. The water is chocolate brown, churned and thrown and roiled into a rich, rapid swell. We pay an additional ten yuan to a woman at the mouth of a wood-and-rope suspension bridge, and I realize that she must climb this trail every day; she wears a knee brace and I am filled with empathy and possibility.

The bridge leads to the Middle Tiger Leaping Stone; it is from here that the tiger made his legendary jump. But there is at least one other Leaping Stone, downriver, where tour busses deposit less ambitious visitors onto a wide boardwalk, complete with handrails. The Lower Leaping Stone is a pulsing mass of humanity but here at the Middle Stone all we feel is the spray from the rapids and the power of the wind and water that has carved this stripe through the earth.

The sun's rays have become long, the blue sky beginning its transition to the pale pastels of evening. Night comes swiftly in these steep mountains. We must begin our ascent. I crane my head back and look up the sheer wall, much steeper than anything we have climbed yet. When we retrace our steps, the woman at the bridge has disappeared.

Climbing up is all about finding the rhythm, rationing energy by moving steadily, neither fast nor slow. *Never hurry, never tarry.* I keep my head down and focus on my footfall. Then I feel my mind float away over the rapids and through the pressure of the canyon walls. This external force has created the energy and power of the water and air in this deep gorge, filling it with life and vibrancy. I feel its raw power and then I, too, am free, free of this body and the worries that weigh down my mind.

We are back on the paved road, "Tina's G.H." painted in simple red block letters on its white cement wall ahead of us. We are crossing a high bridge, spanning a gap above a loop of river far below. I turn my head to marvel at the chasm and as I do so, I catch my toe. I stumble and scramble.

But I do not fall.

My Missing Piece

In the photo, she is smiling so broadly her eyes are nearly closed; she is stretching her arms wide, one extended up, one down, as if the white-bordered photo were too small to hold her, or like a magician who has just finished a performance and wants you to look at them, not the scene behind them. She is in my *Babsci*'s kitchen, when it was newer and maintained, mint-green walls offset with cream moldings, a plain wooden table, a glass Coke bottle, a child's highchair pushed to the edge. The closed door behind her leads to the bathroom, the open one to my grandparents' bedroom, and the one next to that a tiny living room. I knew this place, and these things, but none of them exist anymore. I never knew the woman in this photo. She is young and joyful. In her squinted eyes and rounded cheeks I see a face I recognize.

This is my mother, before she was my mother.

She is alive. She is happy.

◆

As a child, I believed in the power of adults, their infallibility, as though they were magical beings with the ability to solve all problems. Despite evidence of instability all around me, I remained insulated from the truth of a world in which foundations could fracture beyond repair. I was small and quiet. I slid into one of those cracks between the pieces where no one could find me.

What I did not know then is that the adults around me were just as breakable as I was. My mother was like a diamond, beautiful but prone to shattering under pressure. My fractures were simply collateral damage.

If you had asked me to describe her when I was a girl, I would have told you she was confident and strong-willed. She wore bold lipstick, big hats, high heels, and matching jewelry. She taught nursing students at night and was always there to meet me after school. She led my Girl Scout troop, organized the school's book fair, and founded a support group for mothers who had delivered babies by cesarean section. She was generous with her time and her love. On holidays, she made fudge for the mail carrier, sent a package to my teacher, even created large-print, Bible-themed crossword puzzles for my great-grandmother when none could be found to purchase. One Easter, she hid tiny model horses for me to find instead of eggs. She always wanted to get it right, to make everyone else happy.

If you ask me to describe my memory of her now, it is a harder task. I think first of coming home from high school to broken glass, food sprayed along the ceiling and walls. It became routine. I think of cooking for myself boxed mac and cheese for dinner every night for three months, of loading all my clothes into the washing machine on the cold setting, of trying to lift her resistant body off the ground of a parking lot in front of the grocery store, when everyone else just stood by and stared. I think of the boxed wine that lived on the top shelf of our fridge, how she sipped it out of colorful Tupperware cups, cups that would not break if they slipped from uncoordinated fingers.

But mostly I think of the tears. Hers, loud and increasingly public. Mine, quieter and mostly hidden. Maybe we were both grieving; she for a loss so palpable and impending that she was powerless before it, and I, naive, simply reflecting her pain.

◆

In the photo, she wears a blue polyester pantsuit, coordinated with a white turtleneck under an open blazer. Her hair is neatly parted down the middle and clipped at the nape of her neck. On her ears she wears two small clip-on gold hoops. The slightest trace of pale blue eyeshadow dances across her lids. She is smiling, gazing down at the child she is sitting behind. The toddler wears a yellow gingham dress and white bonnet, little white socks pulled up and stopping just below chubby thighs, and white shoes with tongues shaped like cat heads clinging to her dancing feet. The little girl looks straight at the camera, a tiny wisp of tawny hair floating below the brim of the bonnet. She is ready to run; one small foot is already in the air. Her mother's hands help her to stay balanced (the right) and support her tentative steps (the left). Those hands protect and nurture.

This photo is from May 1977. I do not remember this day, but I do remember the woman, her smile, the way those pants made a soft swishing noise when she walked. I remember this woman cared for me fiercely, deeply. She nurtured me and helped me to believe that I was good enough.

She did those things until she simply couldn't. I remember that too.

◆

Her sister Louise is 82 years old now and lives alone in a claustrophobic apartment in a state-supported housing complex for seniors. She has lost her father, younger sister, mother, son, and husband, in that order. The memories, photos, clothing, and furniture she surrounds herself with nearly bury her. I visit her on the day before my mother's birthday. On this year, my mother would have turned seventy-one. She was nine years younger than Louise. Louise says my mother was their father's favorite.

They would go out to chop wood together. I try to picture my mother and my *dziadziu* in their postage stamp of a yard chopping wood, but instead I remember the tiny garden ringed with bricks in which my grandfather grew dill and cucumbers for his pickles. But my aunt remembers them chopping wood. She remembers that my mother was outspoken, could get away with saying and doing things that she herself could not. Louise had wanted to go to college, but money was tight. Instead, she went to work. Because their family didn't have a car, she got a ride from Taunton to Attleboro every day with a neighbor.

Louise married young, started a family, and moved into the apartment above her parents. My mother moved to Boston, becoming the first in the family to earn a degree. There are no pictures of her commencement, because on May 4 of that year, students were killed at Kent State, and her classmates protested, rioted, and closed down the Boston University campus. There are pictures though, from when my mother finished her master's degree five years later. Her long, dark brown hair frames her face beneath a mortarboard, her black graduation gown unzipped, her crimson dress chosen to show school pride. Her heels make her tower over her parents, even my dziadziu. Louise and her husband stand stiffly in the background, hanging on to my young cousins by the hand.

But before all that, my mother and Louise shared one tiny room and their parents another. Their grandparents, the Stadnickis, lived upstairs in the second apartment. My aunt is named for their grandmother Stadnicki, my great-grandmother, and Louise my mother's sister says Louise Stadnicki was a force to be reckoned with. She was married to "Little Dziadziu," a small, slender man, who would one day walk around the block leading Patches the dog and pushing my cousin Mike in a stroller. Little Dziadziu was Louise Stadnicki's second husband; she gave birth to seven children, all but six in her native Poland. Only my grandmother Jennie was born here in the United States. They all spoke Polish and were deeply committed to the Catholic faith. To celebrate the Epiphany, they use blessed chalk to write out the initials of the Three Kings—K+M+B for Kaspar, Melchior, and Balthazar, plus the year—on the mint-green lintel over their front door. *Christ blesses this house.*

On Friday evenings, Little Dziadziu, my dziadziu, and Louise and my mother watched boxing on the television. They knew all the names of the fighters and cheered for the underdogs. My dziadziu gave Louise, my mother, and my Babsci new shoes on their birthdays. He was a weaver at a local mill and my Babsci cleaned houses. My great-grandparents never learned English, and Louise spoke only Polish until she turned six.

We were never poor. We never worried about that.

My mother's sister remembers.

◆

My Babsci made pierogi every Christmas Eve, hundreds of them, stuffed with potato, cabbage, or prunes. They lay across tables and ironing boards and countertops in the overcrowded mint-green kitchen. Everyone took turns helping. People laughed, told stories and made mistakes as they folded the dough. Nobody worried if the pierogi looked perfect. Somehow, they always did.

My mother tried to make the pierogi on her own; my father and I did not help her. I could hear her weeping in the kitchen as she stretched the dough, cut the disks, dropped in the filling and folded, over and over. I thought she wept in frustration over the tedium, but today I see my mistake.

In Polish tradition, the preparation of holiday food is a festive, family affair, not a solo act. Pierogi are produced in quantity to be shared, traded, and frozen. My mother wept because this modern kitchen, with its tan patterned linoleum and state-of-the-art oven and long countertop, could never compare to the one three hundred miles away with faded mint paint and cracking walls.

This was just one of the reasons my mother cried. Maybe she didn't realize that I saw her tears fall, running down her flushed cheeks and dropping to her chest, that I heard her low moans. Nor did I understand that this pain, too, was as real as a disease, that it eroded her and made her vulnerable to other more tangible illnesses. Poverty is not always about material goods.

◆

I was a liar. While my mother taught the nursing students at Russell Sage College, I enjoyed sitting in the college secretary's office, opening and closing drawers, sorting boxes of paperclips, and especially typing on her typewriter. I imagined I was powerful and in charge. I hit the keys with purpose. One time, the day following one of our visits, the secretary called my mother and accused me of trying to change the typewriter ribbon.

I had found the new cartridge in a bottom drawer. It was striped, half black and half red, on twin spools. Office supplies held a special allure over me. For some reason, the cartridge compelled me to reach out, crack open the cellophane packaging, and hold the spools in my hands. Once I started, I couldn't stop. Besides, how hard could it be? I would just pop the old one out and the new one in. No one would ever know.

Almost immediately I recognized that I was over my head. The ink coated my hands and I left red and black fingerprints on everything I touched. The spool unfurled and the ribbon soon twisted around itself, refusing to lay flat in the channel. I shoved the new spools down on their spindles; they refused to latch into place. Panicking now, I took the old ribbon and threw it in a garbage can down the hall, toweled off the ink stains and pulled the typewriter's plastic cover back over the top. No one would ever know who had created such chaos.

The secretary must have always seen the waste and damage I left behind, but this transgression was simply too much for her to ignore. My mother brought the subject up with me, casually and softly, as though she already knew the truth but was in no way going to acknowledge it.

You wouldn't have changed the ribbon, right? She must be mistaken.

I shook my head no—a saintly angel, incapable of wreaking destruction on even a pencil, never mind an innocent typewriter.

She never said anything about it again and I was allowed to stay in the office the next week, though the typewriter was gone, wheeled into a different, locked, room. I wonder now what it must have cost her, to know her daughter had lied and to go along with the deception (she had to have known). But maybe she knew her child needed reassurance that when she was not perfect, someone would stand behind her, no matter what. And I wonder how she could have known.

◆

I try to picture the moment she was told she had multiple sclerosis. I imagine her in her navy polyester pants sitting in an exam room (she never wore jeans), poised on one of the chairs lined up on the side, her mismatched canes leaning up against the wall. Or maybe she was sitting on the opposite side of a large oak desk covered with books, files, and dust, the neurologist peering at her over his glasses. She would have heard the words as if standing at the end of a long hallway, time slowing down, as if it were happening to someone else. She would have nodded her head up and down, her short bob swinging, her red lipsticked smile strained, hearing the words and maybe even agreeing with them aloud, but not in her heart. *But M.S. isn't supposed to cause pain,* I imagine her saying, because she said that all the time afterwards, because the relentless pain made it hard to walk and even get out of bed. But the doctor would have just assured her that the pain was from a confounding condition, like a slipped disc or sciatica and therefore not important. She wouldn't have cried, not then. She would have been conciliatory and agreeable, as if the news the doctor had shared were nothing more important than an affirmation that the day was cold or eating leafy greens healthy.

The tears would have come later, after she had dragged her sluggish legs back out of the office, down the hallway, on an elevator and into the parking lot toward her 1986 Buick LeSabre, the car that would become mine in college. Its maroon interior had small, pilled squares and she would have tried to smooth them out as the tears overwhelmed her and her face crumpled into wrinkles like a withered applehead doll.

She and I cry the same way, our eyes disappearing behind compressed lids, thin lips drawn back into a clear upside-down U. She would not have cried quietly, not then. The sobs would have come, wracked her whole body as she asked:

Why?

◆

We went as a family to pick the Buick out, the last car my mother would ever drive, my father negotiating every small detail, my mother mostly concerned about the color and losing patience with the process, and me rolling around on the dirty carpeted floor, jittery after drinking too much free Pepsi. A few months after getting it home, another driver sideswiped the Buick at the intersection by the local Price Chopper. The passenger side rear bumper was crumpled and my mother was distraught. I was scared because we had been hit; she was scared because the car was damaged.

Cars can be repaired. People cannot.

All witnesses reported that a red car had run the light. Both cars were red. No one was assigned blame. Or everyone was. In the end, is there really a difference?

Years later, hand controls were installed in her Buick for braking and acceleration, a knob mounted to the wheel for steering. The B and the U fell off, leaving just ICK on the rear panel. My mother took private driving lessons, but when she wasn't supervised, she refused to use the hand controls. Instead, she lifted her non-responsive right leg with her hand from the gas to the brake; sometimes her toe caught on the pedal and she pressed both together. Her friends stopped riding with her but I did not. I don't know if I had a choice.

One day she miscalculated the exit ramp from the highway; I could tell the arc we travelled was wrong and I held my breath, waiting for her to correct the line. *She must know we are about to crash.* The front driver's side corner crumpled, sparks flying, a shrill exhalation as the metal contracted from its impact on the guard rail. She jerked the wheel and the ICK wobbled right, then left, before settling itself between the lane lines. She looked at me.

"What just happened?"

What happened was you made a mistake, I think, but don't say. I know that driving is her only remaining freedom.

Later that day, I did not correct her when she told my father that she swerved to avoid something in the road.

Cars can be repaired but people cannot. She was a liar and I was complicit.

In the end, is there really a difference?

◆

"Do you think she was ever really happy?" I ask this of my father one day many years later. He is silent for so long I think he hasn't heard me.

"I think she always knew there was something wrong, even before the doctors did, that there was a reason it so was hard for her to keep up with everyone else."

My girl-self recoils; she remembers my mother as being capable.

"I think she did so much to make up for feeling like she couldn't keep up. So no one would notice."

I think now of my own overly full life and my struggle to attain an ideal only I can perceive.

I think that perhaps my mother felt she had a hole to fill, too.

◆

I am in the yoga studio. I am sweating. My thoughts bounce around in my skull and make concentration fleeting.

Inhale strength, exhale effort.

I squeeze my eyes, shake a bead of perspiration from my nose and flex deeper into the pose. My right knee is bent, left leg extended behind me, left toes pointed at the wall. I reach through my front side body, right arm extended in line with my shoulder, fingers reaching, straining. They are limited by my left arm, stretched behind me, fingers like arrows pulling me both forward and backward. I am caught in the middle.

Inhale this moment. Exhale the world outside. It will still be waiting for you when you are done.

I am forty years old, and I am constantly reaching for a future that I think will somehow make me feel whole again, yet I am weighed down by this past, this hole that cannot be filled. Here in the present, I feel my bare feet slipping slightly on my yellow, pilling, discount yoga mat, the burn in my engaged quadriceps muscle, the increasing strain on my stretched hamstring, the effort of holding my arms in the future and the past at the same time.

And time. This is the real problem. You always think there will be enough time.

I wasted time when I was young, in my twenties and thirties, on frivolous things. Time wasted like sand sifting through your fingers on the beach, as impossible to hold as the tide that turns the sand to mud, weighs it down. Then one day you open your eyes and look in the mirror and see a lumpy middle-aged woman with worry lines creasing her forehead, the corners of her eyes, and the curve of her mouth.

And you see her, the other her, and realize that she thought she had more time too.

You realize there is still so much more to do.

◆

You wonder if it ever goes away. The hole. The search for your missing piece.

There is a woman in your writing workshop and you can hardly look at her. Her face, her voice, her profile, are your mother's. She is right now about the age your mother was when things started to go wrong. Physically wrong, that is. But perhaps they had never been right to begin with.

You visit your father's new home in Florida. He lives there with his new wife, has a new life that includes classes at the local college, a stargazers' club, and a community chorus. You open the closet in the guest room to get another blanket. Even though you live in New England you still get cold here at night. January in central Florida does not mean warmth. You pull back the beige folding door, looking for blankets, but instead you see her rain-coat. It is teal with a broad royal blue stripe. You cannot imagine why your father kept it. And then you remember your last family portrait; you see her, sitting in her wheelchair on the deck of a cruise ship in Alaska. You are standing next to her, your father behind her, bundled up. She is wearing this raincoat, teal hood pulled over her head, and a red plaid blanket over her lap. The three of you look at the camera, faces inscrutable.

You close the closet door. You are shaking, but no longer from the cold.

You wonder if it ever goes away. The hole. The search for your missing piece. And if you find it, how will you know?

TEN PISCATAQUA

We gratefully recognize these Patrons
for their generous support of regional writing and
outstanding regional writers

Martha & Jeff Clark
Rev. Dr. David A. Purdy & Pamela Chatterton Purdy
TVC Systems
Bob & Karen Graham
Kenny & Sally Gilbride
Linda & Cathy

◆